Guardian Angel

Gard tensed as if jolted by electricity, grabbed Desta by the waist, and jerked her against him.

Plastered against his chest, she gasped and twisted trying to free herself. When she opened her mouth to protest, he clamped his hand over her mouth. She aimed a kick at his ankle with her heel.

"Be still," he whispered urgently. "We have a reception committee of goons waiting at our car."

She didn't jam her spiked heel into him. Easing her foot down, she gazed cautiously around his chest toward the parking lot. Two large men were near Gard's car, but they appeared innocent enough.

Gard jerked further back against the shrubbery. "Damn, they saw us. Let's get out of here."

They turned to retreat back into the building.

A large man stepped out of the building and grinned malevolently at them. With a brutal face of ax-hacked angles, he appeared anything but harmless, and he had them effectively trapped. He also had a gun pointed at them.

Bottling them in, the other men lumbered into the shrubbery-lined walk toward them.

Desta stared at the ax-faced man, the obvious leader. Nothing of compassion, humor, or love lived behind his inhuman slate eyes. Only cold. Her hackles rose as she sensed his dangerous reptilian alienness.

He leered, aware of her horror, and reached toward her with a meaty hand.

She backed into Gard's side to avoid him.

Gard glanced at the building they'd just left then grabbed her. In one quick movement, he picked her up in his arms and threw her over the waist-high shrubbery. "Run, Desta. Run."

What They Are Saying About

Marilynn Byerly

"Marilynn Byerly's descriptive phrasing, creative plot lines, and powerful characterizations make reading her stories an absolute addiction."

—Jaycee
Romance Reviews Today

"Ms. Byerly is a wonderful writer, as capable of portraying a tender moment as a brutal encounter, a lingering love scene or a compelling battle, and making the reader feel and believe every word."

—Norah-Jean Perkin
Word Museum

Guardian Angel

Marilynn Byerly

A Wings ePress, Inc.
Romantic Suspense Novel

Wings ePress, Inc.

Edited by: Lorraine Stephens
Copy Edited by: Christie Kraemer
Senior Editor: Lorraine Stephens
Executive Editor: Lorraine Stephens
Cover Artist: mpmann

All rights reserved

Wings ePress Books
http://www.wings-press.com

Copyright © 2006 by Marilynn Byerly
ISBN 1-59705-887-4

Published In the United States Of America

Wings ePress Inc.
3000 N. Rock Road
Newton, KS 67114

Dedication

For my family in loving apology for all those North Carolina vacation moments when I was imagining danger in the sand dunes, mobsters in the mountains, and exploding boats on the lake.

One

"I always wondered what your virtuous soul would cost, and now I know." Lauton O'Brien smiled at the wince Gabriel Gardner hadn't been able to hide, picked up the freshly signed contract from his mahogany desk, and admired it.

"I sold you a few weeks or months of time, not my soul."

"All a matter of opinion. A matter of opinion." Lauton tucked the contract into the file and pulled out the other documents. "And here is the first half of your payment as well as your paid life insurance policy."

Gardner barely glanced at the check, which was considerably more than he made in several years as a Federal Agent, then shoved it into his pocket. The life insurance policy received the same cursory glance before it went into his own briefcase.

"A hard bargain, Robbie, but worth every penny if you keep my little girl safe when the time comes."

Gardner's blue eyes narrowed at the nickname he despised, but he replied evenly, "A hard bargain, but worth whatever the cost to me if it gives my son a new life."

Lauton chuckled to himself. Gardner had read the fine print of the contract with great care, but there was considerably more to this deal than he was aware of, considerably more.

Gardner may not have sold his soul, but his future, if he survived, was now Lauton's.

~ * ~

Gabriel Gardner brushed wearily at the grass chunks the trimmer had garnished his bare calves with, then sauntered from the shed at the corner of his yard down to the dock. Plopping down in a sagging, aged lounge chair at dock's end, he gazed out over the lake.

Early afternoon sun glinted on the green blue water, mud dulling the first foot of water where boat wakes had churned it against the shore. In the far distance, he could just see the deserted houses on the other side of the bay, and on the main channel, no boats darted about. Even in June, this part of Lake Norman was dead on weekdays; the residents at work, the second-homers back in Charlotte, or wherever else in North Carolina they lived.

Ignoring the patter of large feet on the dock, Gard yawned closing his eyes.

A cold dog nose nudged his sweaty bare shoulder for attention.

"Barkley!"

A pathetic whimper answered him.

He opened his eyes. The half-grown German shepherd, a bedraggled red Frisbee in her mouth, gazed at him with huge heartbroken eyes. Chuckling, he stroked her brown throat. "You miss him too, don't you, girl? You don't know how many acres a nine year old fills until he's not around."

The puppy thumped her tail vigorously in agreement.

"We'll just have to manage alone. He needs other people besides us. That's the child-raising theory anyway. It's good for him even if it's lonely for us."

Barkley's ears went up, and she stared at a yacht broaching the bay from the main channel and heading toward them.

Shading his eyes, he studied it. The clean lines of its white hull and distinctive passenger cabin and flybridge spoke eloquently of its identity. He'd only seen one of those restored beauties on Lake Norman, and Lauton O'Brien owned it.

"Damn! Just who I didn't want to see." In the almost two years since he'd signed Lauton's contract, the other lawyer had visited occasionally to annoy him and remind him of their contract. As of he'd forget his deal with the devil.

The yacht turned toward their small cove and throttled down.

A muffled, violent explosion shook the air as fire blossomed out of the stern and shot toward the passenger cabin. The boat jerked to a stop as if a giant had slammed a fist into its hull.

Jumping to his feet, Gard screamed, "O'Brien! O'Brien, get off. It's going up!" He dove into the water.

The unexploded natural bomb of the boat's fuel tank and boiler ticking away in his brain, he swam as hard as he could toward the sinking craft. He'd have to get O'Brien off and away fast, or they'd both be blown to smithereens with the yacht.

He made the fifty yards to the vessel in record time. Treading water, he shouted, "O'Brien! O'Brien. Get off now, damn you. O'Brien!"

An image out of hell, a figure stumbled across the deck, flames behind outlining a woman's curves and long, dark hair, the billowing ends on fire.

"Jump. I'll get you."

Her vacant, pale face regarded him a moment, then she arched off the blazing deck into the water beside him and sank.

Grabbing her neck in a lifesaver's hold, he pulled her back up, screamed "O'Brien" several more times, then began to tow her limp body toward the shore.

He concentrated on moving away as fast as he could instead of on O'Brien, who must have been killed in the first explosion. No one deserved to die like that.

The boat exploded.

Brutal sound surrounded him, the water and the force of the blast buffeting him, then deafening silence fell with burning shrapnel and throat ripping black smoke. He dodged a chunk of debris.

His stroke staggered, and he swayed like a drunken duck, but kept heading for the shore. The burning planks around him were a maze he had to swim through.

Disoriented by his changes in direction and blinded by smoke, he coughed then called out, "Speak, Barkley. Speak, girl."

An intelligent sound beacon who seemed to understand his problem, the puppy began to bark without stopping.

He swam toward the noise.

His feet touched ground, and he stood, picking up the woman, and trudged out of the water and up onto his lawn. His vision cleared in the thinning smoke. The puppy jumped excitedly around him.

Heaving from exhaustion, he fell to his knees on the lawn. The puppy sat down beside him. "Good dog. Good girl, Barkley."

He bent toward the woman he still held. Her head was thrown back against his arm, her throat rippling with pulse and breath. Her chest rose and fell naturally. She mustn't have swallowed much water. "Miss?"

Long brown lashes flickered upward, and she stared at him with stunned chocolate brown eyes for a moment, then closed them.

Pale under her light tan, her face was unmarked. She wore only a bikini bottom, her full breasts bare. Bruises were already appearing on her left shoulder and right thigh, but he could see no burns.

Her hair had been on fire!

Settling her into his lap, he turned her breasts into his chest, her face against his throat, so he could examine her back. Her dripping bedraggled hair was plastered against her back almost to her waist.

The stench of singed hair burnt his nose. He bit his lip, caught the hair at the nape of her neck, and lifted very, very carefully so he wouldn't pull away injured flesh with the hair.

He coiled it around his hand until he uncovered her back. Just a few slightly pink spots and a shallow bleeding cut across her left shoulder blade to her armpit were the only damage. She'd been incredibly lucky. With his finger, he examined the cut for shrapnel.

She groaned and thrust her breasts against his chest to escape his finger.

A bolt of sexual electricity shot from her nipples through him to his groin. His body jolted, his reaction instantaneous.

He closed his eyes, counted to ten, then released her hair. He would tend her back later. "It's all right, miss. You're safe now. Your guardian angel was watching over you." Turning her slightly and cradling her against him, he really looked at her as more than an accident case. His body and subconscious had already recognized her as a sexy beauty, and they were right. Even now, the woman was stunning.

In her mid-twenties, she had an oval face, high cheek bones, and classically perfect eyes, nose, and full lips. Intelligence and aristocratic breeding shown from every inch of her.

Her slender neck extended down to broad shoulders and full firm breasts, the nipples like tiny rosebuds.

He counted to twenty.

Her hips were just full enough, her legs long and supple. She must be only a few inches below his own six feet.

The bikini bottom covered a very nice rump. No, not really a bikini bottom, more of a two-piece bathing suit bottom. It covered too much to be a bikini. The sun lines on her bare breasts showed its companion half, lost in the accident, had been as conservative.

This woman made no sense. She wasn't Lauton O'Brien's usual type of mistress. O'Brien always had some young blonde giggler with an I.Q. smaller than her micro-bikini's bra size with him on the boat. This brainy, classy, dark beauty was more his style than O'Brien's.

No, he'd never accept one of O'Brien's leftovers.

She was staring up at him with liquid brown eyes a doe would envy.

Smiling, he stroked her head to comfort her.

Her voice was husky and cultured but childlike with shock. "Your eyes are as blue as the sky. You're beautiful."

He blushed like an idiot.

"I tingle when you touch me." She fingered his already drying blond hair then his cheek.

He felt her caress all the way down to his toes.

"Who are you?" she asked.

"Gabriel..." He didn't finish; he stared instead as her eyes dilated with wonder becoming giant chocolate disks.

Wonder turning into distress, she blinked tears. "I waited my whole life for a man to make me tingle, and now I've found one, and he's not even a man. It's not fair."

"You're drunk!"

She shook her head solemnly. "Don't drink, smoke, mess with drugs or men. Never met one who made me tingle. Wanted that much from him." She added ingenuously, "I do love chocolate though. Is that a sin?"

"I don't think so. I like chocolate, too."

A smile lit her face and the depths of her eyes. "I'm glad." With an index finger, she traced his lips. "If they have chocolate here, they must have... Pardon me for being forward, but do you have a lady angel, or are you still looking?"

All the clues clicked together, and he chuckled.

She looked away as if embarrassed.

His heart twisted at her pain, and he wanted to hold her and comfort her, wanted to stretch out beside her in the grass and make love to her until she tingled all over, wanted to carry her to his bedroom and never let her out, wanted to... Instead, he said kindly, "What's your name?"

"Desta O'Brien."

"*You're* Dusty O'Brien!"

"Daddy calls me that, but no one else does. I don't like it."

"Desta, you aren't dead. You jumped off the boat, and I brought you to shore. I'm not the archangel Gabriel. My name is Gabriel Gardner, but my friends call me Gard."

She stared blankly for a moment, but seemed to accept being alive as fast as she'd accepted being dead with an angel. Her face relaxed. "Hello. Thank you for saving me. I was supposed to find Robbie Gardner. Are you a relative?"

"Lauton calls me that, but no one else does. I don't like it either. He uses it to make fun of me."

"I'm sorry. I won't then. Why Robbie?"

He surprised himself by telling her. "He was cross-examining me in court. He couldn't make fun of the FBI so he made fun of me. He called me Robert Redford of the FBI like I was nothing but a... I was a very good agent, whatever I look like."

"You do look a little like a younger Redford. But in a very nice sense. Your face has integrity, kindness, and humor like his does, and intelligence."

"How are you feeling?"

"Numb. Even my brain's numb."

"It must be emotional trauma from the accident. You don't have any of the symptoms of concussion. Let me get you inside." He hoisted her back in his arms, swayed awkwardly up on stiffened legs, then turned toward the lake.

Debris and oil still burned on the water where the boat had sunk, but he couldn't see any burning timbers that would endanger his dock or the trees near the shoreline. The wind had changed blowing everything toward open water.

Desta wrapped her arms around his neck. "Poor old boat. Daddy'll hate she's gone. Don't know what I did wrong. Driven it dozens of times before."

"You were alone on the boat?"

"Yes." She rested her face against his throat. "So sleepy."

Barkley at his side, he began to walk toward the house. "Stay awake just a little longer. Why are you here?"

"Daddy sent me. Told me two years ago to go to you if things fell apart. Told me where you lived, who you were. Said I'd be safe with you. He's left... disappeared. Not going to come back."

"Someone wants him dead?"

"Must. Made me leave everything I had and go into hiding so I couldn't be used to hurt him or be killed."

"Who wants him dead? A dissatisfied client? Someone who told him too much under lawyer-client communications?"

"Don't know. He sent you a letter that said. Was in the galley of the yacht. Only knew he wouldn't send me to you unless real danger. He's not stupid." She yawned broadly.

"He's not stupid. You're safe with me, Desta. I promise you that."

"Nice man," she agreed and relaxed against him.

Fear wrenched his stomach. His day of reckoning had finally arrived. He'd hoped it would never come, but now here it was.

Could Lauton be wrong?

No, even without facts, it was obvious someone wanted Lauton dead. It had been a bomb, not driver's error, that made the yacht blow up. Someone wanted Lauton dead, and this beautiful believer in angels could be killed in the cross fire. Lauton probably deserved whatever happened to him, but this wide-eyed innocent didn't.

Gard fought open the screen door and sidled through it with his sleeping bundle, then strode through the living room to the hallway. He chose Zach's bedroom instead of his. His bedroom made her too tempting, better a little boy's room where he could keep his mind on his protective obligations.

He eased her onto the *Star Wars* bedspread. She grumbled when deprived of his warm body and curled on her side as if cold.

With a final lingering ogle at the sexiest spinal column he'd ever seen, he retreated for supplies.

When he returned, Barkley, her eyes on the stranger, sat on the bed beside Desta. Her ears went up at his arrival, and she thumped her tail in greeting.

Fiercely protective of Zach and Zach's personal territory, Barkley probably wasn't happy about Desta being here.

"Don't chew off her throat, girl. She's a guest."

The puppy sniffed her back, thumped her tail vigorously, grinned, then sniffed again.

"You like the way she smells." Bending over Desta, he daubed at her long hair with a towel. "Me too. A very friendly, sexy smell." He tugged at the strands, pulling them away from her body, then wrapped the towel around them. "I'm afraid a good foot of this mane will be cut from the fire damage."

Unbidden, images came. A sultry, beckoning Godiva, Desta standing naked except for her long hair, a curl draped coyly around a full breast, a rosebud nipple peeking through. Desta lying on top of him in bed, their bodies joined in the final drive toward completion, her head thrown back in ecstasy, sweat clinging to her breasts, her hair tangling down on his face, hands, across his chest...

With a groan, he began to count to fifty. His hand shook like a teenaged boy's when he began to blot her face and neck.

Berating himself, he concentrated on being as gentle as possible. He also started some serious planning. The next few hours could make the difference between being murdered or not. If he didn't handle himself just right, Desta, Lauton, and he could end up dead, and Zach's life could be ruined. He must be very, very careful about the plans he made now.

And whatever the cost to him, he had to make certain Desta remained safe.

~ * ~

From his dock end, Gard watched one of the SBI's divers surface and toss a chunk of metal into his powerboat then sink again into the dark lake water. Gard shivered with sympathy. The deep water must be cold and uncomfortable.

Stretching, he glanced toward his lawn at the small mob of local, state, and federal law enforcement and forensic experts. The dozen men all seemed quite happy quizzing each other after pestering him for the last two hours. He liked being the pesterer more than the pesteree, but his days as a special agent were gone.

So they wouldn't realize he was escaping, he engulfed himself in the arrogance of a pesterer and sauntered into the house.

He opened Zach's bedroom door and entered. The quiet eye of the law enforcement hurricane she'd inadvertently caused, Desta curled on her side asleep in bed, her long dry hair splayed around her, her upper arm draped over Barkley's neck. The puppy lay beside her.

Barkley lifted her head and thumped her tail in greeting.

Sitting down on the edge of the bed, he stroked the puppy's head.

Desta stirred at the bed's movement then stilled.

Her long lashes rested against her cheeks, highlighting a Renaissance Madonna profile, and the thin cotton of her tee shirt nightgown was pulled against a full breast, her nipple etched in white.

Lust and tenderness warred inside him for attention, two dull aches in his groin and heart.

No woman had affected him like this in a long time, and he certainly shouldn't feel this for the daughter of a man he despised, the woman he'd sworn to protect. Angry at himself and at her, he turned his back on her and walked out of the room, closing the door on her but not on the dull aches.

In the master bedroom, he cleaned himself up, finally washing off the residue of oil and smoke he'd had since the accident, and changed into jeans, a blue knit shirt, and sneakers. He now looked moderately more presentable and felt almost human.

Nearly cheerful, he stepped out into the hall then froze.

FBI Special Agent Mark Faulkner stood in the hall, his hand twisting the knob of Zach's room. He was the last person in the world who should see Desta O'Brien.

"Don't open that."

Mark jumped at his explosive voice then grinned at him and twisted the knob further. "Why not?"

"The puppy's in there. I don't want her out."

On cue, Barkley began to growl as if she wanted to tear Mark into Alpo chunks.

"Puppy? Sounds like an attack dog." Mark released the door knob.

"She's a German Shepherd, almost fully grown, and she's very protective of us. That's Zach's room. Nobody gets near Zach with Barkley around." Gard sauntered down the hall toward the living room to draw Mark away from the room. Barkley had stopped growling.

"Zach's here?"

"No, he's with a friend's family at the beach. I was wondering when you'd show up. Your forensic people have been here an hour."

"I was far on the other side of Charlotte, but Braggonier knew I'd want to handle a case involving you."

"I'm dying of thirst. Want some tea?"

Mark followed him docilely into the living room. "Love some. About that puppy Godzilla."

"She's a good dog, but she's part puppy and part adult, and she's not straight yet on being a guard dog. All this circus has her upset. I'm afraid she might bite someone."

"You want her around Zachie?"

Gard turned into the kitchen and began to assemble glasses, ice, and the prepared tea. "Zach she's very straight about. The moment those two met I heard violins and everything went to slow motion. Love at first sight for them both. She's been very good for him. He's still too introverted."

"Poor kid. It must be rough losing your mom at seven."

"It's rough losing your mom at any age, but seven is the worst. He's doing much better. His therapist and I think he's over the hump." Gard handed Mark his tea. "Let's adjourn to the living room."

They settled down on the sofa where they could see the lawn and its activity through the picture window. Mark pulled out a notebook, pen, and tiny tape recorder from his suit jacket pocket. He laughed. "Never thought I'd be doing this to you."

"Better my former partner than anybody. Be gentle, it's my first time."

Hooting laughter, Mark ruffled his hair out of his eyes with his fingers. About Gard's thirty-five, he was a dark, slender opposite of Gard—brunet, brown-eyed, and very aristocratic in feature and bearing. Other agents had called them Day and Night for both their looks and their differing but complimentary personalities. "You mean you didn't go all the way with the guys out on the lawn?"

"Didn't ask the right questions. I was waiting for a master."

"That's me." Mark flicked on the tape recorder, spoke the date, time, and interview subject, then asked, "Would you identify yourself please."

Gard told his full name and address.

"Do I have your permission to tape this interview?"

"Yes, you do."

"Tell me what happened."

Gard told the truth about the events, but never mentioned Desta, and again he chose his words carefully so he wasn't lying, but he implied that Lauton O'Brien had been on the boat alone and had been blown up with it.

Mark glanced at his notes to himself. "Why was O'Brien coming to visit you?"

Gard sipped his tea. He'd better be very cautious with Mark who was not only a superb interviewer, but also so close he'd sense lies others wouldn't. "I have no idea. He didn't phone to tell me, and I didn't speak to him when the boat got here."

"But you recognized his boat. You must have seen it before."

"He has come before. Maybe seven times since I bought this house. He'd flounce in with that beautiful old boat and annoy me for several hours, then he'd depart. He liked to rub his money in my nose. After I left the Bureau and was studying for the state bar exams, he asked me to join his law firm."

Mark snorted laughter. "I'm certain you were honored."

"Hardly. I didn't take his offer too seriously. We hated each other's guts in court whenever I gave evidence against his clients, and my feelings hadn't changed. He knew I had no respect for him or the way he trampled on the law."

"Are you ready to confess to his murder? You just gave me a motive."

For a moment he thought Mark was serious, then he laughed with amusement. In the next moment he wondered again if Mark had been serious. "Bombs are not my style. No, I didn't kill him. I had no reason to kill him. I merely told him what he could do with his job offer. I wanted a small town civil law practice. I had no desire for criminal law big time, especially not with him."

"How's your office coming?"

Gard stiffened. Mumbling noises were coming from Zach's bedroom; Desta was having another nightmare. He forced himself to act normal.

"The building's almost done. I'll open up my offices officially in mid-September. Unofficially, I've been handling some cases here. Mostly, I've been enjoying this last summer of freedom with Zach."

"He's at the beach?"

Desta was practically screaming. Couldn't Mark hear it? "For two weeks. He left yesterday. Rebecca's in California. O'Brien blew up deliberately just to ruin my private non-Daddy vacation."

"Wouldn't put it past him. What were your plans?"

"Female hunting. A lifetime lease if I found the right one."

"You always were the marrying kind. Give me short-term leases any day. Are you really ready? Megan?"

"I still love her, but now I can love someone else, too. Zach needs a mother." He relaxed slightly. Desta had shut up.

"The bomb was attached to the throttle?"

"It must have been. The moment the boat slowed, it went off. She probably didn't slow speed from the moment she left the marina until she turned into my cove. If she had, she'd have blown up in open water with no witnesses, and no one the wiser. A perfect murder if that would have happened."

Mark straightened. "She?"

Gard winced inside at his slip. "The nautical feminine. I was referring to the boat. She was a real beauty. It was a sin to blow her up."

"It was damn convenient having that boat blow up in front of you."

Gard stiffened. The comment had the sharp edge of one of Mark's barbed innuendoes. Could he be accusing him of something? "I beg your pardon."

"You're the perfect unimpeachable witness. I couldn't think of a better witness to that boat blowing up. You could even tell the difference between a faulty boiler explosion and a bomb. Are you certain O'Brien stayed on board? Could he have jumped off and swum ashore when you couldn't see him?"

"You mean he faked his own death?" Gard replayed the accident in his head. "It would have been difficult to have avoided me. The boat went up fairly fast. No more than two or three minutes total from the first explosion to the second. He could have gone off the other side of the boat when I went into the water, but he'd have a good distance to swim to avoid my seeing him. I don't think a man his age could do it.

"Plus, how did he know I was going to be out on the dock that day or that time? That would have required a spotter with binoculars and a radio to O'Brien's boat, which would be waiting out on the main channel."

"A very faint maybe then that O'Brien faked his own death. A woman across the bay called the local sheriff's department at 2:15 to report the sound of a loud explosion, yet you didn't call the Sheriff until 2:48. Why is there such a discrepancy in time?"

"It took me that long to get to the phone. I was already exhausted before I jumped into the water. I'd spent the day working around here in the yard, then I swam out to the boat as fast as I could, then swam back toward shore as fast as I could. I was still in the water when the boat went up. It about knocked me silly. The water was filled with burning boards and smoke, and I had to navigate through them. I almost didn't find the shore because of the damn smoke. I crawled up on shore and stayed there for a long time. I didn't know it was as long as half an hour."

Mark's sardonic eyebrow went up, and he drawled, "Real heroic stuff there, Gard. You should sell it to the movies."

"Heroic, hell. I'm embarrassed with my tottering antics. We don't have the stamina we once had."

Mark clicked off his tape recorder. "Speak for yourself. I'm still lean and mean. No geriatrics for me."

"That wild bachelor life will catch up one day, and you'll fall apart completely."

"And they'll find my carcass with a big smile on its face."

"Would you keep me informed on this case. I'd like to know who and why."

"Hunting dogs don't lose their instincts even if they do leave the pack. Why don't you come back, Gard. I miss you. Everyone's dull in comparison."

Gard shook his head. "I won't say I don't miss the excitement, but no. It was best for Zach, and I'm beginning to realize it's best for me, too. There's more to life than chasing possums and skunks, and I'm finding out what it is. Why don't you join me?"

"A small town civil law practice?" Mark shuddered. "I'd die of boredom in two weeks. What's your most exciting case so far? A jaywalking case?"

"I meet a lot of nice people, and I help them. I'm doing something positive, not playing federal garbage man with human scum garbage. When I get my practice going, I'd like to run for city council."

"Ah hah! Political ambitions. State or federal? Senate? Governor?"

"City council. Maybe mayor. End of ambition. I'm just not ambitious in that sense. I want to provide a good life for Zach and myself. Maybe find a very special lady for us both. That's my overweening ambition."

"I don't understand you."

"Your father is a wealthy senator, my father was a poor farmer. You can be the next J. Edgar, I never could. Doesn't that say enough?"

"This is America where the inherited rich get lazy, and the middle class pass them at a run. You're the one who should have ambitions."

"I'm a lawyer in a town the size my parents farmed in.
That's a climb up the ladder. Zach can make the next rung if he wants."

"Night and Day, that's us." Mark stood, filling his suit pocket with his notebook, pad, and tape recorder. "I'll keep in touch on this, Gard. I can already tell it's going to be a major pain to solve. O'Brien's handled the biggest psychos and professional criminals in this part of the country. Whoever blew him up will have covered his tracks well."

"Try his current cases. Maybe one of them told him too much, then decided he couldn't trust O'Brien's lawyer-client confidentiality to keep his secrets."

"Good thinking. I will."

The rest of the afternoon and evening was an anticlimax to Mark's visit. No one else, even the journalists, was as dangerous to his half truths as Mark.

After the crowd left, Gard locked the house, cut on the answering machine for stubborn journalists, and concentrated on Desta. Even awake, she remained in a sleepy daze, her mind and emotions numb from the trauma of the explosion.

He fed her supper then watched her sleep the evening away as he made plans and listened, his pistol beside him, for the bomber who might come to finish the murder he'd botched that afternoon.

Pliant, vulnerable, and innocent as a child, Desta attacked his most basic defenses. His nurturing and male protective instincts were at war with his self-protective desire to avoid Lauton O'Brien's daughter, and his sexual attraction grew worse the more he touched, smelled, and saw her.

Finally, at bedtime, he dragged himself away as if her presence was a drug he'd become addicted to.

He kept her bedroom door and his open, and left Barkley with her on guard, then checked the house and its defenses again. When he'd moved in, realizing he'd left the agency but not old criminal enemies behind, he'd made this house's security tight. Getting in to hurt Desta wasn't impossible, but it would be difficult.

Knowing he'd done everything he could, he went to bed, his loaded pistol under his pillow.

Well after midnight, Desta's terrified shrieks woke him. Gun in hand, he ran to protect her.

Two

A bare male chest loomed out at Desta.

She blinked the sleep out of her eyes and stared at the object almost against her nose in bed. Bare? Yes, definitely, not counting the sprinkling of curly blond hairs. Male? Yes, very definitely male. A very nice male chest. Broad, well-muscled, no fat. It smelled very male too, musky with a whiff of Ivory soap.

A man faced her in bed, his upper arm draped over her ribs, his face so near her head that his peaceful, sleeping breath ruffled her hair. His legs were almost against hers, his leg hair scratchy against her smooth, bare legs. His body heat and scent surrounded her with a greater intimacy than his body.

His presence gave her goose bumps, hot fever, and cold shivers all at the same time, but they were a wonderful combination and only a little scary.

Who was he? The morning light was wrong for her bedroom. Where was she? How did she get here?

Lifting her head, she studied his face. Gosh, he was beautiful. Fairly straight blond hair, a lock tumbled boyishly across a wide brow, a squarish face with well-proportioned eyes, ears, and nose. His generous, sensuous lips seemed to smile even in sleep. The eyes too were just mature enough to have set smile crinkles around them.

Gosh, he was beautiful.

Fighting her inclination to explore his face with her fingers, she eased away from him to get a more complete look. He wore thin white cotton pajama shorts. She wore a man's baggy tee shirt. She was tall; he was taller.

All of him was beautiful, even what the pajamas only hinted at was beautiful. He was also sexy, that primal sexy that had little to do with looks, but a lot to do with male strength, assurance, and magnetism. Even asleep, he was... He was... Wow!

She didn't know who he was, or how she'd gotten here, and she was in bed beside him after a night of God-knows-what activity. He could be a kidnapper and rapist. He could have drugged her, and... She should shriek her lungs out in horror. She should bolt for safety. She should...

Of the emotions she felt, horror wasn't one of them. Most profoundly, she felt regret she couldn't remember last night. It must have been very special and mutually agreed upon. He had the face of a man frightened children would seek help from, not the face of a rapist.

She'd wakened surrounded by a sense of safety and security in his arms, and the feeling hadn't gone away even though she still didn't know where she was, who he was, and how she'd gotten here.

She was an intuitive person, but these feelings had to be more than intuition. They must have remained from the time she couldn't remember.

Slipping from under his arm, she sat up in bed.

The room belonged to a little boy. A *Star Wars* stuffed Ewok, plastic aliens, and the toys of Saturday morning advertisements filled the toy shelves with more traditional balls and books. A small slalom ski leaned against the wall. An elderly teddy bear sprawled on a nearby armchair; a young German Shepherd sprawled at the room's open entrance.

A framed picture sat on the night stand. In it her sexy stranger stood with one arm around a little blond boy as beautiful as he was. A striking Irish blonde with a laughing and loving smile shared the other arm. The little boy had her smile. Husband, wife, son.

Damn, a married man. Maybe she should shriek and bolt for safety.

"Good morning, Desta. Or perhaps I should say nice to meet you. I see you're back to normal." His head propped on his hand, he smiled at her. His eyes were the purest sky blue she'd ever seen, and deep and open with strong, honest emotions. She could fly around for eternity in wise eyes like that.

Remembering terror, she shivered and explored her hair. A good foot of it was gone, neatly trimmed off at the bottom of her shoulder blades. With a gasp, she covered her mouth with her hand. "The boat blew up."

"Yes, it did. Do you remember yesterday now?"

"Kind of. It's like I'm on the very top row of the balcony of a huge darkened theater, and I can see myself and you on stage, and I can hear the words, but it's not me I'm seeing."

"You've distanced yourself from the accident. That's only natural."

She frowned. She'd never considered herself a wimp or a person who couldn't handle reality. She'd handled her mother's death with strength. Why should a boating accident be any different?

As if completely open to her feelings, he chuckled. "It's not a defect in character. I've seen the same thing happen to hardened professional policemen and soldiers.

"It's like a very localized case of shell shock. Your mind and body knew you were safe and protected, and there was nothing they had to do so they numbed to let themselves heal. I'm complimented you felt that safe with me." His face changed suddenly, his eyes flickering over her enigmatically, and he sat up. "I guess I should get us breakfast. We can make plans later." He slid out of bed as if uncomfortable with her.

"About last night."

"You don't remember?" He smiled, the kindness she'd seen in his sleeping face awake and vivid. "You had a screaming nightmare about the explosion. I ran in armed to slay dragons and crooks, but didn't find any." He retrieved an automatic pistol from under his pillow and displayed it. "For a few moments, I misunderstood what you wanted from me, then I realized you just wanted to be cuddled and comforted like a child. I put a brake on my libido, and you fell asleep again, and so did I, still holding you. End of events." He turned and walked toward the door.

"Thank you, Gabriel. Thank you for everything."

"I promised your father I'd protect you, and that includes protecting you from me. I'll bring you breakfast."

She glanced distastefully around the bed. She'd been passive and shell shocked long enough. "I'll join you. I think I should clean up first."

Although he didn't turn around, she felt him smiling with approval. "There's a bathroom across the hall. Help yourself to what you need." He left, the bouncing, now wide awake puppy at his heels.

Half an hour later, she emerged from the bathroom and began to search for her human guardian angel. She checked the bedroom area. A mussed and very masculine master bedroom was at the far end of the hall, across from it a study. Another bedroom, obviously a woman's but not occupied at the moment, was across from the little boy's room. Her father had called Gabriel a widower. Who lived in that room?

Curiosity, definitely not jealousy, prickled her. She ignored it and strode through the living room. This was rather a pretty little house, neatly and competently designed for use, the furnishings attractive, decorated defensively with a young child and the casual, messy lake life in mind, but she liked the informal, almost Early American furnishings, which were both male and distinctive. A woman's hand showed too in the carefully tended, well-placed plants, and handicraft wall rugs. Who was that woman?

The living room blended into the dining room, which blended after a right turn into the kitchen, a kitchen bar separating the two areas. Gabriel, no, Gard, he preferred to be called Gard, sprawled in a chair at the head of the dining room table, a newspaper spread in front of him, a cup of coffee beside him. Already dressed in chinos and a white knit shirt, his chin freshly shaved, his blond hair combed, he shook out the paper in his hand and glanced over the top.

He grinned at her, a dazzling friendly smile that melted a good portion of her insides.

Her bare toes curled with embarrassment, she stopped at the foot of the table. She felt vulnerable and childlike dressed like this. The old but clean man's striped dress shirt had been hanging in the bathroom, and she hadn't anything else to wear over her tee shirt gown. Her wet hair hung around her shoulders, the tail of the shirt hung around her thighs.

"Cutting that hair was a sin, but I couldn't leave the burnt, singed ends on. The smell bothered you, and I was afraid someone would walk in and find you. A sleeping mistress I could explain away, a woman with burnt hair after a yacht had burnt..."

Uncertain whether she'd want to be explained away as a mistress, she fingered a long strand. "I'd intended to cut it anyway. I grew it long out of curiosity, and... You cut it?"

"Yes. I always cut Zach's. He hates the barber. I once worked undercover in a beauty salon, but that's another story. It's just a straight cut above the damaged hair. You'll want someone qualified to do a civilized job on it." He patted the chair beside him. "Have a seat and some breakfast."

"You did a very civilized job on it. Thank you." She took the seat, gingerly covering her rump with the short shirt. "You have a beautiful little boy. I've been admiring all those pictures of him in the hall."

"Thank you. He's at the beach with friends now." Gard poured her coffee. "Sugar, cream?"

"Yes, both." She folded her hands in her lap. Very polite social conversation seemed bizarre while wearing only a man's shirt, especially when you'd just slept, albeit chastely, with your fellow conversationalist.

He placed her coffee beside her. "How do you like your eggs?"

"Scrambled is simplest." She picked up her coffee, glanced at him, then hastily concentrated on her coffee after seeing the odd expression in his eyes. Was he laughing at her?

She kept her eyes down until he left the table then pulled over a piece of the morning paper.

Her father's picture jumped out at her from the front page of *The Charlotte Observer*. The headline read, "Lauton O'Brien Murdered."

The paper fell out of her numb fingers. "No!"

Some time in the dark horror and disbelief, she must have begun to cry because she found herself sobbing against Gard's chest, his arms holding her, his hand stroking her head. Strong, comforting emotions poured out of him into her like a healing balm.

"Don't cry, Desta. Don't cry. It's not true. He's not dead."

She clutched at his chest and his words. "He's not?"

"I swear he isn't." His lips brushed her forehead. "I shouldn't have let you see that until I explained."

Trying to regain control, she sniffed back tears. "He's not dead?"

"Would your hairdresser lie to you? He called last night after I cut on my answering machine. You can hear the tape if you want. People only think he's dead."

Her brain hurt with the same intensity her heart had hurt moments before. Reality had broken apart since yesterday, and nothing made sense any more. "This isn't Kansas any more, is it, Toto?"

"Welcome to Oz, Desta." He chuckled and squeezed her harder. "I've wanted to do this ever since you walked in acting brave and sophisticated but with those lost lamb eyes. Your whole world fell apart yesterday, and now you're as bereft of everything as a newborn child— your father and home gone, all the routine of your life vanished, even your clothes and possessions blown up."

Shocked he'd read her thoughts so completely, she nodded.

"I'll keep you safe, then I'll help you rebuild. That's what I'm here for."

He was a very nice man. Now she knew why her father had been so certain he'd watch over her when danger came. "None of this makes sense. He's dead on page one, but he's not dead? I'm not usually such an idiot, but I don't understand any of this."

"I've been lying like crazy to everyone but you since yesterday afternoon." He straightened away from her and came to his feet in front of her chair.

She brushed away her tears.

"Let me cut off breakfast. You'll be more interested in food later." He walked into the kitchen and removed a smoking frying pan from a stove unit. "Come with me." He led her into the living room to a sofa near the television.

She sat down and scrubbed at her damp cheeks again.

Gard plopped down beside her. "Your father knew that one day a crazy or angry client could decide he wanted him dead. He was especially aware of this danger with the organized crime types he's been so busy with lately."

"When I was a teenager, one of his clients was accused of being a rather sick rapist. The man was acquitted, but he was unbalanced and kept hanging around my house. Daddy had bodyguards for Mom and me for weeks. The father of one of the victims killed the man." She shivered.

"I've read about the case. No other girl was raped after he died. Your father didn't handle the father's defense; he couldn't afford your father's outrageous fee."

Gard's condemnation hung heavily in the air, but she didn't spring to her father's defense. "I love my father."

"And whatever he does, he's still your father. He loves you a great deal, too. He asked me to watch over you if that threat ever came. He was afraid you'd be killed to hurt him, or you'd be kidnapped to be used against him."

She nodded. "Yesterday, he came and told me to get to you as fast as I could and stay until you said it was safe to come home. He said he was going to disappear because someone wanted him dead, and he probably would never be back. He said goodbye."

"And you came. The boat didn't just explode. There was a bomb aboard. A bomb meant for your father."

She blinked, digesting that piece of horror, then shivered violently.

"Let me show you what I did." He flicked on the TV and VCR with a remote control. "I recorded the local six o'clock news yesterday."

On the TV screen, the Charlotte anchorwoman said, "Nationally prominent local defense lawyer Lauton O'Brien was killed today, apparently blown up aboard his yacht on Lake Norman. We switch you live to Lake Norman, and our reporter Blake Andrews."

The young black reporter gave a brief resume of her father's most important cases. Behind him, she could see the cove she'd peeked at through the curtains this morning. Several boats and divers were on the water behind him, and she could see debris from the yacht, but nothing of the boat itself.

Fighting a violent shudder, she hugged herself.

Andrews continued, "Gabriel Gardner, the eyewitness to this tragedy, has agreed to describe what he saw."

In a blue knit shirt and jeans, Gard nodded at the reporter and pointed toward the open water. "Dusty and I were..."

The young reporter snapped at the bait like a hungry trout. He glanced around. "Dusty? There was another eyewitness?"

"My German Shepherd puppy. Dusty and I were on the dock when O'Brien's boat turned toward our cove. The moment it slowed, the bomb exploded just below the water line. I swam out, but before I could find Lauton O'Brien, the flames from the bomb hit the boiler and gas tank, and the boat blew completely up. No one could survive that. The water was so full of smoke and burning debris I had to follow Dusty's barks to find the shore."

Touching his ear like he was receiving a message from the station on his earphone, the reporter asked, "Aren't you Gard Gardner of the Charlotte office of the FBI?"

"I am a former member of the FBI. I left the Bureau to start a private law practice on Lake Norman."

"Then you're absolutely certain it was a bomb. That's your professional opinion?"

"Speaking as a private citizen with that professional background, yes, it was a bomb. I'm certain of that."

"Then O'Brien was murdered?"

"It would seem so."

"I recall you two were fierce enemies."

"In the courtroom, yes, we were on opposite sides. I gave expert testimony against a number of his clients."

"Why was he here today?"

Gard grinned. "That is a question you should ask a psychic with a Ouija board, or investigating officers after their investigation of O'Brien. I have no idea."

Unaware he'd been led by an expert, Blake Andrews nodded, satisfied with the interview, and began to talk to the camera about the investigation.

Gard clicked off the VCR. "Quotes like that are in all the newspapers, too."

Her estimation of Gard going up a thousand times from its already high level, Desta shook her head. "That was brilliant, absolutely the most devious trick I've ever seen. You gave Daddy a safe escape because everyone thinks he's dead so no one will try to find him. You kept my name out of it, but at the same time, you told Daddy I was alive and well and didn't go up with the boat. I'm awed. Daddy couldn't have done any better."

Gard's cheek twitched as if he didn't like the favorable comparison to her father. "My first priority was your safety. If Lauton's home free, then you will be safer."

"You've lied to the authorities about me. Isn't that illegal?"

"I haven't lied, but I have withheld information. That's illegal."

She studied him. He wasn't the illegal type. She wanted to ask why he was doing this for her, but she didn't. Her feelings had come alive again since waking this morning, and most of them involved him. Already she felt a fragile, tenuous beginning between them that could become something enduring and loving. He must feel something, too. Why else would he risk his life and reputation for her?

"Then every thing's all right, and I can go home and back to work now?"

"No, first we check out the territory and talk to some people. It may be weeks before you can return to your own life."

She brightened. Being protected by Gard sounded rather nice. "You said Daddy called last night."

"Yes, I found this among all the calls from the journalists and gossips this morning." He walked over and cut on his answering machine.

Her father's distinctive voice boomed out, "Robbie, you sneaky bastard, bless you." He chuckled. "My love to your *dog* Dusty."

Gard flicked the recording off.

She rubbed away the goose bumps on her arms. "That was Daddy, all right. I'm glad he's fine."

"I wish he'd realized I didn't have that letter from him. I've got to find out who wants him dead. Until I know that, I won't be able to keep you safe."

"Why would they want me dead when Daddy's presumed dead?"

"I don't know, but until I'm certain you're safe, you're not getting out of my sight. We also have to remember your father might reveal himself inadvertently at any time, and the game will begin all over again at the beginning."

Trying to ignore the terror of still being a target after nearly losing her life the day before, she stood. "Well, I'm ready to get started. What do we do first?"

"First, we have breakfast, then we'll make some phone calls. After that, you and I are going to Charlotte to do some investigating. We need to talk to your father's partner, then we're going to interrogate the finest FBI agent in the area while he thinks he's interrogating us."

Her goose bumps reappeared.

~ * ~

Desta glanced toward Gard at the wheel of his car. Gosh, he was dashing in a dark blue suit. It did incredible things to his sky blue eyes and blond hair. Before he spotted her drooling over him, she forced herself to turn back to the passing scrub pines. He had an aversion to being gawked at for his incredible looks. She could understand the feeling. Nothing was more irritating to her than having her intelligence and talent ignored or belittled because she was attractive.

Not that she was attractive at this moment. She had a man she actually wanted to notice her looks, and she looked like a ragamuffin in borrowed overlarge pants and blouse. Letting her eyes linger for a moment on his profile, sun glinting on his blond lashes, she spoke with feigned casualness, "I hope your housekeeper doesn't mind my borrowing her clothes."

As if recognizing her subtle search for information, he chuckled. "I don't have a housekeeper. Those are my mother's clothes."

She froze the pleased smile before it reached her lips; she'd imagined some voluptuous housekeeper. "She lives with you?"

"When my wife Megan and I found out she was dying... Megan asked me to leave the Bureau for Zach's sake. I was traveling all the time, and it is a high risk profession. Zach was losing one parent, and we didn't want him to lose two. I quit.

"After she died, I found this place. I wanted Zach to have a small town upbringing, and the lake and everything. It was ideal for a little boy. My mother, Dad's been dead for five years, moved in to help me with Zach. The finances were rough, but I received a bit of a windfall. It took me over a year to study and pass the state bar, and I'll be opening an office in the fall."

"Is there much call for a criminal lawyer almost an hour out of Charlotte?"

"I'm a civil lawyer—wills, real estate, financial matters."

She beamed; she hated her father's branch of the law. "It must be a nice change helping people rather than putting them in jail."

"You understand my situation better than Mark does. He thinks civil law is boring."

"Your agent ex-partner?"

"Yes."

"Is your mother at the beach with Zach?"

"No, she's visiting friends in California. I was born in California, rural California." He stuck his hand in his pocket, pulled out a quarter, and gave it to her. "Retain my services as a lawyer."

She took the quarter. "I have a... Dunlap Dubois and Porter Alberts handle my..."

"Your father's legal people?"

"Yes."

"Your father pays them more money. Their loyalty isn't to you. Retain me. I'm on no one's side but yours."

She'd be handing him another chunk of herself if she took him as her lawyer. Well, if she trusted him with her life, she certainly should trust him with everything else. She offered him the quarter. "This is a retainer for your services."

With a nod, he put the quarter back in his pocket. "Now I have the ammunition for today."

"Legal services are certainly cheaper outside the big city."

"That was a one time only special for a very special client." He melted another chunk of her innards with a warm smile.

A prickle of doubt touched her. Could he be using her sexual attraction to control her? Well, she could always un-retain him if things got out of hand, and he'd proved trustworthy so far. He'd even refused to take her body when she'd been too numb to say no, and her feminine instincts told her he wanted it, if not the rest of her.

Glancing at his watch, he changed the subject. "I hope Barkley's behaving at the Johnsons. Their twelve-year-old girl adores her so she's probably having the time of her life."

"I'm head over heels in love with that dog myself. Would Zach rent her?"

"Afraid not. She already owns you anyway, or at least she thinks she does. She must have heard that Chinese proverb about saving a person's life. She already owns Zach the same way."

Desta chuckled.

"No, I'm serious. When she wasn't much bigger than she is now, she stayed between Zach and a copperhead snake that had crawled into the yard. Zach was determined to investigate it, and the snake had been badly injured in some nearby bulldozing so it wasn't leaving. She stayed between them and barked her head off for me until I came and shot it. She even nipped at Zach to keep him away."

"A very bright dog. Was she bitten?"

"No. After that, she gave up her role as youngest child of the family and became Zach's owner and guardian. She pretends to be his dog, but we all know the truth about the relationship."

Desta laughed. "Everyone needs a guardian angel."

"You have three—one celestial, one human, and one German Shepherd."

"And I need them all."

"Afraid so." Gard turned his full attention back to his driving. Even the far outskirts of Charlotte were crowded anymore.

She admired the sunny late morning sky and the smell of newly mown grass and pretended she and Gard were on a date. Harmless romantic fantasy was preferable to remembering someone wanted her father, and maybe her dead, and that at any moment another car could pull up even with them and blast away with guns.

"You're certain we can trust the head of security of this place you live in?" Gard asked.

"He'd not let journalists or anyone like that in. A well-
paying hood? Yesterday, I would have said he wouldn't, but now..."
She shrugged.

"You've seen Oz."

"Yes. Take a left up ahead. That will put us at the back entrance of Carolina Pines. Officer Battson promised he'd
be waiting for us there."

When they reached the back gate of the tall security fence that surrounded the property, James Battson was at the guardhouse. He walked up to the car.

Gard rolled down his window.

Battson tipped his uniform hat. "I'm sorry, sir. This is a restricted community. Unless I see a pass..."

Desta leaned across Gard. "Hello, Officer Battson."

Battson's lined, battered face lit up with instinctive pleasure then sorrowed. He hunkered down to car window level. "Hello, Miss O'Brien. I'm so sorry about your father."

"Thank you, James. This is my friend... and lawyer Gabriel Gardner. He's helping me through this mess."

Battson studied Gard. His eyes narrowed with suspicion.

Gard met his gaze. "It's legally registered. Would you care to see the card?"

Battson relaxed. "You're the ex-Fed."

"Yes, and you must have been one of Charlotte's finest."

"Retired." He spat into the grass. "They after Miss O'Brien?"

"I'm not certain, but I don't want to take any chances. Who's tried to get to her?"

"Newsboys with their fancy trucks and cameras. My people." He glanced at Desta.

Gard assured him, "We've got an appointment with the FBI in a bit."

With a nod, Battson motioned beyond the gate. "This is a top notch place, but a determined pro could get through."

"We won't stay. I'm keeping her out of sight until we know more."

"If you need me, call." Battson handed them a key. "The copy of the security key to your door you asked for, Miss O'Brien. You take care now, and come back safe." He tipped his hat at them and signaled for the security gate to open.

Desta waved goodbye as Gard drove through. "Did any of that make sense?"

"A good man. He spotted the slight bulge of my pistol in my shoulder holster. He probably would have spotted any phony journalists, too. Apparently, no one else has tried the front door approach."

"My people?"

"The local police. They were probably trying to reach you for the county people handling the boat explosion."

"Exactly how many law enforcement agencies do I have to lie to?"

"Mark promised to share his interview information with the others. You only have to lie to Mark. He's the toughest of the lot."

She grimaced. "Wonderful. Take a right up here."

Gard whistled with admiration when her condominium unit materialized out of the woodland landscape. The Tudor architecture gave the illusion of a large manor house rather than three condominiums. None of the other units were within sight in the exclusive complex.

"I'm on the far right."

Gard parked in the tiny lot on the far side. "Doesn't look like anyone's at home."

"Middle's a widow who's visiting her sister in Cannes. Left is a stockbroker with delusions of playboyhood."

"And you're not playing."

"I'm not into that kind of merging." She stepped out of the car.

His gaze taking in the surroundings, Gard paused at his door. "Looks safe. These things must cost a fortune."

"Afraid so." When his face hardened with disapproval or some similar emotion, she didn't add she'd designed this unit of the complex herself. "Come on in." She punched in the code that cut off her security system, unlocked her front door, and flicked on the inside lights.

Gard stepped in behind her and shoved the door bolt in. "Stay here." His hand on his holstered gun, he circled her living room, disappeared into her dining room and kitchen, then he headed up the steps.

A few minutes later, he came back down. His face had hardened a little more, another chunk of the emotional openness she'd begun to cherish gone. "No one's tried to break in. The house is safe. You have a lovely place."

"I think so." Smiling, she shifted nervously on her bare feet. Didn't he like antiques or her taste? "This will take some time."

"Take all the time you want." He plopped down in an armchair and picked up the most recent edition of *Town and Country* then tossed it down.

Because of the disapproval so evident on his face, she didn't tell him one of the houses she'd designed was featured in it. With a sigh, she went upstairs.

She changed into her own clothes, fixed her hair, and applied makeup, then packed a week's worth of clothes and necessities as Gard had suggested. Several items she paused over then threw in. Her life had changed completely in two days; who knew what would happen inside her in two more days? She opened her safe.

Inside, she'd always kept emergency items for her disappearance, but she'd been unable to come home for them yesterday. Fortunate for her since everything she'd had was blown up with the boat.

She tossed all the cash, her fake identification and passport, and the credit cards under her new name into her purse with the loaded pistol. Her hand settling down on the extra cell phone on her bed stand, she recalled Gard's warning not to bring anything electronic that could be used to track them so she left it where it was.

Pausing, she glanced around her bedroom at her cherished antique bed, her own paintings, and all the memorabilia of her life and her mother's. She'd only allowed herself a few pieces of jewelry and her parents' photograph, which she'd sewn long before into the lining of her suitcase.

Realizing she might never be back again, she sighed, locked her suitcase, picked it up with a dark raincoat suitably nondescript for hiding herself in, and walked out. She whispered, "Goodbye," and cut off the light behind her.

Shrugging off her grief and loneliness, she walked down the steps. She was not only walking away from the past and all her friends, she was also walking toward the future. Special things could wait in the future for her, too.

Standing in front of the Rembrandt portrait, Gard spun toward her when she came down the steps. His sky blue eyes glistened with pleasure at her appearance then began to harden until a polite stranger stood before her.

Dismayed, she stopped at the end of the steps. After being a barefooted ragamuffin since they'd met, she'd tried so hard to be beautiful and stylish to attract him. Her makeup was perfect, and she'd braided her long brown hair into a sophisticated knot down her back. Her silk dress was dark brown and businesslike yet feminine, her long legs was clad in silk, too. "I'm ready to go."

"You look nice."

"Suitable for a dead father and being interviewed by the police?"

"Yes, of course." He glanced back at the painting. "Is that real?"

"Yes, I inherited it from my mother. It's been in her family for five generations. She loved it a great deal."

"Yes, you are related to the Tylers. Maternal grandfather a two-term governor, great grandfather a Vice President, owners of a tenth of the state."

"Not so much, I imagine."

"The paternal branch of the family isn't exactly poor or unknown either."

Sensing condemnation, she straightened defensively. "They're my family. I didn't ask to be born into them, and I haven't made them ashamed of me either."

"No, you're a fine, strong, courageous woman. None of them would be ashamed." He took her suitcase.

She followed him out the door without looking back at what she was leaving behind. "I have your mother's clothes in my suitcase. I wish I'd had time to wash them for her."

Gard plunked her suitcase into the trunk beside his. "She won't mind."

Desta settled into the car. Tempted to ask what sin she'd committed, she glanced at him but held her peace. He'd been extraordinarily good to her out of his natural

generosity, and she had no right to demand more.

His silence intensified during the long drive through Charlotte to her father's office.

Ignoring her sense of loss, she concentrated on armoring herself for the coming hours. She only had herself she could truly trust now, Gard could leave any time, and she'd best do her best. Her father's life as well as her own hung in the balance.

Gard parked under the big oaks near the side entrance to the huge Victorian house her father had restored for offices. He spoke brusquely, "Let me get out first."

His eyes moving like a Secret Service agent's around the President, he stepped out of the car, then he opened her door.

Coming out of the car beside him, she took a deep, steadying breath. "Opening curtain."

"You'll do well. Break a leg." A breathtaking sexy and kind smile wreathing his face, he took her right hand in his left.

She smiled back at him, and they began to walk toward the office entrance.

A man stuck his head up over the bush by the door as his silenced pistol popped and flashed.

With a thrust of his left arm, Gard threw her backwards and stepped between her and the man, his own body going into a crouch as he pulled out his gun.

<h1 align="center">Three</h1>

Desta caught herself with her hands before she hit the ground, and pulled herself into a low squat behind Gard. Visions of him being shot blasted through her.

He trained his gun on the other man. "Get out of there. Keep your hands where I can see them."

"Sure thing, man." As pale as she felt, the young photographer crept out of the shrubbery, his hands up, his camera swinging around his neck.

"You fool. I could have killed you. Let me see your press card."

Her heart hammering with fear and anger, Desta rose and peeped around Gard's shoulder.

"You okay?" he whispered.

"Yes." She brushed off her dirty, scraped palms.

"I'm just a freelancer, man. Here's my I.D." The young photographer handed Gard a driver's license.

Gard glanced at it. "Well, Mr. Owen, you'd better get out of here, and I'd better not see those shots in the paper, or I'll find you. It's not healthy for Miss O'Brien or you for those photos to be public. Do you understand me?"

"Yes, sir." Owen looked properly submissive.

"And next time, don't do something like that, or you could end up dead." Gard returned his license.

With a nod, Owen trotted off. Gard didn't put his gun into his holster until the other man was out of sight. He wrapped his left arm around her shoulders, and she wobbled into the building with him.

They paused as the door closed behind them. "That was scary," she whispered.

"Very." He wrapped her in his arms and stroked her nape beneath the braid with gentle fingers. "I'm so sorry. I could have gotten you killed. I should have seen him."

"I looked at the spot, and I didn't see him." His heart whamming against her breast, she clung to him. "Don't you dare get yourself killed for me. I won't allow that."

With a chuckle, he rubbed his lips against her neck. "I have no intention of either of us getting killed."

Goose bumps spread down her back and arms from his lips. Lifting her head, she met his eyes. "No, I mean it. Don't you risk yourself. I'm not vital to anyone, but you've got Zach to think about. I couldn't bear for that beautiful little boy to lose you."

His nose bumped hers, their gazes locking like fused lightning bolts. "I meant it, too. I have no intention of dying."

Her breath caught as she felt the incredible primal pull between them, and she willed him to kiss her. If he didn't kiss her, her heart would shatter. She'd waited an eternity already.

His lips brushed sweetly against hers, his hands molding her to him.

A deep theatrical voice boomed, "Desta!"

Jerking apart, they spun as Dunlap Dubois trotted around the corner of the hall toward them.

With his premature gray hair, handsome forthright face, and long slender body, Dun was the embodiment of an aristocratic young defender of justice as he stopped in front of them. "What in the world? My secretary said there was some kind of scuffle outside."

Mentally cursing his bad timing, she brushed back her neat hair with shaking hands. "Hello, Dun. A crazy photographer scared us. He jumped out of the bushes. We thought he had a gun."

"You poor thing. And after everything you've been through." Dun hugged her. "I'm so sorry about your father. He was such a good man and such a good friend. I'm really going to miss him."

She stiffened, but let him pat her back in comfort. "Thank you, Dun. He thought of you as a son."

Dun draped his arm around her shoulder. "Come up to my office, honey, and you and I will talk about this mess."

"Have you met Gabriel Gardner? He's been watching over me."

Dun dipped his head stiffly. "We've met before. Hello, Gardner."

"Dubois." Gard nodded.

Dun turned his back on the other man. "Come on, honey. Let's talk."

Desta meekly walked with him, Gard trailing behind. "Gard has agreed to watch over my interests, Dun. I've retained him as my lawyer."

Dun's face fell as if she'd mortally wounded him. "Porter and I have always handled..."

"I know, and you've done a very good job. But these
are extraordinary circumstances, and I need Gard's legal and law enforcement expertise."

"He's not even a practicing lawyer yet, Desta. Certainly he's fine enough as your bodyguard. He deserves the money Lauton paid him. I thought so when Lauton hired him, but your lawyer..."

Hired to be her bodyguard! He wasn't a nice man after all; he'd just been hired as one of her daddy's flunkies. She'd nearly kissed her bodyguard. Her stomach tightened into a painful knot.

"Let's send him on his way. He's done a fine job taking care of you, but I can take over from here. We don't need him anymore."

She almost agreed, but something instinctive warned her not to give up Gard or his careful plans for her future. Whatever his motives, he was on her side, and she wasn't certain where Dun stood anymore. "He stays as bodyguard and as lawyer."

Dun sighed as if humoring a foolish child. "As you wish, Desta." He patted her shoulder. "I was surprised when my secretary told me you'd called this morning and were coming here. I spent most of last night trying to find you. Things must be settled."

They reached Dun's elegant, stuffy formal office. Desta took the big wing chair in front of Dun's giant mahogany desk, and Gard slipped in the chair beside her. She kept her eyes away from him so he couldn't read her uncertainty of him.

Twisting a brass unicorn paperweight in his hands, Dun stretched back in his chair. "We have to decide on a memorial service."

"A memorial?"

Gard interrupted, "The police divers are still searching for Lauton's body. Perhaps you should wait for a short time."

"Perhaps we should wait."

"As you wish," Dun said. "I thought it might be easier for you if we had the service."

"Who wanted Lauton dead?" Gard asked.

Dun shrugged. "I don't know. For obvious reasons, he remained silent about his more volatile clients. I wasn't aware anything was wrong until I found Lauton's note yesterday morning saying he was disappearing. He also said he was sending Desta to you."

"Yes, and I'll honor my contract concerning her."

"Your second installment is already in the mail. I sent it yesterday."

"Thank you. I'm sorry I'm having to earn it. Who are Lauton's current clients?"

"His secretary could tell you, but she's going over those files with the FBI. Desta, you really must see the police. They're most anxious to talk with you."

"I'm going to talk to the FBI after we leave here. I'm afraid I can't tell them any more than you have. Why would anyone want Daddy dead? Especially one of his own clients. I just can't understand it."

Dun shook his gray head. "Neither can I."

"Will there be any kind of problem with inheritance?" Gard asked.

"I really don't think that's any of your business."

"Please tell him, Dun. He is my lawyer now, too."

"Very well. Very simply put, Lauton arranged a living trust for Desta. He knew he might have to disappear, and he didn't want her inheritance delayed for years. He transferred a large portion of his wealth into this trust, which pays Desta a handsome monthly sum.

"At Lauton's death or disappearance, the control of the trust leaves me and goes to Desta. She should gain control in a matter of months. His personal possessions will have to go through the long legal process."

"The trust's mainly stocks and mutual funds," Desta added. "Daddy explained the trust and its contents very carefully."

Gard nodded. "I'm quite familiar with living trusts. May I see a copy?"

Dun glanced at her then nodded unhappily. "A copy will go in the mail tomorrow." His face softening, he turned to her effectively snubbing Gard. "Desta, honey, you and I must talk. At a time like this... I really believe you and I should follow your father's wishes. It would make him so happy knowing you're being taken care of, and you know how I feel about you.

"Please say you'll marry me. We can wait a discreet time after the tragedy, then we can begin our lives together."

Gard stiffened as if he were going to lunge at Dun then settled back so easily Desta wondered if she'd imagined it.

Coming to his feet, Dun pleaded, "Please marry me, Desta."

Blushing, she studied his handsome honorable face. "My feelings haven't changed either, Dun. Daddy's death changes nothing. I'm a competent adult. I don't need a keeper."

"It's not just that, honey. You know I love you."

Unwilling to say aloud she didn't love him and never could, especially not in front of an audience, she stood. "You're a dear man, but I can't marry you." Leaning forward, she brushed a kiss on his cheek. "Thank you for your kindness today, Dun."

"Where will you be if I need you?"

"We won't remain in any place," Gard said. "Until we're certain Lauton's killer isn't after Desta, I want to keep her out of harm's way. Leave a message with Special Agent Mark Faulkner. I'll remain in touch with him."

"Your ex-partner." Dun nodded. "Very well. You take special care of Desta. She's very precious to me."

"I intend to take very good care of her, Mr. Dubois."

"You are being paid for that, aren't you?" Dun smiled at Desta. "You listen to your bodyguard now, and nothing impetuous. Your father chose a very good one."

With a nod, she turned and walked swiftly down the hall.

Gard caught up with her at the exit and rested his hand on her shoulder.

Jerking away, she eyed him like a servant who'd forgotten his place.

His voice iced with reserve, "Miss O'Brien, don't go outside without my checking the territory. Someone besides a photographer might be waiting."

"Very well," she conceded, a tiny part of her heart aching at his coldness and her out-of-character snobbery.

His hand on his gun in his shoulder holster, Gard stepped outside.

Her heart lurched with sudden fear for him, and she almost followed him outside, but anger ruled her. She stayed, her face impassive.

Gard pushed open the door. "It's safe."

Her eyes warily studying shrubbery and bushes, she came outside and walked to the car. He opened her car door and clicked his heels like a royal coachman. His tone dripped ice, "Your Royal Highness, your carriage awaits."

She slid into the car.

As he drove through town, she kept her eyes on everything but him. Finally, she couldn't hold her anger in. She opened her mouth then closed it. One didn't bicker with servants.

"Your Royal Highness wishes to speak?"

Steam rolled out her ears, but she spoke coldly, "Why didn't you tell me you were my bodyguard?"

"I thought you knew."

"He never said... You're just a mercenary. Another of Daddy's paid flunkies."

Gard's cheek twitched angrily. "I wouldn't do anything for your father except for money. We aren't exactly friends."

"Why?"

"Money. I needed money. Megan was dead, I'd left the Bureau, and I had a little boy to support while I studied for the state bar. Your father offered me a fortune so I sold my soul to him. He wanted my integrity, and he bought it. It was very expensive."

Gard's knuckles whitened on the steering wheel, and he continued, "He wanted someone who couldn't be bought by his enemies and who could outfox anyone after your precious hide. I was perfect. He offered me a huge sum, half on deposit, half on the day you needed protection, to make certain you stayed alive. I also insisted upon a large life insurance policy on me for Zach in case I got killed. He'll be a wealthy orphan if I don't survive this."

"How businesslike of you to sell yourself for so much."

"What the hell do you know about needing money? You're just a spoiled, rich brat who's never had to work for anything in her life. You live off your shyster daddy's ill-gotten gains in your pretty little condo with its antiques and Rembrandt and let the world go by. How dare you judge me. You've never been hungry or gotten dirt under your nails like us peasants."

So he thought her one of the pampered idle rich, did he? Some judge of character he was. She'd tell him... She bit her lip. No, she'd tell him later and scrub his misjudgment in.

Instead, she changed the subject. "We're going to see Mark Faulkner next?"

"Yes, you'll like him. He's one of you—old money, prep and Ivy League schools, and a daddy who's a senator."

"Senator Faulkner? I've met him. A fine man."

"A better senator than father apparently. Mark's not that impressed."

"Movers and shakers rarely are good parents. They do a lot of good for people, but usually leave a wake of disastrous personal relationships behind them. They just don't have time for the private when involved with the public."

"Personal experience, Princess?"

Her heart lightened at his gentle tone. "Yes, personal experience. I had my mother though. She was very special. Many of my friends didn't have that."

With a nod, he became silent. The silence, contemplative rather than hostile, continued through downtown Charlotte, while parking the car, and into the Federal Building where the FBI had its headquarters.

As they strode down the corridors, Gard held her arm with a protective paternal air. Secretaries, coatless men with shoulder holsters, and forensic types all greeted Gard with natural warmth. The women's smiles were either maternal or contemplative of Gard's now single status. He had obviously been very popular and respected among his colleagues. All let them pass with only a word or two as if sensing Gard was there on business.

Finally, Gard pushed open an office door. "Knock? Knock?"

A sleepy voice responded, "Who's there?"

They entered the bland regulation cubicle. A tall, dark man of Gard's age sprawled at his metal desk, a file spread across his chest. His unshaven cheeks and bloodshot eyes were ample evidence he'd been up all night.

He yawned, spotted Desta, his brown eyes lighting up with sexual interest, and came to his feet with an athlete's grace. A dimple at his left cheek, a lock of brown curly hair over his eyes, he smiled. He was almost as astonishingly handsome as Gard.

"Hello." He held out his hand. "You must be Desta O'Brien. I'm Special Agent Mark Faulkner."

She shook his hand.

"And I'm Gard, your ex," Gard drily reminded him.

Mark dragged his gaze away from her face for the first time. "Hello, Gard sweetie. Get your alimony check from me?"

Gard chuckled. "Yes, I did. It wasn't enough."

"It never is." Mark's expression became serious. "I'm terribly sorry about your father, Ms. O'Brien. Thank you for coming in to talk with us."

Desta nodded.

"Please take a seat." Mark motioned at the chairs in front of his desk.

Clutching her purse in her hands, she perched uneasily in her chair although she schooled her face into calmness. Now was her moment of truth, or lies; she had to convince this professional her father was dead, or she'd be in deadly danger with her father.

Mark glanced at Gard. "You can leave now."

"Miss O'Brien has retained me."

"Ambulance chasing already? For shame, Gard."

"I prefer that to skirt chasing. I intend to see Desta protected in every way possible."

Desta started. Was Gard warning off his friend's amorous intentions? Well, that was one situation she didn't need protection from.

"I see." Mark's tone and expression were filled with multiple meanings only an old friend like Gard could understand. "Well, then, Ms. O'Brien, are you ready to answer some questions?"

"Call me Desta. Yes."

"Let's go then." Mark cut on a tape recorder, identified himself, told the date, time, and case subject. "Present are Desta O'Brien and her attorney Gabriel Gardner. Please identify yourselves and give your addresses."

Desta's voice shook slightly, but by the time Gard finished speaking, her heart had stopped slamming against her ribs. He had a calming effect on her when she wasn't furious with him.

"Do I have your permission to tape this interview?"

She nodded then added hastily, "Yes, you do."

"So much for the red tape. Ms... Desta, when was the last time you heard from your father?"

"Yesterday afternoon around one. He came to my office. He told me he was in danger, someone wanted to kill him, and he was going to disappear and might never be back."

"Did he say who wanted him dead?"

"No, he didn't. He didn't want to endanger me. He told me to go to Gard, Gabriel Gardner, who would protect me."

"Gard! Why Gard?"

"He knew he could trust him. If I couldn't find Gard, I was to find you."

"That's quite a compliment. Did he say anything else?"

"That he loved me and to take care. Personal things like that."

"Why do you need protection?"

"I don't know anything about his clients, but perhaps they don't know that. Or perhaps, they thought my death or a threat to me could stop or hurt my father."

Different possibilities shimmered in Mark's eyes. "Why to you, Gard?"

"Lauton O'Brien retained me to protect Desta over a year ago if this ever happened."

"Why didn't you tell me this yesterday?"

"I didn't think it pertinent. I don't want the information public either for Desta's sake."

Mark nodded. "We like to protect the victim's family's privacy. Desta, what happened after your father left?"

"I drove to Gard's home as soon as I could. When I got there, police were everywhere. I parked the car at a nearby vacant house and waited until they left. It was almost dark then. When I found Gard, he told me about the boat exploding, and I fell apart." Her face twisted with grief and remembered terror, and she swiped away a tear.

Mark's expression softened with sympathy, and he turned to Gard. "Why didn't you call me last night?"

"She couldn't help you, the shape she was in. I let her have some peace. She stayed in Zach's bedroom overnight, and this morning, she was ready to face all the questions."

"Why would O'Brien come to you after he'd sent his daughter there for safety's sake? He'd just be leading the killer to Desta. A smart operator like O'Brien wouldn't do anything so stupid."

"But he did," Gard reminded him. "He must have had some reason. Maybe he thought he was wrong about the danger and wanted to retrieve Desta."

"That makes a certain sense."

"I wouldn't be as concerned with that question as the others. I don't think the answer will help the investigation."

"Perhaps you're right. Desta, your father has mentioned no enemies?"

"No. He never spoke of his work. He knew I didn't approve of what he did, and who he did it for so he remained silent about it. He tried to explain what he did, but I've never really understood."

"What did he say?"

"He said it was the same reason some people keep poisonous snakes and spiders, an unhealthy fascination with dangerous, alien creatures."

Mark exchanged a knowing glance with Gard. "I think I understand. Maybe you need a policeman's mentality and experience with criminals to understand."

He examined his notes. "Let me check on my facts about you. You have a degree in architecture from my alma mater, Harvard, and you're a partner in the architecture firm, Designs Alive. Very prestigious."

She beamed at his approval. "Yes, I am. I'm been a successful architect for several years."

"I saw the layout in *Town and Country* of that marvelous house you did for Morgan Sprague. Quite impressive. With its style and proportions, you wouldn't know it was designed for a man in a wheelchair."

"It's quite a challenge making a house both beautiful and accessible. That's why I've enjoyed specializing in such houses. My greatest challenge has been to design a house for a family, all under five feet tall. Everything had to be scaled down, even the built-in cabinets, and at the same time I had to make it visually attractive and comfortable for their larger guests."

"Quite a feat."

He was flirting with her, she decided, and after a glance at Gard's stone face, she flirted discreetly back.

"You also donate time to design low income housing for various social organizations. You must have little time for a social life, Desta."

"I do manage to date on occasion, but I'm not attached. I'm also quite fond of water sports, music, and anything played with a round ball."

"Me, too." He opened his mouth as if to ask what she was doing that weekend, but glanced at a glaring Gard and the tape recorder and changed his mind. He studied his notes again as if to remind himself of what he was supposed to be doing. "You lived with your mother after their divorce. That was when you were eleven."

"Yes. I didn't become close to my father until my mother died five years ago." She shrugged. "He really didn't have the time for me. Mom's death shook him up enough so he started making time."

Mark nodded with understanding. "And you're your mother's sole beneficiary?"

"Yes." She smiled suddenly. "If you are trying to prove I blew up my father for his money, I'm afraid you're mistaken. Mom left me a great deal of money, and I'm successful in my business. Daddy also started a trust years ago for me. I gain little from his death."

"I wouldn't be such a plebeian cad as to accuse you of such a thing." Mark grinned innocently despite Gard's grunt of disbelief.

"Not without a good deal of evidence to back it up, I'm sure, Special Agent Faulkner. I suggest you talk to Dunlap Dubois on the matter."

"I fully intend to. Do you have anything else to add?"

"I don't think so." She met Gard's eyes for the first time. He shook his head no. "I guess I don't."

"Thank you for helping me. You're handling this situation remarkably well."

"Now, I'm handling it well. Later when I don't need to be coherent, I'll find a quiet corner and have hysterics." She sighed. "That's my way of handling disaster."

"If it works, don't knock it."

"How is your investigation proceeding?" Gard asked.

"Slow and exceedingly fine. I haven't been able to pinpoint O'Brien's location from the time he left his home yesterday morning. We have found his Cadillac parked at the marina where his boat was docked, but nothing else to indicate his whereabouts. It being a Monday afternoon, no one saw him or the boat leave."

"Any idea about the bomber?"

"Most of his ex-clients, the ones who aren't in prison, have up-to-date files. Some are dead, etc., etc. We're looking into the most promising. It will take time, but few seem likely. I'm more interested in his present cases.

"Hats off to your instincts again, Gard. You were right on that point. Presently, he has two clients of intense interest. Avery Martin for one."

Gard grimaced. "The Neo-Nazi leader. What a charmer."

"O'Brien was handling his conspiracy charges in the Fayetteville bombing. Martin is psychotic with a fondness for bombs. He looks very promising."

"But he's not subtle. He likes an audience for his mayhem. That bomb had been set to go off in deep water away from audiences. It was very subtle."

Mark disagreed, "You could pull back your throttle going out of the dock. Many do while maneuvering the boat out of the slip. How was the boat parked at the marina, Desta?"

"With its nose pointed out into the water." She winced at her quick answer. Had she given herself away?

Gard interrupted, "Have you tied Martin to yesterday?"

As if he suspected them of collusion, Mark glanced suspiciously from Desta to Gard. "Not yet, but we're working hard at it. We'd love to pin a murder rap on Martin. He's been a pain in the... The world would be a nicer place with him in jail.

"Our other suspect is Cal Ferret." He explained to Desta, "We have him up for racketeering and smuggling drugs. Since Florida's coast has become so patrolled, he's been using the Outer Banks coastline like

Blackbeard did, and he kills anyone who spots his people, or tries to testify against him. Nasty fellow."

Desta shivered. It was like having the choice between a man-eating tiger or a rogue lion after her, both men were deadly and determined.

"I'm keeping Desta with me," Gard said. "We can't guess what either of those will do."

Clicking off the tape recorder, Mark smiled intimately at her. "I'd volunteer for special guard duty myself, but I'm needed to chase down these two lunatics and figure out which one did it."

"Do that." Gard came to his feet. "I'll keep in touch."

"Do that," Mark agreed lazily, unperturbed by Gard's irritation at his flirting. He cut on a megawatt smile and took her hand. "You take care, Desta. Don't let him bully you. He's a terrible bully; the smugly virtuous always are."

She returned his smile. "I won't."

"I look forward to seeing you again in happier circumstances."

"I'd like that." She followed Gard out of the office. As they walked down the hall, she offered, "You're right. I do like him."

"He's never stayed with a woman longer than a month. He doesn't want a permanent relationship."

"How interesting, but people change. Thank you for telling me."

"I am being paid to protect you from dangerous situations."

"Mark's a dangerous situation? That makes him even more interesting." Her goading words surprised her. She didn't know why she'd flirted with Mark. He was extremely attractive, intelligent, and well-bred, but, emotionally frivolous, he lacked the special feelings she sought in a man.

She'd thought Gard had the special caring that denoted a passionate and great heart, but his passion had proved to be for her father's money, not her.

"I've never seen him do such a bad interview. He could have cut us to pieces half a dozen times, and he never went for serious blood. His hormones, not his brains, did that interview."

She glanced around the corridor, but no one was within earshot. "He seemed suspicious of us. Could he suspect?"

"Mark's suspicious of the sun coming up in the morning. It's his nature. That's why he's such a good cop. Don't worry."

Desta worried. Gard was deliberately glossing over Mark's reactions.

"Why was your father's Cadillac at the marina?"

"I drove it there. My car is in the shop, and Daddy insisted I drive his."

Gard made a considering "mmmm," but said nothing else as they passed through the back entrance of the building and walked along the shrubbery-lined sidewalk to the parking lot. "That was convenient for Lauton. His car at the marina, his boat blown up with no witnesses. Lauton O'Brien dies aboard his yacht, but he's not aboard.

"Could he have sent you out on that boat deliberately to give himself a convenient death?"

Red fury blurred her vision, and she jerked to a halt and swung at him.

Smiling grimly, he caught her wrist before her palm met his cheek. "I assume that means no."

"Don't ever say anything so vile about my father. He loves me." Angry tears burned her eyes.

"I hope so, Your Royal Highness. I hope so. But like Mark, I've learned to be suspicious of the sun's motives. I've personally seen the death and destruction a 'perfect' father or husband can do to the people he's supposed to love."

"Well, my father didn't." She yanked her wrist free.

He tensed as if jolted by electricity, grabbed her by the waist, and jerked her against him.

Plastered against his chest, she gasped and twisted trying to free herself. When she opened her mouth to protest, he clamped his hand over her mouth. She aimed a kick at his ankle with her heel.

"Be still," he whispered urgently. "We have a reception committee of goons waiting at our car."

She didn't jam her spiked heel into him. Easing her foot down, she gazed cautiously around his chest toward the parking lot. Two large men were near Gard's car, but they appeared innocent enough.

Gard jerked further back against the shrubbery. "Damn, they saw us. Let's get out of here."

They turned to retreat back into the building.

A large man stepped out of the building and grinned malevolently at them. With a brutal face of ax-hacked angles, he appeared anything but harmless, and he had them effectively trapped. He also had a gun pointed at them.

Bottling them in, the other men lumbered into the shrubbery-lined walk toward them.

Desta stared at the ax-faced man, the obvious leader. Nothing of compassion, humor, or love lived behind his inhuman slate eyes. Only cold. Her hackles rose as she sensed his dangerous reptilian alienness.

He leered, aware of her horror, and reached toward her with a meaty hand.

She backed into Gard's side to avoid him.

Gard glanced at the building they'd just left then grabbed her. In one quick movement, he picked her up in his arms and threw her over the waist-high shrubbery. "Run, Desta. Run."

Four

Surprised but clearheaded from adrenaline and panic, Desta landed on her feet, stumbling forward, then with a glance backward began to flee around the building toward the main entrance and help. They wanted her, not Gard, and maybe she could draw them away.

The sickening smack of flesh against flesh slowed her, and she turned her head.

Gard punched the ax-faced man, dived over the shrubbery, rolled, and came to his feet. He charged after her.

Ignoring the naked feeling of her back to the men's bullets, she ran as hard as she could so Gard wouldn't have to slow down when he reached her. Her heeled shoes built for elegance and comfort, not speed or cross-country conditions, she concentrated on the placement of each foot on the lawn.

So far, the goons hadn't used their guns, and she couldn't hear pursuit behind them. Maybe she and Gard were home free. She raced around the corner of the building.

A tall, chain-link, barbed wire-topped fence stretched from the side of the building, effectively trapping them.

"To the right," Gard called.

Hoping for an exit and not another dead end, she turned right angling away from the fence.

The sound of heavy foot tread behind them spurred her forward.

A tall, scraggly boxwood fence now blocked their path. One of the shrubs had partially died, the damage cut for regrowth, leaving a small hole.

The practical everyday portion of her brain thinking of ruined hose and dress, she shimmied through the hole then pulled it to let larger Gard through.

"Don't wait for me! Run, dammit." He pointed with his gun's barrel.

Following his direction, she darted across the narrow apron of grass toward the tree-lined street.

A bullet smashed into the tree beside her, bark flying everywhere.

Gard's gun exploded twice behind her. One of the pursuers howled with pain, then Gard caught up with her, his free hand catching her right, and he tugged her across the street toward the old storefronts renovated into specialty shops on the other side of the street. "We need cover."

No one else was in sight, the area deserted. Gard dodged past the Chocolate Shoppe and dragged her through the open door of The White Rabbit's Hole—*Children's Books A Specialty*. He slid and Desta staggered to a halt, her legs almost giving out on her. Slamming the door closed, he bolted it.

The proprietor, an elderly woman with bright red hair,
spun at their running entrance. She peered at them over her wire-rimmed glasses. "Gard?"

His gun at the ready, Gard glanced back at the door. "Alice, help."

With as much aplomb as her Wonderland namesake, Alice nodded easily as if this happened every day. "Through here."

She ushered them past neat shelves of brightly colored books to a hallway. "It leads out. He's in now. My love to Zachary."

Gard nodded. "Watch out for them."

"I'll lock myself in the office and leave the back door open to lure them out. Police?"

"Police. Bye, thanks."

"Come again," Alice told them cheerily as if they were regular customers when they charged away.

A bullet shattered the front door's glass.

Trusting Gard's supreme confidence in the woman who seemed well able to stay out of the goons' way, Desta trotted beside Gard down the long, neat alleyway behind the specialty shops. Four doors down, Gard stopped, glanced back for emerging goons, and knocked loudly on a metal security door.

The door swung open, and a man with a fat, rough face stuck his head out, regarded them with suspicion, and drawled in a thick country accent, "What you want, boy?" His eyes lit up with recognition. "Why, Gabriel, you old son of a gun."

"Trouble, Bubba." Gard motioned backwards. "Someone's after us."

"Come on in then, son. Come on in with that pretty little lady." Bubba swept open the door.

Desta darted through with Gard.

A bullet hammered into the door, but Bubba eased it closed as if things like this happened every day and bolted it shut. "That sucker's made of steel. Take a Howitzer to bring it down." He wiped his huge hands on the clean chef's apron stretched across his pot belly.

They were just inside a small restaurant kitchen. Pots boiled and simmered with interesting smells, but Desta couldn't identify any of the dishes in preparation. Her stomach rumbled with hunger; she hadn't managed to have lunch today. On a nearby preparation table was a menu with the unlikely name of "Bubba's Fine Swedish Food—We Cater" imprinted in elegant gold letters on it. Big Bubba looked more like a local tobacco farmer than a Swedish restaurant owner and chef.

"They'll circle back around and come from the front," Gard decided.

"Let 'em try." Bubba unlocked a cabinet, pulled out a sawed-off shotgun, and strode toward the dining room.

"These are pros," Gard warned and followed him. "Don't be foolhardy. Let me take care of them."

"Hell, boy, I was dealing with pros before your pretty momma had you. You take the left, and I'll take the right." He hunkered down in a little alcove on the right.

Desta trailed after Gard. The small dining room was empty of customers, the dozen tables cleaned up from the lunch crowd. With white linen tablecloths, candles, and elegant homey details, it was a charming place, probably popular with trendy area executives.

Wooden with a lattice covered glass window, the locked front door rattled violently.

"Get into the kitchen," Gard ordered and slipped into the small vestibule to the restrooms.

"I won't wait like a helpless mouse for them to find me. I'll stay with you."

Gard opened his mouth to protest, but the door shook with the loud crunch of someone's foot battering against it. Grabbing her wrist, he yanked her behind him. "Stay out of sight."

Scrunched into the space between his back and the front wall of the vestibule, she rubbed her wrist. She was getting extremely tired of him throwing and yanking her around, but now seemed a bad time to mention it.

Gard tensed, his gun hand going upright parallel to his chest in a marksman's stance, and he peeked around the door frame toward the front of the restaurant, then he jerked back.

Her heart whammed so violently with terror it threatened the structural integrity of her ribs. She whispered a little prayer to her celestial guardian angel for his human counterpart and her. Life had introduced too many sweet possibilities in the last two days, and she didn't want to die, and she especially didn't want Gard to die.

She added a quick prayer codicil of protection for Bubba the Swedish chef good ol' boy.

Someone huge battered into the front door. The door's window shattered.

Jumping, she fumbled around inside her purse. Until that moment, she'd forgotten her pistol. Her hand wrapped around its handle, and her finger found the trigger, but she left it camouflaged within the purse. She had no intention of surrendering meekly to the ax-faced man with his psychotic killer eyes or of letting Gard face him alone.

"Bubba, get back into cover, you idiot," Gard whispered loudly.

The door smashed open.

Bubba's shotgun blast was followed by its second barrel.

A whimper of panic escaped, but Desta remained still, her hand firm on the gun.

A pistol shot from outside followed the shotgun in quick succession, and male voices shouted on the street.

Gard peered around the door frame.

Silence was deafening and lasted a hundred interminable years while they waited for the goons' next move.

"They've gone," Bubba announced cheerfully and strode into the restaurant dining area and toward the front door.

"Get back!" Gard motioned toward safety, but he was too late.

A scuffle shook the room as someone attacked Bubba. A lot of someones. Furniture crashed everywhere.

Gard jerked back into hiding, shoved Desta into a corner, his body shielding hers, his gun at the ready, and waited for them to come to him.

She could feel sweat dripping down Gard's neck and the ragged whisper of his breath.

Someone finally came.

Gard spun, his body going into a gunman's crouch as he aimed his weapon.

The other gunman reacted as quickly, his body a mirror image of Gard's deadly ballet-like grace.

Both men froze, their fingers just squeezing the trigger.

Desta peeped around Gard's shoulder to see what held the men from firing. The other gunman was Mark Faulkner.

Mark unthawed first. With a grin, he lowered his gun. "Faulkner's rule number five—"

"Never shoot the cavalry coming to your rescue." Gard lowered his own gun. "What took you so long?"

"Even impromptu rescues take time. Lucky for you Peggy Altley lusts after your body and was watching you leave from the second floor, or we'd have never known." He peeked around Gard and offered a deadly lady-killer smile. "Hello, Desta. Nice seeing you again."

"Hello, Mark." Her hand slid away from her gun, and she pulled a hankie out, and daubed at the rivers of makeup and sweat running down her face.

Gard walked out of the vestibule. "You can let Bubba up, Al. He owns this place. He's on our side."

Three large men sat on Bubba's prone body in the midst of broken and fallen tables, chairs, and debris. They eased off as if dismounting an untamed lion and backed away.

Unscathed, Bubba stood and shook himself. "Must be getting old. Used to take four or five to do that."

She staggered to the nearest surviving table and chair, plopped down before her legs gave out, and took stock of herself. Her sodden hair had escaped her braid in places, what little makeup she had left was smeared, and her dress was ripped down the side and on the sleeve, but she seemed moderately intact, no major pain claiming her attention. She was alive and well, but damnably back to ragamuffin status again.

As her wet, hot body felt the air conditioning for the first time, she shivered violently and hugged herself. All was safe and calm now so she could have a private case of hysterics.

Distant police sirens moved toward them.

Mark pulled up a chair beside her and sat down. "There's our local brethren. Jose, you and Al go back to headquarters and report to Braggonier. Bill, go meet the police officers and explain the situation. Ask for suitable plainclothes liaison, if you would. It's time for questions to be settled for both parties. Now, Desta, could you—"

Bubba patted her shoulder. "Boy, leave this poor gal alone for a bit. Let me get some of Bubba's Swedish magic in her tummy, and something to drink, and she'll be ready to face all of you."

"Thank you." She flashed Bubba a grateful smile. "Could I also have some plain paper and a pencil?"

"Sure thing, gal." Bubba disappeared and returned with a pad and pencil.

Mark glanced at Bubba's threatening face and didn't press his luck or his questions. He turned to Gard, who'd folded into the other chair at the table, his head sagging with weariness.

Bubba placed water glasses and a big pitcher before them and glared at Mark as if to include Gard in his circle of protection.

With a sigh of resignation, Mark picked up his glass of water.

Gard lifted himself from his exhausted stupor. "Bubba, Alice okay?"

"Just fine, she stuck her head in a moment ago to check on you. Drink that water."

Gard drank his water.

Desta finished two glasses, then cutting off the outside world and remembering, she tucked the pad like an easel on her stomach and the table edge and started drawing. She'd just finished when Bubba set a plate of food in front of her. Her stomach grumbled happily at the wonderful smells. She flipped the pad face down on the table. "Thank you. What is it?"

"Ask that fellow of yours. He knows." Bubba smiled mysteriously and shuffled back into the kitchen.

Not knowing if she liked or disliked having Gard considered her boyfriend, she studied him shyly.

"My mother's parents emigrated from Sweden." Gard glanced toward the kitchen and whispered, "Bubba is sweet on Mom."

Remembering the elegant, beautiful blonde from the photos in Gard's home, she couldn't see his mother with Bubba. "Really? How does she feel?"

"She says she'll never love any man but Dad. Bubba is heartbroken. He's been a Swedophile since he married his first wife, a real Swedish bombshell in World War Two."

Amused at the idea of young farm boy Bubba in a wild romance with an exotic foreign lady, Desta grinned.

Gard tapped his plate with his fork tines. "The meat is *kalvrulader*, parsley-stuffed veal rolls, the vegetable pie has onions, caraway, chives, and bacon. I believe you recognize the carrots."

Her stomach rumbled for attention so she hastily gave it some *kalvrulader* with creamed gravy on it. She closed her eyes in ecstasy. Her taste buds had loved it, too. She sampled the onion pie with its flaky crust, sour cream, and bacon. Eighty zillion calories, but who cared? That was wonderful, too.

With as much well-bred daintiness as she could muster, she wolfed down her food. Near death gave one a good appetite.

Gard, whose appetite had been as good as hers, put down his fork and accepted a cup of coffee and a plate of cookies from Bubba. He stretched wearily in his chair. "Nothing like a good run with the hounds at your heels to improve the appetite."

She smiled her own thanks at Bubba for her own cookies and coffee. Her butter cookies were shaped like the letters "S," "O," and "U," and the thin circles beside them tasted like gingersnaps. She offered Mark a cookie since he hadn't been included in Bubba's largess.

Mark grinned taking an "O." "Thanks." None the worse for the long run after them, his hair in place, his skin unsweaty, and his suit morning fresh, he would make a perfect movie action hero—great looks and an unmarrable surface.

Gard didn't look a tenth as bad as she must, but he was charmingly human with his damp rumpled locks and his wrinkled suit. His gaze met hers, and she lost herself sailing into his blue sky eyes. She forced herself to break contact. Leaning across the table, she brushed near his ear at his left cheek with her finger. "You have a slight bruise here."

"He just barely connected with his fist."

His patience at an end, Mark demanded, "Who?"

"Him, I think." Desta handed Mark the drawing she'd done of the three men and pointed at the ax-faced man.

"Him," Gard agreed and stared at the picture. "That's incredible. Like a photograph. You didn't miss a detail on any of them. You even got the tallest one's mole."

"A good memory for visual detail's a necessity in my profession. It's not as easy as you think being one of the pampered, idle rich."

Gard winced at her jibe. "Touché."

Mark tapped one of the two goons. "I know him. He's minor league, freelance muscle. I'll remember his name in a minute or two."

He didn't have a chance. The Charlotte investigative people arrived, and the questions began. Letting Gard field them, Desta remained silent through most of the questions. From his professional background, he had a more complete view of their little chase than she. She only corroborated what he said, and offered her sketch as evidence. He skillfully avoided lying about her situation, but at the same time hinted strongly that this attack on them had been related to her father's murder.

"They were trying to kill me," Gard said. "All the shots were aimed at me. Either they thought Miss O'Brien was harmless, and I wasn't, or they intended to kidnap her. Either way, they were desperate to stop us. It takes desperation and gall to attack someone outside the FBI building."

"Why would they want her?" Mark asked.

"I don't know, but they aren't going to get her." As if in deep thought, Gard scowled at the table.

The questions continued. Fortunately, thanks to Mark's intervention and her excellent sketch likeness of the three men, she and Gard didn't have to go to police headquarters. When the police left, she excused herself, and with Bubba's safety pins, she salvaged her dress as best she could, combed and rebraided her hair, and wiped off the last smears of makeup. She doused herself with perfume to mask her stench and came back out.

Gard, Mark, and Bubba waited for her. Gard appeared more presentable himself, his hair and suit straightened as if he'd cleaned up, too. He came to his feet at her entrance.

Still sitting, Mark ogled her. "What a beauty you are."

She grimaced. "You'll never make it in politics. You can't lie with a straight face. Bubba, I'd like to speak with you." Taking his hand, she led him into the corner.

Bubba grinned at the other men. "When you've got it, you've got it." He gazed down at her. "What can I do for you?"

"I wanted to thank you for your kindness." She handed him Dunlap Dubois' business card. "This is my lawyer's card. Please send him the bill for all the wreckage. Get Alice to, also, for that broken window. Tell him it's out of Desta's account. My name's Desta O'Brien, by the way."

Bubba shook her hand with his giant mitt. "Bubba Henson. Thanks most kindly. It was worth it. Not often these day I have so much fun." His gaze flashed toward Gard then back to her. "You remember me now for your wedding. Swedish food for a Swedish groom."

"It's not that way between us. He's my..." She couldn't say "bodyguard" which made Gard a servant. "He's protecting me."

Bubba winked broadly as if he didn't believe her protest. "Sure thing, gal. He's a good man, be a good husband. I make a mean smorgasbord for a reception. You remember Bubba."

She brushed a kiss on his cheek and admitted, "Bubba I'll never forget."

Mark and Gard escorted her out of the restaurant and down the street toward Gard's parked car. She glanced nervously around the quiet city street. Like a young bunny whose mother had just explained predators, she could feel wolves, hawks, and foxes behind every bush and tree. Goose bumps slithered down her spine.

"Relax," Mark told her lazily although his hunter eyes studied the terrain. "They're in South Carolina by now."

"Sure thing," she replied with Bubba's disbelief. "What happens next?"

Gard examined the bushes for predators. "You and I are leaving now, and getting far away from here, out of target range before they find us again, and we're leaving the detecting to Mark in his infinite wisdom."

"Who won't leave a stone unturned," Mark assured her. "I have better plans for you than solving your murder."

Gard's gaze hardened as if he gave Mark wolf status. "Just do your job, and I'll do mine protecting her."

Mark beamed as if amused by the implied threat.

Weary beyond belief of being chased, questioned, and argued over, Desta said nothing until they reached Gard's car. He unlocked the passenger door and opened it for her.

As his back turned, Mark caught Desta's shoulder and pulled her into his embrace with practiced ease. His lips
blended with hers.

Too surprised to protest or jerk away, she let him kiss her.

It ended as quickly as it had begun. Freeing her, he murmured, "Take care, honey."

Stepping back, she resisted her urge to glare or hit him in his presumptuous teeth. Despite his obvious desire to sleep with her, he had meant that kiss more for Gard's reaction than her seduction. He'd coldly and secretly studied Gard during the whole supposedly passionate exchange. She shoved the car seat forward, his Machiavellian maneuvers beyond her comprehension at the moment, and slid into the back seat. "I'll sit in the back."

~ * ~

Gard forced his right fist back into a hand before he knocked Mark's teeth, or the side of the door in, and pushed the front seat back into position. He locked and closed the door, then nodded curtly to his former partner. "I'll call you."

Mark grinned slyly. "I'll wait breathlessly. Take care of the lady, will you?"

"I won't forget that's my job." He stalked over, opened his own door, and slid in without looking at either of them.

"And take care of yourself, too."

With another nod, he drove away. He concentrated on his rear view mirror, and busy city streets, until he was certain he wasn't being tailed, then he took the fastest route out of Charlotte and concentrated on putting as many miles between him and them as he could. Finally, even the crowded intrastate couldn't divert him from the knot of anger in his gut. He twisted the rear view mirror searching but couldn't find his silent passenger. Her Royal Highness was keeping a low profile. The knot twisted again. He was her bodyguard, not her damn chauffeur. Couldn't she even sit or speak with him?

No, she only communicated and socialized with Ivy League princes like Mark.

The knot twisted again.

Miles and hours passed. The last of the long summer day disappeared over the nose of his car and the horizon, and he realized he couldn't make his planned destination that night. Bone weary, he was losing both his protective edge against attack and his driving sharpness. He had to stop.

He parked by the office of a family-style motel in Whiteville and got out. This small town and motel weren't exactly suited for the royalty in the back seat, but he didn't think he could find a palace or a Hilton in this rural neck of the woods. He awaited her outrage.

She didn't protest. In a cozy little ball on her side, her magnificent legs curled almost to her stomach, she slept peacefully, Zach's pillow for naps under her head. Her bare toes curled, too. A run in her hose stretched sensuously from a hole at her ankle to her thigh then disappeared under her ruched dress.

Why did she have to look so damn sexy and waifishly innocent when she slept?

Tenderness and desire gouged at his insides, already made raw from anger. Grinding his teeth and concentrating on the anger, he locked the car door and stomped into the motel office, then stomped back out, and moved the car to their room.

Sleeping peacefully through his grumpy bear histrionics, Desta didn't wiggle. Gard grinned suddenly at that image of himself. To tease him out of bad temper as a child, his mother had always called him Grumpy Bear, and when history repeated itself in his child's behavior, Zach had become Grumpy Bear, Junior.

His anger relegated to minor irritating status replaced by weariness, he opened his motel room and flicked on the light, then returned to his charge. She'd had a lousy day herself, and maybe he could get her into bed without waking her.

He leaned toward her, slid arms under her shoulder and thighs, and lifted her.

As he stood, she sighed, her arms entwining around his neck, her body nestling comfortably against his. The scent of her gardenia perfume filled his nostrils. She murmured sleepily, "I didn't ask him to kiss me."

"I'm sure you didn't. A beautiful princess must attract lots of pushy princes... and toads."

"Lots." Her chocolate eyes glistened as sleep left them.

He stared into them, more tempted by them than by any piece of Godiva chocolate he'd ever craved. With a will of its own, his face bent toward hers.

Her lips parting, her face gravitated toward his.

"Mr. Lunderson, is your wife ill?" Ready to run for the police, the elderly suspicious-eyed desk clerk gawked at him as if trying to decide whether he was a nut, an adulterer, or a kidnapper-rapist with a drugged victim.

Desta jumped at his voice, her eyes flashing discreetly at the motel and the little man in the plaid vest. Yawning, she snuggled against Gard. "Are we at the hotel yet, darling?"

Gard glared at the little man. "You woke her! It's all right, honey. We're there. Go back to sleep now."

She rested her face against his throat. "See the kids again tomorrow. Can't wait."

"I can't either, darling," Gard assured her solicitously and edged through the motel room door as the clerk disappeared, disappointed by another dull married couple. Gard closed the door with his foot. "You're one heck of a quick study, Princess. You just saved our bacon."

"You're welcome." She examined the tiny hotel room from his arms.

"A married couple causes less notice than a man and woman with separate rooms," he explained, "and I can't protect you in another hotel room."

She made no comment about the shared room or its cheapness as he put her on her feet. Her hands over her head, her bodice tight against her full breasts, she stretched sleepily. "One minute we were in Charlotte, then poof, it's night and we're here. I must have really zonked out."

He'd spent the whole afternoon angry at her for being in the back seat and for not speaking to him, and she'd only gone back there to stretch out, and she'd been asleep the whole time. Somehow that made him even angrier. "I hope you can sleep tonight."

"I will. I could use another twelve hours. You look dead. I could have driven, too."

The friendly intelligence of her assessment made him nervous. He brushed back his hair. "When you've taken the driving lessons I've taken about avoiding capture, gunfire, and being run off roads, you can."

"Sign me up tomorrow. Sounds interesting."

She seemed sincere. She'd probably handle tactical driving with the same aplomb as she did everything else, even sharing a motel room with a relative stranger. "Let me get the bags."

When he returned, he dumped their suitcases on the bed by the door. She was in the bathroom. He went out and carried in the cardboard box of supplies, then fed quarters to the drink machine at the motel office.

When he came back in, she was sitting on the edge of the far bed. He plopped the cold drinks on the tiny dining table and locked the door, chaining it. "I hope you like ginger ale. I didn't think you'd want any caffeine."

"I love ginger ale."

"Peanut butter and jelly sandwiches are the only items on the menu tonight." He hauled out a loaf of bread from the box. "Fathers of nine-year-old boys carry them everywhere. I hope you find that satisfactory."

"Most satisfactory. After Bubba's rich meal, I'd prefer a sandwich." She stood. "Why don't I make them, and you can clean up."

With a nod, he retreated into the bathroom. He'd expected her to nervously start making ground rules about which bed was which, and how she expected to sleep alone, and he was to be a gentleman about it. Instead, she acted as if they were at a bloody tea party. He was the one acting like a blubbering, nervous virgin at an orgy.

Waiting at the table, she had the sandwiches placed on napkins at their dining chairs, their drinks beside the sandwiches. Her eyes didn't even widen when he sat down at his place, his suit jacket and tie gone, his shoulder holster still in place. She picked up a rectangle of sandwich and ate with relish.

He chewed on his sandwich then washed it out of the roof of his mouth with ginger ale. "You act like you enjoy that."

"I do. This is a real treat."

"Plebeian food for a change?"

"Calories for a change. Peanut butter is fattening, and even when I do indulge, the jelly is low calorie. Grape Smuckers is a treat." She smiled, bit, and chewed dreamily.

She was so calm and even-tempered he wanted to start a fight, he wanted to make her nervous, he wanted... His gaze flicked over her body. "You don't have an ounce of fat anywhere. I looked."

An eyelash or muscle didn't tremble at the innuendo. "There would be if I weren't careful. I spend most of my work week sitting down. Even a weekend of sports can't handle too many peanut butter and jelly sandwiches." With a long delicate tongue, she licked at a grape smear on her index finger.

He squirmed, his body reacting to the unintentional eroticism of the gesture. "Why don't you take a day off and play. You can afford it."

"I can, the firm couldn't, until recently. We've finally established a reputation, brought in some talented people. I enjoy work, especially the creative element. I won't leave it just to play."

"What would you leave it for?"

"I want children. I'd rearrange my work around that." She studied him with unnerving forthrightness.

"You're lucky you can. Most women don't have that choice."

"Megan worked?"

"She was a research chemist until she became pregnant with Zach. She quit then to protect him from side effects. She intended to go back when he started the first grade. She didn't have that chance."

"Life can be absolute excrement sometimes."

A swallow of ginger ale caught in his throat. When he stopped coughing, he agreed hoarsely, "Very adequately expressed."

"Where are we?"

"Whiteville, North Carolina."

"I've been through here on the way to the beach."

"Holden Beach. Your dad has a condo there."

Her placidity rippled a moment in her eyes. "How did you know that? It's a great secret."

"A... girl named Ginger told me. She was visiting me with your father, and she mentioned it to your father's displeasure."

Desta grimaced. "I didn't know she could complete a sentence."

"With great difficulty. She was trying to impress me with her intelligence and sophistication."

"You would be the type she'd like to impress. I'm sure Daddy loved the competition."

"He was rather... amused."

Desta twisted her head in question. "Did she?"

"Did she what?"

"Impress you."

"No. My tastes have never run toward mental and sexual bunny rabbits. I don't understand your father's fondness for them. Your mother obviously wasn't one."

"How do you know?"

"Beyond being a Tyler... You don't have an ounce of bunny in you."

"That's the nicest compliment you've given me. Thank you." She beamed at him.

A corresponding circle of warmth settled in his heart, but he forced himself to break eye contact. He picked up his drink and sipped. "Where is the condo?"

"Are we going to hide there?"

"We need to find your father. It would be insane to go after whoever's after us. We'll leave that to Mark, but we can even our own odds of survival by finding your father. He can tell us who's after us."

She shook her head. "No, we'll lead those people to him. Everybody thinks he's dead."

"If everyone thinks he's dead, why were those men trying to kidnap you?"

Her eyes widened. "They know he's not dead, and they wanted me as a hostage."

"Exactly."

"We still shouldn't lead anyone to him."

"Your loyalty is admirable, but wrong. Who will warn him they're after him if we don't?"

For a long minute, she ruminated over that question and her sandwich. "Very well. I'll show you."

Before she saw it in his expression, he staunched his sense of victory. He didn't give a damn about that pig Lauton's safety, but nothing on Earth was going to hurt Lauton's daughter, and something deeper inside than a desire to honor a contract motivated him. Even if she was an unattainable princess, he was her liege man, heart and soul.

"Which bed shall I sleep in?"

For a moment, he thought she said "whose bed." He bit back the "mine" that almost slipped out. He'd better control his libido with her, or he'd be in misery in such close quarters. "I'll take the one closest to the door."

"Barkley guarding the door." She grinned teasingly. The comment stung anyway.

She finished her peanut butter sandwich as if an exquisite pastry then began to lick her fingers clean with her tongue.

He shivered, his body reacting instantly to the sensual exploration of her tongue. She had to know what that did to a man.

Maybe she did know. The rich brat must be teasing him deliberately. She knew he couldn't respond because of his position so she was teasing him like a tiger in a cage.

As if she felt his burning gaze, she smiled like a child caught being naughty. "Sorry about the bad manners. I have a sweet tooth. I have a terrible time controlling my appetite."

His voice was hoarse. "Me, too."

She missed his sexual meaning or chose to ignore it. "Why don't you have the shower first. I'm certain you must be exhausted."

She'd offered him a cold shower so she had understood his meaning. He'd dearly love to strangle her spoiled neck. No, actually, he wanted to carry her to bed and make slow, gentle love to her. Cover her face and breasts with kisses, tangle his fingers in her long hair, thrust deep...

Definitely needing a cold shower now, he swiped at the sweat running down his neck. "Thank you." He grabbed his suitcase from the nearby bed and made it to the bathroom without letting her see how easily she got to him. She wouldn't receive that satisfaction from him.

When he came out of the bathroom, she was sitting cross-legged on her bed brushing her long hair, her eyes on an open *Newsweek* in front of her. She glanced toward him, stared a moment at the bare chest and legs exposed by his thin white terry robe, then forced her gaze back to the magazine.

He chuckled to himself. She wasn't exactly immune to him either. Let her take a cold shower.

"Bathroom's yours."

"Thank you." She retreated into the bathroom with her suitcase.

He cleaned his automatic, then placed it on his night stand within easy reach. Fluffing up his pillows behind him, he settled back against the headboard and picked up the James Michener novel he'd been wading through for the past few weeks. He waded back in.

Almost a chapter later, Desta interrupted softly, "Gard?"

She stood at the bathroom door, clutching a hotel towel around her bare breasts, thin pajama bottoms shadowing her long legs. Her hair cascaded seductively over her right shoulder onto her breast.

The white hot knot of desire, tenderness, and anger burned at him again. She was teasing him once more. He spoke coldly, "Stud service wasn't included in the contract, Desta. Forget it."

She gawked a moment as if he'd hit her for no reason, then bright red spots of fury appeared in her cheeks. He expected her to clobber him with the nearest available object or bolt back into the bathroom, but she did neither.

Advancing to his bed, she handed him a bottle of hydrogen peroxide and a cotton ball. Although the fury had not faded in her cheeks, her voice was regally calm. "I can't reach the cut on my back. Would you please do it?" Turning, she perched on the bed beside him, her bare back to him.

Cursing himself and her, he said nothing and saturated the cotton ball. He paused before daubing at the long cut that ran from her left shoulder blade to her armpit. "This is infected! Why didn't you tell me?"

"I've been called a whiny rich brat enough today, thank you." When he patted the cut with the peroxide, she didn't wiggle or complain although it must burn like the devil.

"This is my fault. I never did get this cleaned completely yesterday. Between dodging the police and..." He couldn't say he'd been afraid he couldn't keep his hands off her so he'd stayed away.

"Quite all right. I'm certain that wasn't in the contract either."

He winced at the brittle hurt in her voice. "I'm sorry, Desta. I had no right to say what I did. I've had a bad day, but I shouldn't have taken it out on you."

"I had the same day you had." She started to rise off the bed, but he caught her shoulder.

"Stay. I want to do this again." He explored the central plane of her back with a careful finger. "You had some mild burns..."

"I don't feel them. Just that cut."

He stared, but all he could see was the graceful curve of the sexiest spine he'd ever seen, the beginning curve of her breasts peeking from the towel she clutched so desperately, the pale shadows of her firm buttocks through her pajama bottoms, a slender neck still stiff with hurt and aloneness...

He wanted to comfort her in his arms and tell her he wanted her so much he was going crazy, but he knew he couldn't have her, and that knowledge made him even crazier. He wanted to say he'd felt the same fear and anger as he'd felt when Megan was dying when those men had tried to take her away from him, and he hadn't wanted to feel that ever again, and that fear had made him even angrier.

Instead, he daubed at the cut. "I've admired your savvy and courage all day. You've handled everything remarkably well from lying to Mark to being chased across Charlotte by a bunch of hoods. You've acted with as much calm as a professional would. I have nothing but respect for you."

"Thank you." Desta's neck didn't relax. "I don't need to pay for stud service. I had offers today for marriage and a fling from two handsome, intelligent, successful men. I've had considerably more offers than that." Standing, she faced him, her expression impassive. "But since you're always so eager to sell yourself for the right price... You are very tempting with such a lovely son to prove your stud qualities, and you're so pretty. If I ever change my mind about a stud, you and I can discuss a new contract."

She ruffled his hair like he were a pet and strode into the bathroom.

He gawked this time, torn between anger and admiration at being so thoroughly retaliated against.

Five

Desta stirred restlessly in the car, glanced at the House of Pancakes where they'd just eaten breakfast, then back toward Gard who stood at the phone booth, the phone at his ear. In his white tennis shorts, sky-blue knit shirt, sunglasses, and Reeboks, he looked like just another hunk on the way to the beach, not an armed bodyguard. He nodded to accentuate a point then hung up, bought a *Charlotte Observer* from the stand at the front of the restaurant, then slid into the driver's seat beside her.

Ignoring her, he frowned and fluffed open the paper.

Wonderful, he was heading into another foul mood. Since yesterday morning when she'd wakened beside him in Zach's bedroom, he'd gone from a kind friend to a cold stranger to an insulting grump. She couldn't understand him, and she wasn't certain she could stand him much longer either. Last night, she'd tried so hard to be agreeable and friendly so they could at least be civil together, but then he'd said that ugly thing without provocation, and with that O'Brien temper of hers, she'd stabbed right back. He'd been dispassionately businesslike ever since.

The loneliness and the fear were far worse without that kind man beside her; she'd missed him desperately since he'd gone. All she asked for was casual friendship, not his bloody hand in marriage. Couldn't he give that much of himself, or wasn't that in the contract either? She smiled brightly, determined to keep being nice to him until he thawed. "Any news from Mark?"

"Bloody hell!" Gard stared at the front page.

Leaning toward him, she examined newspaper pictures of her with Gard. They were standing by his car, smiling at each other, holding hands. The other photo was slightly blurred. Gard was pulling out his gun, his eyes blazing, her form almost hidden as she fell toward the ground. She whispered, "Bloody hell." The headline under the photo said, "Lauton O'Brien's Daughter Chased by Armed Gunmen."

Gard swore again. "I hope the photographer has life insurance for his survivors. I'm going to kill him if I get out of this alive. That photo makes us ten times easier targets than before." He shoved the paper toward her. "Read it to me. I'm getting us out of here before someone spots us." He pulled his clip holster from under his shirt at the small of his back and tucked the gun into the seat beside him, then started the car and maneuvered out of the lot.

Smoothing the paper, she studied the pictures. In the first photo Gard's eyes were filled with kindness; she looked like a lovesick adolescent. "Story on page one of the local news." She found the local news section and glanced over the story. "The story is pretty bare bones. You and I were chased by three armed gunmen from the Federal Building to Bubba's where they tried to shoot their way in. The intrepid FBI came to our rescue.

"The reporter asks Mark if this has anything to do with Daddy's murder. He says, 'It is a possibility that someone believes she has dangerous information her father may have been killed for, but I'm absolutely certain Ms. O'Brien has no information. We questioned her extensively, and she was quite honest with us on this point.' He goes on to say the investigation is progressing nicely. What does that mean?"

"He hasn't learned a damn thing. Well, Mark tried to cover our tracks although he couldn't fool a nun with that assurance of your innocence."

"But it's the truth."

"The fact someone's after you refutes it to the general reader, and the gunmen won't believe it for their own reasons. How does it describe me?"

"Handsome, gallant... It doesn't."

"How did it describe my relationship to you?"

"You 'accompanied' me to the Federal Building. It points out you witnessed Daddy's murder, and you used to be an agent. Nothing more."

A short tight laugh caught in his throat. "That photo says it all."

Recalling her infatuated expression, she blushed.

"It shows I'm guarding you, and I'm wearing a piece."

"Oh, you mean a gun. Well, after yesterday, they know all that anyway. You shot one."

"Yes, but no one else did. Your father has more than one enemy. Most wouldn't have given you a second thought, but now they will. Someone believes you have valuable information, and now the others will, too. They'll come after you. As an ex-agent with close ties to the Agency, I make you even more tempting. They'll think I'm protecting you for the Agency because of information you have."

For a moment fear overwhelmed her, but she struggled back onto rational solid ground.

"But maybe that first photo will throw them off." He scowled. "It gives the false impression we're involved with each other."

"They'll think you're smitten with my face and forget us."

"As well as your great body, legs, and perky ponytail." He caught her ponytail and trailed it gently through his fingers in an almost caress as if comforting the terror she couldn't quite hide. "You're a lovely lady, Princess."

He fished around in his shorts pocket and brought something out in his fist. "I wanted to give this to you."

Surprised by the present, she blinked, and held out her hand. He dumped the contents into her palm. It was a necklace with a chubby black plastic disk and sturdy, cheap metal chain. She paused, trying to think of a compliment for such an ugly present. "It's charming."

His sky eyes flickered with lightning surprise as if she'd said something strange and unexpected. "It's a homing device. Megan's parents gave it to me for Zach last Christmas. He wears it when he's outside. It has a range of half a mile. With my tracking device, I've found him when he's been stranded without wind on the sailboat."

"Oh."

"I want you to wear it. Don't take it off for anything. If we get separated, it could be our only link."

She slid it around her neck and tucked it under her shirt. The disk, warm from his body, rested just above her cleavage.

Gard caught her left wrist, pulled it toward him, and glanced down at her fingers. "Where did the wedding band come from?"

Her pulse accelerated the moment he touched her. Afraid he'd feel her sexual reaction, she pulled her hand away from him. "It belonged to my mother. We're a married couple. I wanted to be authentic."

"Nice touch. The small touches make a lie believable. I hadn't even thought of that." He lifted a much nicer golden chain with a gold wedding band on it from around his neck and handed it to her. "Unstring it for me, please."

"You still wear your wedding ring?"

"You don't stop loving someone when they die. I knew it was time to go on with my life so I stopped wearing it on my finger, but I don't think I'll take it off completely until a woman matters enough to spend my life with her. Megan wanted that for me and for Zach."

The wedding ring burned her fingers. Inside the band were the words "Always, Gabriel" and a date almost twelve years before. Desta's throat caught painfully, and she handed him the ring and the chain. "She sounds very special."

"She was." He slid the ring on.

Hurting inside, she turned toward the hot, dry landscape outside her window and fought her desire to cry.

The flat, straight two-lane intrastate stretched blandly ahead of them; flat, cultivated farmland planted in cotton and soybean extended beside them. No one else seemed to be going to or from anywhere, the road empty.

Almost an hour later, Gard's "damn" jerked her out of her contemplation of the coastal landscape and the dire
possibilities of the dangerous future. She spun around.

Gard motioned toward the huge bridge, which arched over the Intracoastal Waterway to Holden Beach. "I'd forgotten it's an island. Is this the only way out?"

"Except by boat. It has one marina I know of. Plenty of private docks."

"That's splendid. Absolutely splendid. It just about makes my day."

"What's wrong?"

"One way in, one way out. A few men on the end of the bridge and at the marina, and they'd have us trapped. We're driving into a deathtrap."

Her hackles rose as she remembered being bottled in by tall shrubs, the ax-faced man with killer eyes reaching toward her. "No one could possibly know we're here. We've told no one but Mark."

"If we thought of this place, someone else must have. Your father couldn't keep this place much of a secret."

"All the Gingers couldn't be discreet. They aren't the type." She paused. "Take a right at the end of the bridge. His condo is a good distance down."

Gard scanned the end of the bridge for watchers then followed her directions. They turned onto the two-lane highway that bisected the long, narrow island. "All the Gingers?"

"He's always had a fondness for the type. Even before Momma divorced him. I'm older than the average Ginger now, and he still collects them." She looked past Gard at glimpses of the Atlantic, the water the hazy blue-green of a sunny June morning. Tightly packed shore front houses, and his profile stole most of the view.

"That must be difficult for you."

"I try to ignore them. I refuse to come down here when he's got company. He keeps them away from me. Momma couldn't ignore them. It hurt her; she's a Tyler through and through."

"Pride."

"No, heart. Momma's people are very emotional and loyal. They fall deeply in love and stay that way. They don't divorce, they don't play around, they don't play games with people's emotions. When you're a Tyler and love a man who has none of those values, you're in deep trouble."

"You have surprising perspective on your parents' marriage."

"When Momma found out the cancer was winning... You know how that gets. She wanted to give me everything she could because she knew she wouldn't be there when I needed the advice. She wanted me to find the right man so she told me about her own mistakes."

"What did she say?"

"To physically hold off sex until I found a man who made my body light up inside; to emotionally hold off love until I found a man who could do that and make my heart light up, too, to hold off marrying until I found a man who could do all that and who could honestly return my love and our children's."

"Wise advice, but there aren't many people like that."

"No, there aren't."

"Which are you, Tyler or O'Brien?"

"A bit of both. I like to think of myself as a Tyler. I hope I am one emotionally. I've got Daddy's temper though."

"His sharp tongue, too."

His amused rather than angry reaction to last night's insults eased some of the intolerable tension inside her. She smiled cautiously in response. "I'm not very good at this game you all play—moving people around like chess pieces, pushing emotional buttons just to see them react. You, Daddy, and Mark play that game with such clever ease, but I can't."

"I don't play with people's emotions, Princess. I can lie and manipulate with the greatest of ease for a good cause, but I don't try to hurt anyone, especially not you."

She wanted very much to believe him, she wanted to tell him she trusted him and that she was afraid and alone and she desperately needed a friend, but she didn't. He could still be playing games like he had last night, and besides they were almost at her father's condo. "Take a left past that gray multi-gabled house ahead. His condo unit is the second one." He followed her directions, but kept going past the condo. "You missed..."

"I know." He turned into a deserted house six doors down and parked as much out of sight as he could under the pilings that lifted the house above the beach and the waves, which rushed underneath it during storms. "We'll go in on foot in case the place is being watched. They won't be watching the beach front." He clipped his gun holster into his waistband at the small of his back under his shirt and slid out of the car.

She got out and smoothed her tennis shorts and pink shirt, then readjusted her tennis visor's band under her high ponytail. Her dark sunglasses completed her face's camouflage.

"Take what you need out of your purse, and we'll lock it in the trunk. You'll look conspicuous with it."

Since she didn't have a holster, her gun would have to stay in the purse. "I guess I don't need anything. I'm afraid I don't have keys to the condo. I always borrowed them when I needed them."

Gard locked her purse into the trunk. "I came prepared for the problem." He held out his left hand. "Ready?"

"Yes." They climbed the steps under the house up to the porch then down the wood walkway that extended across the dunes in front of the house to the beach, then down the steps again onto the beach.

The tide was low, the long white beach smooth and hard. No more than twenty people were in sight, mainly small family groups with young children. A Golden Retriever, a dirty tennis ball beside it, helped one of the children dig a hole. A jogger moved away from them at a steady pace.

As they strolled down the beach like a pair of newly arrived tourists who couldn't wait to hit the sand, Desta stared longingly at the ocean, which rolled in just a few feet away. "I'd love to get my feet wet."

"Me, too." He squeezed her hand. "It would be fun just to play in the surf, build a sand castle. I guess I've never really had my heart in adventures. I'd rather do normal family stuff than chase criminals."

"Or be chased by criminals. I build a good sand castle. I'd like to build one with Zach when all this is over."

"He'd like that."

A light wind from the ocean ruffled her ponytail and the blond lock across Gard's forehead.

He tensed slightly, all play gone, as they approached the steps up to the condos. Gazing upward as if trying to peer through the dunes themselves to the lower ground beyond, he dropped her hand. "Up we go slowly."

She followed him as he walked with seeming casualness but with the caution of a stalking cougar. When they reached the top of the steps and were on the walkway, he studied the four balconies of the ugly block of condo units. No one was on them, and pulled blinds gave them the appearance of being unoccupied.

"Which one?" he asked.

"Top floor left. We go up the steps from inside the hallway."

His gun in hand, he entered the dark entrance between the two bottom floor units. The other open entrance to the front parking lot was empty. He crept forward. With a sudden dart he leapt into the stairwell, but no ambush awaited him.

Sweat running down her neck, Desta stayed at his back. She'd never dreamed she'd ever be terrified walking here where she'd strolled dozens of times before.

As they reached the second floor, Gard paused, his eyes checking all corners, then knelt in front of the apartment door. He holstered his gun and brought out a small plastic kit from his back pocket. "Lock picks. Watch the entrance to the stairs."

Her back to him, her eyes on the stairs, she asked, "Isn't that an unusual talent for a federal cop?"

"Federal cops get training in this. It's surprising how handy it is." The lock went *snick*, and he pushed the door open. "With search warrants, of course."

"Of course. I own this place now, or will soon. You have my permission."

"Thanks." He pulled her in quickly and locked the door behind her. His gun out again, he crept toward the kitchen. "Stay."

Her back to the door, she stayed until he returned from checking the kitchen and two bedrooms.

"No one has been here for some time."

She sniffed judiciously at the stale air and cleaning solvent odors. "It smells empty. Maybe a month. What now? He isn't here, and hasn't been."

"We look for clues to where he could be. Where would he keep papers?"

"In there." She led him into her father's bedroom.

Gard glanced around at the fashionable pastels of the furniture and the brighter splashes of art posters some decorator had foisted off on her father, then went to the Swedish modern desk and began to rifle the drawers.

"Why didn't we do this to his office or his house in Charlotte?"

"Mark got them. Besides, a smart operator like O'Brien... your father wouldn't leave anything there. Here's the place he'd be careless. This is his retreat, his private place."

She examined the intense curve of Gard's neck as he bent over his task, his face a study in concentration. Seriousness roughed away the boyish handsomeness and left strong character and classical symmetry. He would age like that, character replacing youth but taking away none of his beauty.

With that honorable face and straightforward blue eyes, he wouldn't betray her because of that precious contract, but she wasn't fool enough to believe the contract extended to her father. Gard wouldn't have included him in the deal for any money, especially if her father's safety might cause danger to her. Neither man would. Whether Gard could accept it or not, her father loved her and wouldn't risk her life for his, nor would he have wanted Gard to.

She couldn't betray her father either. Would helping Gard find him be a danger or a help? Certainly her father would read that article in the paper and understand the implications. Yes, and he'd try to find her to protect her so he'd follow Gard's trail. Knowing how she detested emotional games and considering her incompetent at them, he would expect her to meekly help Gard find him without question. So she should help Gard because Daddy thought she would so...

Her temples ached with the quandary. She would help Gard find her father. Was it because of all that circular logic about devious men, or because she was so drawn to Gard? Her head throbbed again.

Leaving Gard to his treasure hunt, she walked into her bedroom, opened her medicine chest, and took some aspirin, then raided the kitchen refrigerator for drinks. She walked back into her father's bedroom and put a cola by Gard, who sat at the desk, his head in his hands, studying the letters and other loot from the desk.

"Anything?" she asked.

"I don't think so." He tipped his head in thanks and sipped the canned drink. "Financial junk mail mainly, a few personal letters."

"Daddy loves high finance. It's as devious as the law."

"The law isn't devious, only some lawyers."

"Whatever." With a sigh, she knelt at Gard's feet at the desk.

His shocked expression showed that considerably fewer woman had thrown themselves at his gorgeous feet than she'd expected. "Move over please." When he complied, she crept under and probed the desk with her fingers. Finally, she found the indention she was looking for, pulled out the hidden drawer, and plopped it on Gard's laps. "Here. I figured he'd have one of these."

"How did you..."

"When I was a little girl, he had one at home in his study. I discovered it during my junior spy period when I was about ten."

"Zach's just starting that." His surprise changing to clue lust, he began to sort systematically through the papers she'd given him.

Perching on the end of the bed, she consoled herself with the sugar in her cola.

"Desta, who's Adam Rountree?"

"Don't know."

"Your father has his credit card slips, some brochures for resorts addressed to him, things like that here. All addressed to a post office box in Charlotte."

"Let me see." She studied the address on a MasterCard bill. "That's where Sarah Winslow gets her mail."

"Who?"

"I'm Sarah Winslow. My credit cards and... Is this in confidence between me and my lawyer, or between me and ex-agent Gardner?"

"Your lawyer, if you prefer."

"I prefer. Daddy had a fake passport made for me and got credit cards under the name Sarah Winslow as part of my exit plan if I ever had to disappear. I use the cards occasionally, and Daddy gives me the bills later. They come to this post office box."

"Then Adam Rountree must be your father's new identity." He stood and shoved the papers into his pants pocket. "We should go, we've been here too long already."

"I'm ready, my captain."

He circled the apartment and peeped through cracks in windows. "I don't see anyone, but they could be hiding. Stay behind me until we reach the beach."

Pulling out his gun, he jerked open the door, peeked out in both directions, then sidled outside, reconnoitering the hallway in both directions, then motioned her toward him.

She closed the door behind her and followed him into the stairwell. His body humming with a hunter's intensity as he listened, he paused, then crept down the steel steps. She mimicked his quiet placement of feet, but hers thudded with each step.

Stopping at the stairwell's door, he listened and concentrated again as if his senses were radar, then he stepped into the open.

He jolted to a halt, grabbed her in his left arm, and melted into the tiny alcove of the caretaker's supply room.

Plastered against Gard's side, she couldn't see anyone, but she could hear men's leather-soled shoes where only tennis shoes and bare feet normally trod. They walked from the street parking lot toward them.

Her heart lurched with terror, and she pushed harder against Gard to take up less space. This alcove didn't really shield one person, let alone two.

His lips touched her forehead in a message of comfort and reassurance, then he seemed to forget her, his radar tuned to the approaching feet. Lifting his gun, he waited.

A man chuckled, the soft amused sound of a cat who'd trapped a mouse and was ready to kill.

Her hackles rose as she recognized the cold essence of the ax-faced man.

Gard's pulse fluttered wildly in his throat, but he remained still. She was supernally aware of him, his woodsy cologne and sweat, the way their bodies meshed perfectly, her breasts against his chest. The distant ocean whispered and surged with Gard's pulse, the salt air tasted of his skin.

She prayed urgently, "Don't let us die," then concentrated on the approaching feet.

Miraculously, the gunmen paused before reaching the alcove and turned into the stairwell. They stomped upward, unconcerned about noise.

Her breath caught and trembled, and she fought her desire to bolt.

Gard waited thirty seconds then peeked outside. "Now."

He ushered her out of the alcove, his hand clamped on her shoulder as if aware of her panic. They walked swiftly out of the building. Gard glanced up at the empty balconies, then at the empty walkway to the beach, and urged her forward.

Needing no urging, she kept fast pace with him, her back warm with imagined bullets heading toward it. Her legs shook going down the steps to the beach.

His gaze examining every family, teenager, and dune for an enemy, he sauntered casually toward the edge of the water. "We're going to jog now back to our car. Slow and easy. We'd be too obvious even from a distance if we run." He started to jog.

Matching his easy stride by concentrating on not running like a scared bunny and not staring about wildly for enemies, she even managed a smile at a five year old in pigtails who was demolishing the sand castle she'd just finished.

Gard ran four sets of steps past the house where their car was hidden, but she'd learned enough of his methods not to point out his mistake. Slowing to a walk, he trudged in the softer sand to the fifth set of steps, and climbed. Almost at the top, he leaned forward and crawled up onto the walkway. Belly down, he peered toward the house where they'd stashed their car. He whispered, "There," and pointed at a dune just beyond the house.

She crept up beside him and studied where he'd pointed. Finally, she saw a man in a white shirt and dark pants hunkered down in the dune, his gaze on their car. She whispered, "One?"

"One. I'll take care of him. Come." He slid under the railing and jumped four feet to the dune below. She followed him landing easily in a crouched position. "We'll get close, then I'll take him. You stay hidden."

"You need a diversion. I'll give it to you." She picked up a battered welk shell. "I pitch in softball."

Their eyes met, all arguments silent, but when hers didn't waver, he nodded as if defeated by her logic and determination. "You provide the diversion then hide. If I go down, you make a run for it. That's an order." He gave her the car keys.

Sticking them in her pocket, she nodded meekly and followed him as he began a devious hidden path among the dunes, and under the other walkways toward the gunmen at their car, but she collected considerably more large shells than needed for a diversion.

Halfway up a dune, Gard slid awkwardly in the loose sand to avoid the cutting edges of a stand of sea wheat and hit sand burs instead. She couldn't hear, but she could feel him swearing as he jerked his hand away. He plucked a bur out of his left palm and sucked the wound.

She grimaced with sympathy and slid into the sea wheat. Her bare ankle sliced with tiny blades, she cussed in eloquent silence but kept pace.

Almost at the crest of a dune, he paused, then crept upward on his hands and knees and motioned she follow him. As she crawled upward, the hot sand seared her bare hands and knees. They paused near the top. Just below them at the crest of a much shorter dune, the gunman waited in ambush. On his stomach, he peered over his own dune at their car just beyond him. Swatting at a fly on his neck, he revealed a pistol in his right hand.

Desta recognized him. He was the biggest of the goons from the parking lot the day before. Gard was big, but this man carried sixty pounds and half a foot more on an average gorilla's frame. Her heart landed in her stomach at the thought of Gard taking him on in unarmed combat. She was all for shooting him in the back now. It wasn't sporting by male standards, but it made perfect sense by pragmatic female standards when one of the males was hers. She touched Gard's arm and mimed shooting the other man.

Gard, bless his fellow pragmatic heart, shook his head no regretfully, and pointed toward the condos then at his ear as if he feared the other men would hear the shot and come running.

He pointed at her then mimed tossing to the left of the gunmen, then motioned to himself and pointed at another dune to the man's right. When she nodded understanding, he caught her wrist, glanced at her watch and his, then pointed at the next five minute segment past the present 1:10 and mimed tossing again. She nodded again, and gave him a thumbs-up and a big smile for luck.

His eyes flashed with warmth, and he caressed her cheek with his right finger tips, then he was gone.

She shifted her shell ammunition into comfortable range of her right hand and waited.

The dunes were miserably hot, the ocean breeze blocked by higher dunes, the sun directly overhead. Sweat streamed down her face and body. She swiped carefully to keep it out of her eyes.

The sand flies found her bare legs and ankles.

As they bit, she twitched miserably, but fought her desire to swat and glanced at her watch. A minute to go.

Below her, the gunman remained still, patient and comfortable in his role of professional hunter. From Gard's dune, a large ghost crab sidled toward the gunman, its stalk eyes studying the unmoving hulk as if it were a dead whale washed in by the sea. Its claw reached toward the bare flesh of the man's arm and pinched.

The goon jerked and spun. Man and crab eyed each other for a long moment.

Desta covered her mouth to hold back an hysterical giggle.

Swearing, the gunman smashed at the crab with a massive fist. The crab dodged and took off toward Gard's hiding place.

Bent on revenge, the goon scuttled after him on his knees. He stopped in mid-lurch, his gun aiming, not toward the crab, but higher. He'd seen Gard!

Sitting up, she hefted the welk and threw it against the gunman's head.

Dazed, he touched the blood trickling down his temple.

Gard leapt down onto him.

Bashing at each other with fists, they grappled and swayed in the sand, then the gunman swatted Gard's chest. Gard went down.

The goon stood, his foot raised to crush Gard's face.

Desta beaned him with another shell.

Roaring with fury, he pulled out his gun and aimed it at her chest.

She ducked behind the ridge as Gard kicked the semiautomatic out of the man's hand. When she peeked back over again a few moments later, both men were rolling in the sand at the top of the ridge as each tried to hit the other. Gard had technique and skill, and the gunman didn't, but with his gorilla size he didn't need it. He casually took the punishment Gard heaped on him and bashed back.

They fell over the sharp incline of the dune toward the house.

She collected her remaining ammunition and charged over the top of her dune, down across the earlier battleground, and up the gunman's dune.

On their feet Gard and the gorilla circled each other in the smooth sand below the house. The gorilla swung, and Gard dodged. If the massive gunman ever really connected with Gard, he'd go down completely. When Gard punched him, he barely flinched.

Heaving like an asthmatic, the goon swung again. Desta clipped him in the back with a shell. He jumped, and Gard punched him in the jaw. He staggered but didn't go down.

Below, where both men had fallen from the dune, Gard's automatic rested, its barrel buried in sand.

Gard deserved all the noble, brave words one usually heaped on a fair damsel's champion, but he seemed to be getting nowhere with King Kong. It was time for the damsel to even up the battle.

She dove over the dune and did a forward roll.

Gard must have seen her because in his moment of inattention, the gorilla smashed him backward into a wood piling and the steps into the house. Gard's body twisted as he hit.

His pained intake of breath was more terrible than a scream, and he just lay there.

Chuckling, the gorilla picked up a weatherworn board used for cleaning fish.

Gard pulled himself upright on the steps with his hands then struggled to stand, but his left leg seemed broken. His hand
sought the gun that wasn't there in the small of his back.

The big man swung at Gard's head.

The board exploded in his hand, and he stopped in mid-swing.

Both men gaped at Desta and the gun in her hand. She didn't know which one of the three of them was more surprised. The gorilla grunted unhappily and surged at her.

Ready to put as many shots in his middle as she could before he tore her apart with his bare hands, she aimed and began to squeeze the trigger.

As he charged, Gard reared back on the steps and kicked him in the leg. The bone cracked, and the gorilla fell. Gard punched him in the jaw on the way down.

The other man didn't get up; he didn't move.

Tucking the gun in her waistband, Desta ran to Gard and knelt by him on the steps. "Is it broken?"

As if groggy, he shook his head and explored his injured leg. "Dislocated knee."

"I hope that means I can move you. We can't wait around here after that gunshot. Can you get in the car if I help you?"

"Try."

She wrapped her right arm around his waist and his left hand around her shoulders. They swayed upright. Gard hopped on his good leg toward the passenger side of the car. His face turned powder white under his tan, and an awful catching groan escaped at each jolting hop, but he kept going. They paused at the door, and she released him to open the door.

"Lucky shot. Thanks," he offered in a careful approximation of his normal voice.

"Lucky, hell." She shoved the passenger seat back as far as it would go to keep him from bending that knee too much then tilted it back. "My cousin Billy Bob taught me how when I was eleven, and I keep it up. Killed more targets than you have. Take you on any day."

"Oh." The sound was more of agony than understanding. Clasping the car frame above the window, he eased himself into the seat.

With a glance back at the unconscious gorilla, she knelt and cradled his legs into the car.

Tears streaming down his cheeks, he groaned and thrust his head back against the head rest.

"Sorry." Blinking her own tears, she closed the door, rushed around to the driver's side, and slipped inside. Her hand shook so badly she almost didn't get the key into the ignition.

As she backed out into the street, he studied the road. "I don't see anyone."

"I'm getting us out of here before they figure out we're gone, then I'm getting you into a hospital. Shallotte has a good one."

"No. Stop before you get to the bridge. See if there are guards."

"Okay."

She concentrated on the road and the rear view mirror, but couldn't see any form of pursuit. Finally, she turned into a real estate company's lot that offered a good view of the bridge.

Gard pulled out some small binoculars from the glove compartment and studied the other bank of the bridge. "Damn!"

"Are you sure?"

"Tuesday, I put a bullet in the man leaning on the blue Ford."

Lifting the binoculars, she saw a man who wore a sling and a sour expression. She remembered his ugly face, too. Another man sprawled in the car. "Can we get past them and make a run for it?"

"We might get off the bridge, but they can stop us in the empty countryside before we reach Shallotte."

"Well, boats are out. You couldn't handle the jostling."

"They'll have that covered anyway."

"How stupid of me. I can walk right into that real estate office and call the local sheriff and an ambulance."

"Cal Ferret operates his drug ring in this area. The local cops could be in his pocket. We can't trust any of them." Gard's head sagged back against his headrest, and he closed his eyes.

She fought sick panic. No way off the island, and no one here she could trust. One group of goons in front of her, another behind her, and her professional guardian angel nearly unconscious. She was very alone.

<h1 style="text-align:center">Six</h1>

Hopelessness nearly overwhelmed Desta.

Glancing over at Gard, she remembered promises she'd made yesterday to a little boy in a picture. She couldn't give up; she had his safety as well as her own to think about. What to do? What to do?

Billy Bob's name resurfaced in her memory, and she grinned suddenly. She might be alone, but she wasn't alone. There were people in the world she could trust, and memories she could trust, too.

When the car began to back up, Gard sat up. "What?"

"I'm getting us out of this mess." She turned onto the main road and headed back in the direction they'd just come from.

He opened his mouth to protest, then closed it as if too weak to argue, but he began to watch for the enemy on the road around them.

Although on the same slow two-lane road the ax-faced man was on, they were heading in the opposite direction from what he expected them to travel, and they were in a ubiquitous steel-gray sedan like eighty million others. He also expected Gard to be driving. She prayed for another
miracle of escape.

Her hands clinched the wheel as the miles crept past. Finally, when she didn't think she could bear more tension, she turned into a small residential road toward the Intracoastal Waterway. It was just as she remembered it. Four houses down, a tiny gray beach house stood out like a shanty among its more expensive unoccupied neighbors. Smiling, she drove under its pilings to the hidden garage behind. No one could see their car now from the road.

She cut off the engine.

Gard straightened. "Desta?"

"We'll hide here." In the half-darkness of the garage, his white face glowed with pain and shock. She brushed damp sandy hair out of his eyes. His forehead was cold. "I'll be right back. I need..." Her hand slid to his thigh.

He lifted his hip to let her take his clipped holster, but she took his lock pick kit instead. He blinked with surprise. "You just can't..."

"I'll be back in a minute."

"You can't break into a strange house, Desta. Someone could be there. It took me bloody weeks to learn to use those things. Desta..."

Walking up the back steps to the house, she let him rave. That might keep his mind off his knee and the killers behind him. Reaching the back porch, she knelt at the door and opened the pick kit. She'd never used these things before, but... She chose two long slender picks with a tiny hook on their ends and probed. After several careful probes and twists, the old lock went *snick*, and she opened the door.

Exploring the shabby bedroom-living room, tiny bath
and kitchen, she found the expected elderly folding wheelchair nestled in a utility closet by some well-used fishing tackle. She pulled it out and opened it, then rolled it out of the house and down the opposite side of the porch to a wheelchair ramp.

The ramp lead into the garage. She blinked a moment at the darkness. Gard had hopped out of the car and was clinging to the rail of the steps. He spun reaching for his absent gun, but stopped when she rolled the chair over to him.

"Thank God. I thought you'd..."

She felt mean seeing his concern for her, but she wasn't quite ready to tell him everything. "Look what I found. Isn't this handy!"

Holding him at the waist, she helped him into the chair. "Is the leg better bent or straight?"

"Straight."

When she lifted his damaged leg onto the chair leg, he gasped with pain, and shook his head as if fighting passing out. She belted him in then began to back the wheelchair up the ramp. Even with its gentle slope, he was a heavy passenger. Her legs ached with strain and tension when she finally reached the flat porch area.

A surprised grunt escaped when he saw the open back door. "How in the..."

"Thanks." She handed him his lock pick kit. "That made it so simple."

"I've been had. You have a key."

"I didn't have a key, Princess' honor. I opened it with your kit."

"Then you have the speed of a professional cat burglar. An architect, Princess?"

She backed him over the door sill, relocked the door behind her, and rolled him to the double bed. "Let me get you cleaned up and in bed."

"Dirty, me?" He ruffled his hair, making sand fly everywhere.

Laughing, she made a quick journey to the bathroom for comb, wet cloths, and towels. She also cut on the decrepit window air conditioner. When she returned, Gard had pulled his shirt off, and leaned forward raking sand out of his hair with his fingers. "Here." She knelt beside him and offered the comb.

He studied her a moment through his hair, his eyes intense, then accepted the comb.

As he combed, she daubed away the sand stuck on his sweaty face then down his neck and shoulders. Dark bruises were already appearing across his arms and chest. "Do these hurt?"

"The ribs seem whole, and no internal damage, but I'll feel these tomorrow. Let me do that." He took the cloth and rubbed briskly where she'd only daubed.

She untied his Reeboks and pulled them off, leaving piles of sand on the wood floor, then toweled his legs and feet staying carefully away from his injured knee. Eying his shorts, she decided to leave them on for several reasons. "Let's get you stretched out."

As she pulled back the bedding, he unhooked his seat belt and slid-hopped from the wheelchair into the bed. His face was as white as the pillow he rested against.

"Do you know what to do to a dislocated knee?"

He shook his head.

"Me neither. I guess I'll treat it like a bad sprain." Ten minutes later, she'd covered him with a sheet, dosed him with arthritis-strength aspirin from the medicine cabinet, poured more water into him for shock, had water boiling to warm a hot pack, elevated his legs by raising the lower half of his mattress with the letters "A-G" of the 1968 *World Book Encyclopedia*, and wiped his sweaty brow several times.

Finally, she couldn't avoid splinting his leg any longer. As she brought out the wood slats and Ace bandages she'd found and knelt by his leg, he studied her with the hunter eyes, which had followed her since he'd stretched out. He appeared no happier about what she was going to do than she did.

Breaking eye contact, she examined the leg. The knee area looked... wrong. On some TV show she'd seen, two men had relocated a shoulder of another man, but they'd known what they were doing, and she didn't. She'd best leave it as it was for more competent types.

She put the slats on both sides of his injured leg.

Sitting up, he held them tight as she taped them on with elastic bandage. His voice was hoarse with restrained agony. "Tell me about your life as a cat burglar, Princess."

As much to keep her mind as well as his off how she was hurting him, she told him. "When I was ten, I believe I've mentioned my famous junior spy period, I found the neatest book in Dad's library. It was called *Lock Picking and Housebreaking* by one of Daddy's ex-clients. The book was dedicated to Daddy who got him off with only five years."

Gard sucked in his breath in pain as she tightened the bandage around his knee area. "Standard reading for a federal cop."

"It was magical stuff for a junior spy. My cousin Sheila Tyler and I worshipped it. We collected nail files, letter openers, and whatever else we could find, and applied ourselves as only ten year olds can for most of a summer. Nothing in our houses was safe. We opened doors, windows, security boxes, files... We didn't steal anything, just snooped. Unfortunately, Momma caught us one day practicing dismantling the burglar alarm, and..."

Gard chuckled. "Your life of crime ended."

"Abruptly." She grinned at him. "The book was thrown away. However, the skill remained. It's like riding a bicycle. The memory stays in your muscles. Over the years, I've opened locked car doors and houses when the key was missing. Those picks sure make it easier though. I'll have to get a set."

"I know a legal source if you promise not to use them like you did today."

She almost told him the truth about the house but didn't; instead, she hooked the bandage closed. "Done. I'm sorry I hurt you, Gard."

"Thank you, Desta. Thank you for everything. You saved my bacon a dozen times, and I appreciate it. You also risked your own neck to do it and disobeyed orders. Don't do that again. I'm here to keep you safe, not vice-versa."

"I'll obey you when I can, but I won't let you get killed. That's not in my contract."

"Desta," he said as if starting a long lecture on the proper behavior of a guarded person.

"I made a promise to a picture of a little boy named Zach that I'd send his father home safe again, whatever contract the father signed. I don't matter as much as that promise to Zach."

Gard caught her hand, but his eyes refused to meet hers. "You matter to me."

Pulling away, she retreated toward the kitchen. "Oh, do you get a bonus if I come out of this alive?"

"Desta!" He sounded genuinely shocked.

Retrieving the hot pack from the hot water, she wrapped it in a towel then returned and placed it gently on his knee. "I hope heat helps."

Pulling out the gun from her waistband, she headed toward the door.

Gard jerked upright. "Don't... Where are you going?"

"I'm going down to the car. I need my purse. Then I'm going to cover the car with a tarp to hide it even better. After that I'm coming back up, and I'm going to call for help. There's a working phone in the kitchen."

"Good. Mark'll take care of things. He'll watch over you while I get my damn knee fixed." He stretched back out.

She nodded noncommittally although she had no intention of calling Mark Faulkner.

"Take care outside."

"I will." Hardening herself inside and opening her senses like the hunter she now protected, she lifted her gun, peered out the door, and stepped out.

~*~

Desta replaced a warm hot pack with a hot one then stretched wearily, rubbing her neck. Sprawled on the big bed, one arm across his eyes, the other across his bare chest, the fist knotted, Gard didn't move or open his eyes during the process, but she sensed he wasn't asleep. He hadn't been able to sleep all afternoon. Every time he drifted off, he wiggled just enough to make his knee flair with pain.

He looked bad, his color and eyes pale, his skin sweaty despite the elderly window air conditioner chugging away nearby. She'd been lucky to get some canned soup in him an hour before. He really needed a doctor. When would help come?

Fighting tears, she breathed shakily. If something should happen to him…

"Princess?" Peering at her from under his wrist, he studied her with those kind hunter eyes.

Swiping at her cheeks, she smiled. "Just a mild case of post-disaster hysteria."

"You deserve more than a mild case. We both do. I never had such a lousy, dangerous day in years as an agent."

"You had better backup back then."

"You did fine. More guts than a Marine. Did you really dive, roll, and shoot that damn gun, or is my knee hallucinating?"

"I really did. I saw too many John Wayne movies as a little girl. They warped my tender psyche."

"Your famous cowboy and Indian stage. Did you practice that, too?"

"Yes, I—"

"Someone's coming."

A car, no, something bigger than a car drove down the street toward them.

Her heart hammered with terror, but she forced herself over to the window facing the road. She peeped out of the closed Venetian blinds.

A small motor home pulled into their driveway, and a tiny blonde with tight poodle curls stepped out of the passenger side and melodramatically peered around for the enemy.

Happiness and relief exploded within Desta, and she charged toward the back door. "It's help!"

Gard shouted behind her, "Desta, wait. Take the gun. Look first."

She ran down the steps, threw herself into the blonde's arms, and would have sobbed happily on her shoulder, but it was a foot shorter than hers. "Oh, Jeri!"

Jeri gave her a python squeeze of a hug. "Are you all right, Des?"

"It's been awful..."

A tall man with hunter eyes and a pistol in his hand at his hip stepped around the motor home's front bumper.

Realizing what a careless idiot she'd been, she opened her mouth to scream a warning to Gard.

"This is Andy," Jeri gushed and included him in the hug with her other arm.

Andy smiled, his brush mustache curling upward into shaggy brown hair, his dangerous hunter eyes becoming Cocker Spaniel friendly. "Hi."

All Desta's earlier images of Andy vanished. "So you're Andy. Hi." A medic's bag with a large red cross was slung across the shoulder without the gun. "I'd forgotten... You're a doctor!" An even greater relief burst inside her. "Thank God! Come on. He really needs you."

Spinning, she charged back up the steps with the same fervor she'd come down them. Gard leaned against the railing at the top, his gun trained on Andy, who'd come up behind her. They jerked to a halt. Desta said, "They're help, Gard."

He shook his head marginally as if trying to remain conscious. His voice was whisper weak. "Where's Mark?"

"I didn't call Mark. I called people I could trust. This is Jeri McDermott, she and I were roommates at Harvard, and this is her..."

Jeri finished, "Fiancé, Dr. Andy Anderson. Hello, Gard. Gosh, you're pretty."

Too pale and weak even to blush, Gard stared blearily at them. "Trust them?"

"Very much." She took the gun he gave her. He sagged against her, his head against her breast, and she caught him with both arms before he went down. "Gard?"

"Let me." Andy hefted Gard into his arms.

Desta rushed to open the door for them and trailed them into the room, then locked the door behind Jeri.

Gard lay on the bed, his head thrown back, sweat pouring down his face, his breath a loud rasp.

She moaned with his distress.

Andy glanced up from pulling the contents of his bag onto the bed. "A little privacy please, ladies."

Desta sleepwalked into the tiny kitchen and plopped down at the two-person table. She rested her head on her arms on the table. All the carefully controlled feelings and tensions of the last days broke loose inside, and she began to sob.

Jeri let her cry herself out and handed her a tissue when she'd finished. She swiped her tears away and blew her
nose. "Thank you."

"You're welcome," Jeri assured her easily. "Sorry I took so long, but I thought having Andy here was worth my waiting for him."

"Bless you. Bless you both for coming." She sniffed. "I was so scared for him. It would be all my fault if..."

"All that stinky father of yours... I shouldn't speak ill of the dead." Jeri changed the subject. "What a handsome, sexy fellow Gard is, and what fiery eyes. Mmmm. They give me goose bumps. No wonder those pretty, bland college boys never interested you; you were waiting for somebody dangerous."

"He's a very nice man—kind, intelligent, tender, and... He has a lovely little boy, too, with big blue eyes and blond hair. A puppy named Barkley, and a nice house and civil law practice, and..." She blew her nose again. "I'm not making much sense."

Jeri beamed. "Perfect sense. You've finally met someone to make those cold Tyler toes tingle. You're falling in love with the man." Her blonde curls bobbing like springs, she bounced with delight in her chair. "Hurrah, at last."

"Am not," Desta protested, refusing to admit how right Jeri was, as usual. "A little smitten maybe."

"A lot smitten."

"A lot smitten. But he doesn't like me, and he despises Daddy. He's only protecting me because Daddy paid him to."

Jeri smiled smugly. "Money didn't buy those fiery eyes when he thought you were in danger."

"He's a nice man. The only things between us are physical chemistry and a bodyguard contract."

"Is he good?"

"I told you he's a nice man."

"No. I mean is he *good*?"

"We've never... It's crazy. I've shared the same bedroom, the same... I know how he likes his eggs for breakfast, the sounds he makes when he sleeps. Seen how much he loves by the light in his eyes when he speaks of his son... We've fought with each other, and together, against others. I've seen him cry with pain, laugh, and be so angry he... I almost killed a man to save his life. We've been so damn intimate together; I don't think I've ever known anyone so well in my whole life, and I don't know what his lips taste like."

"As long as you know what the rest of him tastes like... Never mind, dirty mind and comment. Forget I said it, Destal Vestal Virgin."

Desta smiled wearily at the old joke between them. "Fiancé?"

Glowing with happiness, Jeri extended her left hand where a tiny perfect engagement diamond sparkled. "Last week. Isn't it gorgeous?"

"It's beautiful. He seems like an extraordinary man."

"He is. He's so sweet and such a big puppy dog. I just love him."

With the knowledge she'd gained in the last few days, Desta knew that Andy was a gentle Cocker Spaniel with a dangerous hunter beneath, a doctor with a medical bag in one competent hand, a loaded gun in the other, but Jeri apparently hadn't seen both sides yet. Well, she might one day, and he'd be good for her until then, and especially good on that day when she really needed him.

"Desta." Andy's voice brought her out of her chair and into the other room at a run.

A stethoscope dangling from his neck, Andy stood by Gard's bed. Stretched out as before, Gard stared at him with the stubbornness she'd become very familiar with.

"What's wrong?" she asked.

Andy cursed softly. "He won't let me put him out so I can manipulate that leg back into place. We can't wait to get to a hospital. It could cause permanent damage."

"I said you could put it back in without knocking me out. I can handle the pain."

"Your muscles are tied into knots. I have to relax the muscles."

"I won't be put out."

"Why not?" Desta asked.

Gard huffed as if she'd said something idiotic. "I can't protect you if I'm sleeping."

"You can't protect me with a bad leg, and I refuse to let you cripple yourself over that stupid contract. Besides, Andy can protect me until we reach safety. He has your eyes."

Gard studied Andy's brown eyes, then her as if certain she was crazy.

"I mean he... He obviously knows how to handle himself. A former policeman, or soldier?"

Andy chuckled. "A very observant lady. I was a Green Beret before I decided I liked putting people back together more than taking them apart. I won't let anyone touch your lady, or mine, Gard."

Gard examined him again, their hunter eyes locking. "Green Beret?"

"Decorated and everything."

"Mmmm."

"Put him out, Andy."

"Desta!" Gard protested.

Sliding onto the bed, she lifted his head and shoulders onto her lap. "The princess is pulling rank. I don't want a guardian angel with a gimpy wing. Hush now, or I'll pin you down until he does it." She motioned to Andy to give the shot.

With a hypodermic, Andy bent toward Gard, who didn't protest again.

She stroked Gard's hair. He jerked as he was jabbed then relaxed under her caress. After several minutes he blinked sleepily. He searched his chest for her hand, then surprised her by twining his fingers with hers. "Stay."

Her fingers joined his as if part of the same hand. "I won't leave you."

He sighed at her reassurance and slid all the way under the drug's control, sagging against her.

Andy checked his pulse, heart, and eye reflexes. "Let's get this done, and him to a hospital."

"Is there something else wrong?"

"Don't think so. You hold his shoulders still. Jeri his thigh. It won't take much. It's not too badly dislocated."

"Lucky me," Jeri chortled with a lusty wink as she wrapped her fingers around Gard's thigh. Her hands tensed with a sculptor's strength.

"Okay." Andy leaned toward Gard's knee.

Although her role was more honorary than real, Desta clung to Gard's shoulders, and bent her head almost to Gard's face. She refused to look at what Andy was doing. After several long moments, Jeri inhaled sharply.

Andy straightened. "There, all finished. Well done, ladies. An easy job. It went in so smoothly he shouldn't have much muscle damage. Maybe only a mild limp for a time."

Desta released the breath she'd been holding.

Jeri poked her playfully on the shoulder. "You can let him go now, Des. Only smitten, ha!"

Brushing away the giant tears splattering down her nose onto Gard's peaceful, sleeping face, she sat up.

Andy finished wrapping Gard's leg back into the stretch bandage then stuffed his medical equipment into his bag. "Stay here and get ready to go. I'm going to check out the neighborhood for ambush." He pulled out his gun, checked beyond the door, then disappeared outside. A moment later Desta heard the soft thud of him jumping to the ground below.

Desta eased Gard's head back onto the pillow, straightened the rooms as she could, cut off the air conditioning, and left a note on the refrigerator— "Dear Aunt Toot, Sorry about the mess. Please don't tow the car. It belongs to a friend. Love, Desta."

As silently as he'd left, Andy returned. "All safe. Let's go."

"I'm ready."

"Take the point. I'll carry him. Jeri can put your luggage in the van."

Desta handed Jeri her pocketbook, the car keys, and Gard's shirt and shoes, then unholstered Gard's automatic. She stepped outside. Watching for enemies, she concentrated on the dunes, now dark with evening sun, and the houses around them, and not on Andy hauling Gard down to the van. She walked toward the van. Jeri closed the beach house door and scuttled after Andy, then opened the motor home door for them all. She emptied the car trunk's contents into the van.

When everyone was inside, Desta stepped up into the motor home and locked the door. She glanced around. The front area was like a plush van with chairs for the driver and passenger. The middle had a tiny table and four chairs for meals, a kitchenette, and a bathroom. A private little nook in the rear had a double bed.

Andy settled Gard in the bed and tucked up the covers. "Des, you keep an eye on him, and keep him still. Don't show yourself in the windows until we get well away from here."

With a nod, she perched on the bed by Gard's ribs. As Andy backed up, she lifted Gard's hand, settled it into her lap, and cupped it in her own hands to assure him she hadn't left him so he'd sleep quietly, and to assure herself they were going to escape the island alive.

The spring within her tightened more and more as the minutes and miles passed although she knew the ax-faced man couldn't possibly guess she was in this van. How could he? How had he known they'd be at her father's beach condo?

Jeri shouted victory.

They must have passed over the bridge off this deathtrap island, but Gard had said ambush would come after the bridge in the rural desolation before Shallotte. She almost got up to tell Andy but decided against it. He would already know.

The spring tightened a little more. Would they shoot the motor home's tires then come and finish off the passengers, or would they run them off the road? Why had she gotten Jeri and Andy into this? Why had she gotten Gard into this? Why the heck had her father gotten her into this? Couldn't he have chosen a safer occupation?

The motor home swayed, and she knew disaster had come. It didn't.

The motor home stopped, and she was certain they were dead, but they started again.

The friendly street lights of Shallotte eased some of the tension, but she didn't accept their complete escape until they were part of the relative anonymity of traffic on I-17 heading south. She thanked God, Jeri, and Andy, then sagged as weary as if she'd run all those miles on foot.

Undisturbed by the trauma of the last hour, Gard slept, his chest rising and falling quietly, his lids and blond lashes quivering with gentle dreams.

Last night, his dreams hadn't been so happy, and she'd wakened to hear him thrashing in bed and mumbling unintelligible words punctuated with Megan's, Zach's, or, infrequently, her own name.

With her index finger she traced the generous curve of his upper lip. If she kissed him now, he'd never know, and she'd finally learn what he tasted like. She'd probably have no other chance because, despite all the sexual lightning and thunderclaps between them, he didn't like her.

She stretched out beside him in bed and bent toward him, her lips almost touching his, but couldn't force herself any closer. If he wouldn't kiss her back... A one-sided kiss was as bland as kissing a reflection in a mirror.

Disheartened, she sighed, and rested her head on his bare shoulder. The motor home's wheels droned soporiferously beneath the bed. The cozy bed nook was so sheltered from view she felt as if she and Gard were alone.

A nap was an excellent idea. She might not get another chance tonight after Gard went into the hospital. The air conditioning chilly, she slid under the covers against him. His skin was as warm as hers was cold.

The flat area between his arm and breast seemed custom-made for her head. She wiggled to make herself comfortable, careful to keep away from his injured leg. His whole body seemed custom-made for hers, the parts meshing perfectly in sleep, play, and survival. Would they be as perfectly meshed in love?

Her heart fluttered erratically, heat flushing her skin, as she fantasized. The warmth of his big gentle hands as they held her hips, his lips on her breasts, those tender sky blue eyes glowing down at her, a passionate sun in their depths. The heat, weight, and fullness of him on and in her...

"Oh, hell," she moaned as a knot of twitching, demanding agony developed in her lower regions, her nipples aching. "Hell."

This wouldn't do. She imagined the dimensions and details of the Abram Poteat house she'd been designing before this mess began. The bedroom with the huge fireplace and bay window, the big round bed... Gard lying on the bed above her, sunlight across his magnificent bare chest, his lips trailing down her stomach... No, the master bathroom with the sauna would be a safer subject. Sweat running down his chest as they rocked together, steam rising around them and from them...

Lord, she'd just invented erotic architectural design.

She squirmed uncomfortably in bed, her lower body rubbing against his thigh, but it made the agony worse.

Gard stirred, his breathing deepening.

Horrified she'd wake him and he'd recognize her problem, she turned to stone.

His hand sleepily explored the back of her head down her ponytail, and he questioned her presence, "Princess?"

"I'm a human paperweight, and you're the paper. I'm supposed to keep you quiet and unjiggled by the motor home's movement."

"Oh." His arm sagged against her shoulder.

Lifting herself, she studied his face. In the passing headlights' glow, his lids were only half-open, his eyes unguarded and serene. "How are you feeling?"

"Floating. Don't hurt." He rolled to his side so he faced her. His legs twined with hers as he bent his legs. "It bends again."

"Careful!" She caught his shoulder to still him.

"Not going anywhere. Like it right here." He stared into her eyes, his nose almost against hers.

Trapped by the power of his eyes, her heart stopped.

"You have the look..." He shifted, the points of her hardened nipples rubbing his bare chest. "And the feel of a woman who wants to be kissed."

Too mesmerized to lie, she nodded like an idiot and leaned closer.

His lips caught the bridge of her nose between her eyes and pinched softly as his hand traced her hair downward and flipped open her hair clip. Her hair spilled out. He fluffed it around her shoulder.

She froze as he kissed each lid, a cheek, and her chin as if teasing them both with the terrible suspense.

His arms tightened around her as he finally lifted his face. His eyes met hers, the primal pull drawing their lips toward each other. When his lips almost touched hers, he whispered, "If someone interrupts us this time, I'll kill him."

"Me, too." She brought her lips against his, one arm clinging to his chest, the other pillowing and holding his head. His lips were hot and hard, but gentle against her lips. Exploring the curve and bow of her upper lip, he nibbled then caught her lower lip between his.

Unable to return the maddening, exciting kiss, she inhaled sharply, and contented herself with thrusting her breasts into his chest, her fingers wandering along the curve of his jaw and ribs. Stubble and beach sand rasped her finger tips. He smelled of ocean spray, medicinal alcohol, and her gardenia perfume.

He released her lip, his tongue nudging.

She opened her mouth to him, her tongue joining the subtle dance of discovery. He tasted of Campbell's Chunky Vegetable and Gabriel Gardner. His taste. She now knew his taste and would never forget it, and it was as unique and as sexy as his tender hunter eyes, the crinkle of his lips when he smiled, his...

His fingers tangled in her hair, holding her head, as he deepened the kiss even more, his weight shifting against her.

Moaning, she forgot to analyze and dissect his essence for future memories.

When he finally pulled his lips away, his heart was chugging as madly as hers, but his body relaxed against her. He murmured a satisfied "mmmm" and nibbled a kiss on the lobe of her ear. "What a wonderful dream this is, Princess."

"I'm awake. Or at least I think I am."

"It's a dream, or we can pretend it is tomorrow. I've ached for you so long... But I can't touch you."

She didn't want to dream; she wanted to start building a physical and emotional foundation between them, but he didn't even like her very much, he just desired her body. Well, a dream was better than nothing if he couldn't return her growing love. "A dream then. A wonderful dream."

"You're so beautiful. All woman." He raked through a long strand of her hair. "Your hair is so... I want it against my skin, in my fingers. And those luminous chocolate eyes." He licked her lids. "You taste of salt. You've been crying again."

"Standard Desta post-disaster hysteria. I don't want you hurt." Her fingers tightened around his upper arm. His muscles were corded steel, but she'd discovered how fragile even his strength was against violence. "I don't want you hurt."

"Why didn't you run when he knocked me down? Why don't you ever run like you're told to?"

"I didn't even think about running. The possibility never crossed... I run when I must; I stand and fight when I must."

"And throw welk shells when you must." He chuckled, the sound low and sexy in his chest. "You've one hell of an accurate right arm, lady." Leaving goose bumps in its wake, his palm stroked down her bare arm then back up again to the sleeve of her shirt then curled under her breast.

His hand was custom-made for her breast, too.

She questioned whether she should protest that intimacy, but forgot the question when he kissed her. His lashes fluttered against her skin as he pressed closer trying to possess her whole mouth with his tongue.

She opened herself wider for him.

His tongue flicked around her teeth, caressed the roof of her mouth, then stabbed under her tongue thrusting in and out in primal rhythm as if trying to mimic a greater desire that couldn't be satisfied.

Surprised by the sudden blatant eroticism, she tensed.

As if he sensed her discomfort, his mouth released hers for a moment then returned more gently, his lips only exploring hers, his thumb feathering her nipple. She relaxed against him and answered his fleeting kisses with her own.

The tip of his thumb circled her nipple, which grew harder, the ache more intense and exquisite. She pressed against his hand. He responded by kneading cautiously, two fingers tugging at her nipple.

Her breasts swollen and hard, she whimpered and rocked against him.

He kneaded harder.

Clinging to him, she covered his face with loving kisses as she tried to say with her lips what she couldn't allow herself to speak. Explosions spread through her from her breasts, the liquid center of her desire throbbing for him.

He kissed her, his tongue now thrusting tenderly to the rhythm of his hand. "Scoot up."

She didn't think, she was beyond thinking, she scooted up.

He nuzzled her breast through the soft cotton of her shirt, opened his mouth, and covered the crest of her breast. His mouth still open, he blew, the warm, wet sweetness of his breath penetrating the fabric.

Her nipple tightened, and she groaned, her arms encircling his head. He breathed again then licked her, the fabric an erotic extension of his tongue.

She jolted so that she almost jerked herself out of his mouth.

His tongue paid erotic homage to that breast and the other, then his lips and teeth closed against her nipple and tugged, the tip of his tongue caressing.

Her finger tangled in his hair, she moaned and kissed the top of his head as he tugged and laved her again.

His hand cupped her buttocks bringing her against him.

The heat and fullness of his desire shocked her for a moment, then she nestled against him. If this "dream" of his was all she'd ever have... She slid her hand between their bodies and stroked gingerly then caught the snap of his shorts. She begged, "Please, Gabriel."

His mouth left her breast, and he rested his head against her for a long moment, their bodies still twined, hot pulsations shuddering through them.

Remembering his injured knee suddenly, she stiffened with worry and caressed his head. "Are you all right? Are you hurt?"

"Scoot down."

She slid down until they were face to face.

"I didn't mean for this to go so far. One of my instructors in training warned that danger and death were powerful natural aphrodisiacs, and that you could dosomething under their influence you'd regret later."

He hadn't really wanted her. She blushed with humiliation and rolled over onto her other side to hide her face. Her voice was tiny and flat. "Oh."

He caressed her temple, but she didn't react. Her body had gone from singing with desire and the happiness of having him want her to shaking with cold. Her stomach knotted with nausea.

"Desta, I know this isn't a very fashionable thing to say, but I've never slept with a woman I didn't care for a great deal. It's just not my nature. I don't think it's your nature either."

She shook her head no, blinking tears, and refused to say she already cared a great deal, and finish the humiliating demonstration of how little she mattered to him.

Seven

The hot water sluicing around his body, Gard rested his head against the rim of the whirlpool and wiggled comfortably. A guy could become very used to this tub. It would be great after yard work, a hard run, or a game of touch football with Zach. He wondered how much Jeri paid for the whole setup. Probably too much for a small town lawyer to spend.

He could live without it, and if he survived, most of the money he garnered from the second payment for Desta's protection would go into investments for Zach's future and college education.

Frowning, he rubbed his injured knee. He'd known from the beginning he might get killed protecting Desta, but he hadn't considered permanent maiming. Andy and the orthopedic doctor had assured him he'd suffer no permanent damage to his knee, but... His fist clinched and unclenched. His heart and his pride had suffered permanent damage over Desta herself, the unattainable princess who wielded a pistol, a lock pick, and an artist's pencil with equal skill.

He'd expected to put up with snobbery and spoiled unpleasantness from O'Brien's blue blood daughter; he'd never expected to fall in love with her. God, what a fool he was.

Sharon had taught him that an old money blue blood never settled for a peasant when she'd left him for a member of her own social class. It had been his first and biggest heartbreak, and a lesson he'd never forgotten. His brain remembered it well, but his heart developed amnesia every time he saw beautiful, brainy Desta with her innocent chocolate eyes and feisty courage.

Desta's voice questioned from just outside the open bathroom door, "Gard, are you all right?"

Scratching his four day beard, he assured her, "I'm fine. Haven't drowned or turned into a prune yet. Come on in. I'm almost ready to get out."

With all the caution of a nervous animal, Desta eased in. She hadn't gotten used to barging into his bathroom although he wore swimming trunks to save her embarrassment during her lifeguard duties. She undraped his bath towel from Jeri's coral sculpture in the corner. The sculpture was entitled "Woman with Child," but it looked to him like giant cold scoops of pink Spaghetti Os piled on top of each other. Desta and Andy had told him Jeri was a world-famous sculptor and dealer of regional art works; he had to take their word for it.

Desta twisted her fingers spasmodically at the edge of the towel. "Can we talk?"

"Sure. Pull up a seat." He patted at the tile beside the sunken tub.

She folded the towel in half, spread it out, and with one smooth movement sank down, her legs comfortably Indian-style. Sweat dripped down her face and dampened her ponytail, white tee shirt, and running shorts.

He forced his eyes away from her exquisite legs, glistening with moisture, and the curve of her heaving breasts to her face. Her eyes were downcast and hidden. When she didn't say anything, he asked, "Have a nice ride on that stationary bike?"

She nodded.

It was obvious she wanted to say something serious. During his eighteen hour stay in the hospital, and their three day stay together in Jeri's house in Myrtle Beach, they'd talked a great deal, but only about ordinary things. He's spoken of his childhood on the farm, his weird adventures as an FBI agent, and of Zachary. Mostly of Zach. She actually seemed interested in his nine years with his son.

She'd told him of Great Aunt Toot Tyler, the elderly eccentric owner of that beach house, whose passion was surf fishing, and of her fun cousins Sheila and Billy Bob who'd shared her serious childhood let's-pretend with real lock picks and loaded pistols. Now, she seemed at a loss for words when she hadn't before.

Her chocolate eyes met his with candor and intelligence. "Why do you dislike me?"

The question was so far from his thoughts and his true feelings he blinked stupidly. "Dislike?"

"Would hate be a more fitting term?"

"I don't hate... How could you have gotten such an absurd..."

"I've been trying to figure out what I've done wrong, but..." She shrugged helplessly. "I gave up and decided to ask. I've told you I'm not very good at game playing."

"I don't dislike you, and I certainly don't hate you. I admit I dislike what and who you are... I despise your father, but I certainly don't hold that against..." Agitated, he raked his fingers through his hair. "I know I've been grouchy at times, but the pressure of protecting you and this damn knee, and...

"Hell, it's the chemistry between us, too. I'm a healthy male, and frustration comes out sometimes as anger or..."

Pain and hurt shimmered deep within her eyes as it had many times since he'd stupidly let things get out of hand between them in the motor home. He cursed himself for a fool for the thousandth time. On the day they'd met, she'd confided to her guardian angel she hadn't much sexual experience, and he shouldn't have taken advantage of that, but he had anyway. She'd been saved from the inevitable conclusion of their overheated necking by a return to his senses when she'd used his given name and reminded him of that innocence, but he'd humiliated her by stopping.

"I like you, Desta. I really do. You're intelligent, brave, funny, resourceful... You've saved my life risking your own. I can't tell you how touched I was that you never left me in the hospital, the moral support and hand holding during all those tests... You gave considerably more of yourself than a bodyguard expects."

"You aren't just a bodyguard to me," she admitted shyly.

For a moment, he considered the wild possibility that a princess might be interested in marrying the captain of the guard, but he forced himself to accept reality. "And you're more than just a body that needs guarding. Friends then? I feel like we're already good friends."

"Yes, we're good friends already." She smiled wistfully
then straightened as she lifted her shoulders with new determination. "I've been thinking a great deal about my situation, our situation. I've decided what I'm going to do.

"Daddy got himself in this mess, and he can get himself out of it. He's as capable of that as he was of screwing up his life and ours. We aren't going to look for him anymore. Instead... Jeri has this friend, a reporter for a local paper, and...

"As soon as you're able to travel, I'm getting on a plane to Europe, and you're going home where you belong. The reporter will take pictures of me going, and by the time the story hits the papers, Desta O'Brien will have disappeared in Europe, and Sarah Winslow will be born. I can stay gone until you say it's safe to come back."

His stomach twisted with panic. "You can't..."

"I know Europe very well. Daddy and I spent lots of time there together after they were divorced, it was my annual summer visit with him. I've been over there by myself, too. I won't have any problems living there, and I've enough money to stay well out of sight until it's safe to come back. Europe is a big place."

"You can't go to Europe alone."

"Do you want to leave Zach indefinitely? Or take him with you? Uproot him and stop your new life for years? Be sensible. Even Daddy couldn't pay you enough money for that, and I'm certain ruining your life wasn't included in that stupid contract."

Her certainty about her decision was stonewall unshakable. He thought like crazy for a way to tunnel underneath the wall. He couldn't think of a way so he used an old lawyer's trick, he stalled. "Ultimately, that might be the..."

"Ultimately, hell, I'm leaving now. I'm afraid, Gard. I don't want to die. The ax-faced man is a psychotic killer, and he wants me. He'll get you too, and enjoy it. I'm afraid for you too."

"I won't let him—"

"You're good at this, but our luck could run out any day. It nearly ran out in those dunes. You're one man against a whole gang of criminals. Have you thought about Zach? That man could grab Zach and use him against you like he's trying to use me against Daddy."

Desta had as little mercy in cross-examination as her father did. "I've thought about it. Zach's safe where he is. I've warned the Nivens to take care, and only my mother and I know where he is. She's been warned not to tell anyone else."

Desta swiped away the sweat from her eyes. "How long will that last? He comes home a week from tomorrow. We'll need time for my disappearance to be publicized. I should have left yesterday."

"Mark says—"

"You promised you wouldn't..."

"I haven't told him our location. I promised I wouldn't get Jeri and Andy officially involved in this mess, and I haven't. Besides, Mark warned me... Obliquely, warned me. Very strong hints, but not outright statements—"

"I know what obliquely means. What sneaky game is he playing now?"

"He's my friend. Yesterday, he warned me. Because of obvious orders from higher up, Mark couldn't tell me this
outright, but we know each other very well, and—"

"I've never known you to maunder before." She cut off
the whirlpool. "Is the hot water affecting your brain?"

The only thing affecting his brain and the rest of his body was her, and the thought of her walking out of his life forever. "Very well then. Someone higher up in the agency, maybe someone in another government agency, is very interested in our situation and location. Mark doesn't trust them with our safety so he'd prefer not to know our specific location so he won't have to lie about it."

"Mark, the bureaucrat, is protecting his rump."

"Ruining his career when he doesn't have to isn't in his contract with me either. He did warn me."

She waved her hand in placation to avert the argument building between them. "So Mark warned you. What does that have to do with my leaving?"

"Nothing. It was off the subject. Mark says they've had a major break in the case, and it could be over very soon. It would be foolish for you to leave for Europe when you'd just have to fly back again."

"What's his definition of soon?"

Gard shrugged, his shoulders rippling the water around him. "At least stay a few more days. We haven't followed the clues we found at the beach house to your father's possible location. If we can find him, we'll be home free, and this nightmare can be over for us both."

"And set ourselves up for the ax-faced man again? No way. I'm leaving."

"He hasn't found us here, has he? He's lost our trail."

"How did he find us at the beach?"

"It's an obvious enough place to look if you know about it. Like us, he might have come to find a clue to your father's location, and just happened to find us. Mark says someone broke into the condo after we left and ripped the place apart looking for something."

"And the ax-faced man found the same clues you have and will meet us there." Desta shivered. "Europe is lovely this time of year."

"He couldn't find the clues. I took them with me. The location we'll check out is as safe as this place. I have reservations and everything. We can leave tomorrow. Please, Princess. Stay a little longer, and see this through with me." He gave her the winsome smile that had turned his mother, Megan, and every other female he'd ever conned into agreeable mush.

Spotting his maneuver, she huffed and tossed her ponytail. "And you said you never use your looks to get your way."

Chuckling, he smiled harder. "This isn't looks, this is dependable adorableness I'm offering. Would I lie to you? Have I ever? Have I deliberately put you in danger?"

Her lower lip quivered with indecision as he melted her into a puddle with his smile and sincere blue eyes. Finally, she shrieked with mock horror and covered her eyes. "Cut it off. Cut it off. I can't take it anymore. I'll stay for a while. Mercy."

"I knew you'd see it my way."

She groaned with dismay, but grinned at him as if she wanted to stay.

His smile brightened even more as he had a new thought. He'd easily melted her marvelous brain with its humane, sensible strategy. Could he also melt that patrician heart of hers with something more than his smile?

~ * ~

"I'm sorry I can't carry you over the threshold, love," Gard murmured apologetically at the door of the hotel honeymoon suite.

The college student bellboy eyed Desta, stunning even in short brown wig and owl-rim glasses. "Hey, I will."

One of Desta's eyebrows rose icily above the edge of her glasses, but she assured her gawking young admirer, "It wouldn't be the same thing."

Leaning on his cane, Gard limped into the suite.

Desta followed him. "Careful, Eric, darling."

For a furious moment Gard thought she was talking so lovingly to the bellboy then realized she was talking to him. "Yes, love."

He waited until the bellboy, never taking his eyes off Desta, had plopped their luggage down, taken his tip, and closed the door behind him before settling down on the day bed in front of the empty fake fireplace in the sitting room.

Desta pulled off the wig and glasses, unpinned her sweat-dampened hair, and shook it around her shoulders. Her eyes without her glasses were huge as she studied the lush surroundings. The suite looked like part of a Nineteenth Century robber baron's mansion. She walked into their bedroom to their huge canopied brass bed and nudged. It sloshed under her fingers.

After examining the gilt-edged mirrors that covered the wall, the Cupid candle sconces, and the landscape reproductions, she said, "This place looks like a Victorian bordello."

He choked on his unexpected laugh. "Well said as always, Princess."

She wandered into the bathroom. "More bloody mirrors. The tub is big enough to swim laps, or whatever."

With a brutal mental shove, he drowned the image of them locked together in "whatever" in the bath.

"The honeymoon suite?" she asked as she reentered the room.

"It was the only way I could get reservations on such short notice. I convinced the lady we were marrying unexpectedly and..."

"She just happened to find an empty honeymoon suite in June, the marrying month. I didn't know that smile worked over the phone lines."

"My charm does. Blushing, fumbling bridegroom and all that. Plus, I think the whole damn place is Victorian bordello honeymoon suites."

"I can see why Daddy and the Gingers like it." Desta strolled back over to him and sat down on the day bed beside him. "How's the leg? Your limp is more obvious."

"Tired from the ride up. The muscles aren't too sore. You should be the one who's tired after the long drive up here."

"I do a lot of driving going to different house projects. What do we do now?"

"A rest, then maybe a swim. Andy said I could start swimming to get the soreness out. We can't do any serious snooping for your father until everyone's gone to bed."

"What are we going to do? Peek in bedroom windows until we find him?"

"You noticed how we were checked in?"

"Yes, and I noticed your discreet noticing."

"We're going to break into the office behind the main reception area and sneak a peek at their computer files."

"And the receptionist will be at the door the whole time. That sounds simply charming."

"Doesn't it."

"While you rest, I'll hit the boutiques." She fluffed her drying hair. "The brochure said they're open on Sunday. I didn't pack with swimming and Victorian bordello vacations in mind."

"I think we should be safe enough here. Even if they track us here, the security is impeccable for all the rich types who frequent the place. Reservations are full so they can't check in as guests either." Glancing at his watch, he stood. "Let's go."

"I've got my gun, Gard. Why don't you..."

"I'm certain you're capable of protecting yourself, but I need a few things, too. It will be closing time in an hour."

She shrugged as if unhappy to have him along on a private female jaunt and began to pin up her hair. "Well, back into the hot disguise."

"Do you need money?"

"No, I got some money off Sarah's credit card in Myrtle Beach, and I can always use the card. How about you?"

"I have a card, too. Eric Lunderson is my uncle. He took the card out for me a few years ago. I sign and pay."

Her disdainful eyebrow went up as she studied him. "So Gard the Smugly Pure isn't so pure. Why were you so huffy about my fake cards?"

He flushed with anger. "The fake card was a precaution, just for protecting you. I knew I couldn't use my own name. The cards didn't bother me. It was the fake passport. Do you know how many years you'd get for that?"

"I'd be too old to have children so don't squeal on me, Eric, or our children won't be around to carry on the Lunderson name." She jammed on the wig and the glasses. "Let's go."

Following her into the hall, he limped along beside her. "Eric has six children and eight grandkids. You don't have to worry about your obligations."

She surprised him by laughing and twining her fingers with his. "You tell your young bride the most unexpected things about yourself, love."

Arms around each other, a young couple walked down the hall toward them.

Gard forced himself to smile with besotted amusement. They said nothing else as they took the elevator down and went out the back exit toward the other buildings, tennis courts, and pools.

When they reached the outside, he squinted in the bright sunlight at the lush valley around them then up at the Appalachian Mountains. The air smelled sweetly of new mown grass and mountain pines. The thud of tennis balls echoed beyond them. Filled with the peace of the place, he grinned. The soft-edged green mountains were protective, not entrapping. "Zach would like it here."

Her own forced smile softened into a natural smile. "Does he like Victorian bordellos?"

"I hope he doesn't know what they are. I was thinking about the pool, the courts, the horses, the... this whole place."

"It's perfect, isn't it?" They stopped under a tree near a cluster of small Alpine-style shops, and she wrapped her arms around his neck. "Have a nice shop, Eric love. I'll meet you back at the room." Her eyes glinted wickedly as she lifted her lips to his and just touched them pretending to kiss him. "Your brown eye contacts give me the creeps. I like blue better."

"And the mustache?"

"I haven't made up my mind yet. I think I like it. The strawberry blond hair and the middle part are interesting. They change your whole face."

"Did my face need changing?"

"Of course not, you pretty thing. Didn't Jeri tell you how pretty you were often enough?"

Despite Jeri's instinctive flirting, she'd been too busy telling him how wonderful Andy was and how perfect Desta was for him to go after him herself. Jeri had the sledgehammer talents of a natural matchmaker, even if she was wrong about the subjects of the match. Saying nothing, he left Desta's illusions alone to save her the embarrassment of knowing Jeri had assured him of Desta's household skills, good nature, virtue, passion, love of children, and large dowry.

Teasing, Desta brushed her lips back against his in another pretend kiss. "I've never been kissed by a mustache before."

"Let me expand your education." His kiss wasn't pretend. His lips caught hers, his tongue discovering entrance.

Her shudder and moan shook through his muscles, and she relaxed against him, her arms clinging. He caressed the inside of her mouth then rubbed his mustache against her lips and cheeks. He would have taken more, but people approached. His eyes opened seeing gawkers, not goons, then closed again as he nibbled her lips with his. His nose bumped into the lower rim of her glasses. He pulled his lips away. "And I've never kissed a woman with such huge glasses. Both of us have learned something."

Her eyes dreamy, Desta drooped against him. "We sure have."

He let her straighten. "See you in the hotel, Sarah. Take care."

~ * ~

The moment Desta disappeared into the bathroom to change for dinner, Gard made his secret call, then stretched out on the day bed. Grinning to himself, he remembered the black bathing suit Desta had worn that afternoon, the sides slashed up her thighs, the scant curves around her breasts, and the bare back. He sighed in remembered ecstasy.

She'd assured him it was the most conservative suit she could find, but it had sent his blood pressure sky-high along with every other man's who'd seen her. He hadn't cared for the audience. He had enjoyed cavorting with her like a pair of newlyweds who couldn't keep their hands off each other. It was odd, but oddly safe, only allowing himself to touch her in public.

He'd even enjoyed their friendly fight over who would be the noble one and sleep on the day bed instead of the regular bed. Female stubbornness and practicality about an injured male had won over male chivalry, but he really didn't care. When friendly, fighting with her was almost as exciting as kissing her. What spirit she had and wit.

And since they'd cleared the air yesterday about his seeming dislike of her, how comfortable they'd been together. They really were good friends. He and Megan had started as friends, and even after love and marriage, they remained friends as well as lovers. If he could only have that with...

Someone knocked softly on the door.

He peeked through the spy hole then opened the door letting in the hotel people. He motioned them to silence, gave them a quick thumbs up of approval when they finished, and passed large tips around as they headed out the door.

Straightening his suit, he chuckled. He really did love being devious, especially in a good cause.

When the bathroom door jiggled, he lighted the candle on the table.

Desta stepped into the sitting room and stared at the darkened room, the candle lit, elegant table, and the nearby potted tree with its white twinkling lights.

She wore a long satin sheathe dress the color of her eyes. One shoulder and her back were bare, and tiny diamonds twinkled in her ears. Not even her short wig or owl glasses could hide her beauty. "You're stunning."

"I thought we were going to eat out."

"I thought you'd prefer something quieter. Somewhere you could let your hair out."

"I would." With a happy laugh, she disappeared into the bathroom then came back a minute later, her own hair around her shoulders, and her glasses gone.

He held out her chair. "Care to join me."

Sitting down, she beamed at him. "This is beautiful. Just beautiful."

"Yes, you are." He joined her at the table.

Her eyes flickered shyly in the candlelight, and she examined the potted Japanese maple. "What a charming idea to decorate a tree like that for a meal setting."

"I thought of that one myself."

"It's wildly romantic, Eric love. Nice small realistic touch to the lie."

He pulled the chilled bottle out of the champagne bucket and poured it into the wine glasses. "Your favorite beverage—diet ginger ale. It's a very good year."

Laughter bubbled in her eyes like carbonation as she took a sip. "Yes, a very good year."

He shifted the covered food plates from the nearby cart onto the table. "I knew you liked fish so I chose a local specialty, Rainbow Trout Something-or-other."

Her face glowed with sensual delight when she lifted the cover and sniffed. "Oh!"

They chatted through the meal like old friends until Gard returned the fish bone-littered plates onto the cart then brought out another covered plate. "And now for dessert. I had this made especially for you because you so bravely went through sweet tooth hell at Jeri's without sugar."

"I only crawled the ceilings and walked the walls five times a day during withdrawal. I don't know how she can live without processed sugar."

He pulled up the cover.

Staring at the small chocolate torte with its whipped cream decoration, Desta began to cry.

Dumbfounded, he circled the table and hugged her. "What's wrong, Princess?"

"It's so beautiful, thank you."

He chuckled and rocked her against his chest. "Who would have guessed it. A sentimental chocoholic."

She hugged him back. "Would you like a piece of my cake?"

Kissing the top of her head, he released her. "I'm honored. I'd love one."

She ate her piece of torte with a sensual relish that was positively erotic, and he finally understood that old folk song about wanting to be the glove that touched the lover's hand. He'd give about anything to be the cake she ate so he could receive that much passion.

As she licked away a final smear of chocolate on her fork, he squirmed miserably. One day, he'd have to explain the sexual suggestiveness of her eating habits to her.

She pointed at his half-finished torte. "Don't you like it?"

"It's wonderful. I was just admiring your mastery of the sport." He lowered his eyes and concentrated on his cake.

Sighing happily, she leaned back in her chair. "That was wonderful. Bless you, Gard."

"You're quite welcome." Drawing more on his courage than he had when he'd faced the goon in the dunes, he fumbled around in his suit pocket and pulled out a tiny jeweler's box. "I bought this for you today." He handed her the box.

Her face flushed with the same childlike delight Zach's would have receiving a present, and she opened the hinged box. Her smile frozen, she stared down at the engagement ring with the tiny, perfect diamond.

He wanted to say something like "I love you. Would you marry me? If not, could you love me one day?" He chose cowardly silence instead letting her put her own definition on his motive for the ring.

After a great deal of consideration, she lifted her head, her enormous eyes meeting his, as if trying to decipher the secrets behind his eyes. Certain of rebuff, he smothered the longing and love before they answered her. Her voice shook. "It's lovely. Sarah thanks Eric."

Relieved and immeasurably wounded that she'd taken it as another small detail in their marriage charade, he joked, "It's much prettier than that ugly necklace I gave you."

With a brittle smile, she slipped it on her trembling finger beside the wedding ring. "It fits perfectly."

Eager to finish the scene before he humiliated himself with a confession of his feelings, he glanced at his watch. It was after midnight. "We can go burgling anytime."

She escaped the subject as eagerly as he had. "What about the food? Won't the waiter come for it and find us gone?"

"We're newlyweds. They won't bother us. We can put the cart in the hall so the room won't reek of trout all night."

"We can leave the torte here for our post-burgling snack. That should worry them. They'll think we're smearing chocolate over each other and..." Blushing, she covered her mouth. "Excuse me. Jeri is a bad influence."

"She didn't rub off at Harvard. I think the influence is minimal."

"She tried. I was hopelessly dull."

"You were true to your honest nature. There's no dullness or shame to that. The shame comes from pretending to be what you're not."

"You're absolutely right." She stood. "Let me change into my burgling outfit, if I can fit in it after that glorious meal." Gard pushed the cart into the hall then slipped out of his jacket and shirt and pulled on a dark jersey and his tennis shoes. He collected his burgling supplies.

Her hair coiled on top of her head, Desta came out dressed in black too. "Do we need to blacken our faces?"

"I don't think so. I hope we don't run into any burglar alarms."

"I know how to..."

"That book you read is fifteen years out of date."

"Not if you've read the fifth edition. It came out last year."

"Desta!"

"Some people do crosswords. I pick locks and dismantle burglar alarms."

Wrapping his arm around her shoulders, he chuckled and jiggled playfully. "Let's go."

"Your cane?"

"I can walk without it. The limp's much better after resting the leg. We're going for a stroll if anyone sees us."

"The moon is almost full." She took his hand. No one noticed them, the halls empty of guests and staff, until they entered the lobby. The night clerk sitting at the desk glanced over the top of her paperback romance at them, nodded slightly, then went back to the book. Behind her, the door to the office they were to burgle was blessedly closed.

Reaching the outside, they turned to the right on the walk. A night guard passed them going in the opposite direction. With a night stick, gun, and walkie-talkie, he appeared far more formidable than the average night watchman.

Desta's breath caught slightly as if she got the same impression, and her hand tightened in his. Gard kept his pace easy and unsuspicious until they reached the office side of the building. Just past the lobby-office area, the building became a right angle wing of rooms. Within the angle were shrubs and several small Bradford pear trees. He slipped through the bushes to the office window. If someone spotted them, they'd be hemmed in by the building, easy prey for the guards.

Desta's gaze shifted around as if she recognized the danger, but she straightened with interest at the double-hung window. The office within was dark, a blind hanging over the window. He ran his fingers around the frame, searching for burglar alarm wires then with his penlight, he studied the inside of the window. No wires. The window lock was of the common household variety. The resort must depend more on the guards than on devices around here.

He offered the penlight to Desta, and she examined the window with even greater care. She gave a thumps-up to go ahead. He stuck a rubber suction cup on the window glass several inches above the lock then cut the glass around it in a semicircle large enough for his hand. Holding the suction cup, he tapped the cut glass free, then pulled the cut semicircle attached to the suction cup out of the window. Unlocking the window, he shoved it upward. It squeaked in protest all the way up.

Wincing, he tugged up the blind, then peeked within the office again. It was dark, the door to the lobby reception area closed. He gave Desta a foot up into the window then came in beside her. To hide them, he reclosed the blinds then shown the penlight around the office. The monitor screen of the small computer glowed with friendly light in the corner. Sitting down at the computer, he handed Desta the penlight. She nodded understanding and began to check over the room for more clues.

The system was on, and fortunately for him, very user friendly with no code words so he began to trace the whereabouts of Adam Rountree.

When Desta gasped with apprehension, his concentration was so intense that he jumped four inches. He swiftly returned the screen to the main menu to disguise his trail for anyone who came in later. She bent toward him and whispered, her breath a soft caress, "I just found the clerk's work schedule. She's supposed to start work in here in five minutes."

He helped Desta out of the window, came out himself, then lowered the blind and window. He smeared the semicircle glass's edges with clear glue then tapped it back into place in the window. When it dried, only a careful look would show the break in the glass.

Light flooded outward from the office.

Both threw themselves to the ground.

The suction cup was still on the glass and in plain view. Gard cursed his carelessness. On her stomach Desta glanced up as if with the same thought.

The soft static of a walkie-talkie erupted almost beside them, and a man whispered, "I've got intruders cornered

against the west wing. Get your ass over here and help."

Burrowing his head in his arms, Gard groaned. Breaking and entering was the obvious charge when the security guards saw the suction cup and his burgling tools. He'd

have to take out this guard before the other one got here.

His upper body low against the ground, he eased up on his knees.

Desta shook her head no, sat up, and pulled off her dark tee shirt.

He stared stupidly as her bra came off next, the light from the window shimmering across the full curves of her breasts.

She slid her hands under his shirt and tugged upward.

Understanding at last, he tugged the shirt over his head. By the time he had it off, she'd slipped off her pants. She lay down, the clothes beneath her and opened her arms to him.

Her eyes glittered with fear as he covered her with his body, his bare chest rubbing her breasts.

When his weight settled on her, she inhaled sharply, but she wrapped her arms around his shoulders. "You animal, couldn't you wait until we reached our room?"

"Oh, darling." Groaning with need, he pillowed her head beneath his arm and kissed her. Her stiff body gradually relaxed as it reacted to the chemistry between them. Her tongue met his, and she began to answer his passion. Her hands traced the muscles of his shoulder blades, her nipples now hard against his chest. Her next soft moan wasn't acting.

"How I love you," he mumbled and nibbled kisses down the column of her throat. Her pulse throbbed wildly against his lips, her neck muscles straining. She smelled of gardenias and the humus beneath her.

The guard whispered, "Shhh! Listen to this."

After a count of twelve, Gard moaned soulfully.

Her fingers tightened around his upper arms, one of her bare legs wrapping around his. "Do that again."

The guards shuffled closer.

With an instinct of its own, his hand cupped her breast to shield it from the others' sight. The nipple grew harder against his palm.

Muffling a wail of delight against his shoulder, she jolted.

The other guard whispered in a strong mountain accent, "Damn kinky rich folks. Look at that!"

Gard peppered kisses across Desta's sweating face as he listened for them to leave. They didn't. Rich folks might be kinky, but the local guards were even kinkier.

He groaned a few more times as if dying then buried his head against Desta's throat to think of a way out of this mess.

Clinging to him with her arms and bare legs, she whispered only for his ears, "I don't think they'll leave."

"Damn voyeurs."

Her pelvis nudged against his groin in a message as old as man and woman. Even through her panties and his pants, it had to be obvious how much he wanted her. He throbbed against her in response. She whispered, "I trust you."

His heart twisted. She'd offered herself to him to save them from this awful mess. He'd be damned though if he'd possess her like this with a leering audience.

"Get this over with before I die of embarrassment."

He lifted himself slightly with his arms to see her face. His finger pricked against a fallen holly leaf. Clutching the leaf, he settled back against her. His fingers found hers and gave her the leaf. "Ouch," he whispered and thrust his body against hers with passion.

She wriggled wildly beneath him then yelped with misery.

"Darling?" he asked.

She jerked upright, his own body coming up with hers, his chest and hands still shielding her from view, and whined, "Damn sharp leaves cover this place. My back's all cut up."

"But, darling," he begged. "I want you."

"Idiot, you don't have to lay on those things. You have nice soft me."

"But, darling." Bending toward her, he covered her sweaty shoulders with kisses as he secretly found her shirt.

"Don't you darling me." Using him as a screen, she wriggled into her shirt in his embrace then tugged it over her thighs and squirmed into her pants and shoes. "Stupid, oversexed, insensitive jerk! My momma warned me about you, but I didn't listen." She bolted to her feet and stormed out of the bushes toward the hotel entrance.

His clothes clutched under one arm, he scrambled to his feet. "But, darling..." To distract the eyes not on Desta, he waved her bra, a white flash in the darkness, and with his other hand pulled off the suction cup from the window, then comically tripped after her while fiddling with his zipper and wiggling into his shirt.

The snickers of the night watchmen followed him into the hotel lobby. He brushed back his hair, hid Desta's bra underneath his shirt, and strolled with dignity to the elevator and into his room.

Her shoulders shaking, Desta hunched on the day bed.

His heart aching at her misery, he sat down beside her and pulled her onto his lap, his arms around her.

She settled against him, her cheek on his shoulder, shaking with silent laughter, not tears. He laughed too and rocked her.

They finally quieted, Desta curled against him.

He stroked her head. "What a team we make, Princess."

"A new Bonnie and Clyde."

"I was thinking of Laurel and Hardy."

"I was so embarrassed."

He brushed a kiss on her head. "There's nothing to be ashamed of. They saw less of you than that new bathing suit shows. I made damn certain of that. Everything they heard was playacting. What really passed between us remained private, between friends, and friends aren't embarrassed with each other."

As if uncertain whether she believed that, she shook her head no. "Did you find Daddy? Is he here?"

For a moment, he wondered if he should lie, but knew he couldn't. "He left Wednesday."

"We've lost his trail then."

"I'm afraid so."

She sighed deeply. "I'm leaving for Europe. Tomorrow."

He tried to think of some way to stall her, but could think of nothing.

A cold, desolate land, the future without her lay ahead of him. He'd gained her trust and friendship, but had run out of time to win her love.

Eight

They were both clutching at straws, very fragile straws.

Desta leaned her head on her hand against the car's passenger door and stared disconsolately out at the breathtakingly sheer drop off from the mountain road to green valley and mountains below. Morning mist still covered the mountain peeks above, although June sun had burned away the mist below them. Slashing through the cow-filled valley, a creek splashed swiftly through large boulders.

Gard's eyes, as blind to the beauty around them as hers, never left the road as he negotiated a sharp turn. For reasons vastly different from hers, he was no more eager for her to leave his protection than she.

After their burgling the night before, they'd slept fitfully, both haunted by the next day's leave-taking. At breakfast that morning, he'd handed her another of Adam Rountree's credit card slips he'd found at Holden and asked if it meant anything to her. The gas station had been fifty miles away from their resort, halfway between the resort and the cabin. She'd mentioned the cabin, a slim lead to her father's location that probably led nowhere but promised another day together before saying goodbye forever.

But another day—perhaps to find another fragile straw clue to her father's location, or learn the identity of the killer after them, or to discover a way to make Gard love her, or to draw him into her arms so she'd have some memory of him to hold in exile.

"Princess?"

Jerking herself out of her funk, she noticed their location, and pointed toward the left fork just past the tiny mountain community she'd used as a final map reference point for their trek deep into the Appalachian Mountains.

Gard turned left.

"The next turn is a dirt road, right past that little church up ahead."

He slowed to a crawl and turned onto the stony, rut-ridden road that wandered up a mountain. His face tightened with concern as their rented sedan shook violently in the holes. "Looks like an old creek bed instead of a road."

"Probably is."

His knuckles whitened on the wheel as he avoided a cave-in on the edge of the road that spilled down to a creek and pines. He swore under his breath. "We need a jeep."

"Oh, I've seen it much worse. We'll make it."

He glared at her breezy confidence and concentrated on his driving. Sweat trickled past his ear down his neck onto his white knit shirt despite the cool mountain air pouring in the cracked windows, and she realized with a spooky sort of intuition that he had a strong aversion to mountain heights.

Regretting her breeziness, she bit her tongue and wished she'd been more insistent about driving to ease the strain on his bad leg. Well, she'd drive back down.

As they negotiated a hairpin turn so narrow her side of the car seemed to hover over the ledge, his breath caught then released as the road widened and smoothed. "What happens if two cars meet going in opposite directions?"

"Few cars come here, but I imagine one will have to back up until the other can pass him."

"Damn!"

Their road peaked and began to trickle downward.

They passed a tiny mountain cabin. A toddler played in the dust by a tree-tied mongrel while a woman in a faded floral dress hung clothes on a line between the house and the tree.

Desta waved at her, and she waved back with a sparse economy of motion and emotion. "That's Betty. She and her husband watch after our cabin." She paused. "See that big oak. The road to our cabin is just past it."

Its shocks moaning with protest, the car climbed upward again. Their private road was even ruttier than the one they'd just left with trees lining it on one side and valley spilling underneath them on the other side. The cabin was perched within a tiny valley overlooking the larger, rich valley below. She said, "The valley the cabin's in is called God's Hands because my great grandmother thought it was shaped like open, cupped hands."

When he ran out of road several hundred yards away from the old cabin, he parked the car under an oak, which had been there when Leif Ericsson had landed in America, and got out of the car. He studied the little cabin with its sagging front porch and hundred-year-old natural stone chimney then glanced at her with surprised hunter eyes. "This belongs to the Tylers!"

"The Morgans, my maternal grandmother's people. She was born here. Momma loved it so much Grandma Beth willed it to her." Distressed, Desta joined Gard. Her father wasn't here either. There was no choice anymore. She'd have to go into exile and away from Gard. She tugged unhappily at her braid. "They spent part of their honeymoon up here."

"I can't see Lauton enjoying this place."

"Neither can I." She strode toward the front steps. "This is the only thing Momma willed to Daddy. The only thing, although he hates it, and I love it as much as she did. She asked that he leave it to me, but it still makes no sense to leave it to him when he hates it." She stopped in front of the steps, knelt by the latticework around the porch, then found the key underneath some stones. "You might as well see the place since we're here."

Testing the boards with his weight, Gard followed her up the steps. "He might hate it, but he's kept it up. The house looks weather tight, and this porch has been shorn up recently. This place has considerably better maintenance than the house we just passed."

With a nod, she unlocked the padlock at the front door. "He does that. I think it's the only reason he comes up here. He and the Gingers wouldn't be caught dead in a place like this." She pushed open the door with a vicious shove.

Gard gaped like a tourist at the hardwood floors with their handmade rag rugs, the plastered white walls, the rockers, and the huge stone fireplace. He walked into the kitchen. The sink had a hand pump for the well water, and the stove was heated with wood.

A tiny refrigerator sat incongruously in the corner.

"There's a generator in the shed," Desta explained. "A few lamps, the refrigerator, and a heater are our only concession to the times."

"And I thought you'd have hysterics staying at a cheap hotel."

"You're going to have to stop watching television for all your information about rich folks. Some of us even like to camp out and have no desire to ruin anyone else's lives, including our families."

He grimaced at her teasing jab. "I'll remember that."

"Let me show you the bedrooms." She led him into the master bedroom. An ornate brass bed with a handmade star quilt took up most of the tiny room. "We're lucky the route is so inaccessible. Many old home places have been looted and vandalized."

"The bathroom?"

She knelt by the bed, pulled out a chamber pot, and offered it to him. "There's also an outhouse."

With a chuckle, he shook his head in refusal. "Never—"

Explosive noise surrounded them.

Once more, Desta relived that moment on the boat when the whole world had demolished around her.

The cabin shook and collapsed like a match stick house smashed by a willful child. Knowledge so ingrained it was almost instinctive took over. Desta grabbed Gard's arm and jerked him into the outer corner of the bedroom.

The chimney exploded, and the house and Gard fell over her.

She floated in a blackness as warm, sweet, and thick as human blood coursing through veins. Someone called her. On the boat, it had been Gard's voice that had dragged her out of the darkness and into his waiting arms in the water. Now, she recognized her mother's voice and felt her presence. "Momma? Momma, this is Gabriel, and I love him. You'd love him, too." The darkness smiled then tattered away.

His breath filling her, Gard's lips covered hers in an openmouthed kiss. She inhaled sharply, and her arms drifted up and around his neck. Her tongue probed his as she began to return the kiss.

Hovering above her on the floor, he jerked slightly and pulled his mouth away from her. "Desta?"

Her eyes crept open at the shaking hysteria in his voice. He bent toward her, his face caked with dust, his eyes like flares in the faint light. Tears streaked his dirty cheeks. Smiling, she tightened her arms around his neck fearing he'd disappear and lifted slightly to brush a kiss on his lower lip.

He laughed as if she'd done something bizarre and brushed at her face with a shaking hand. "Oh, Princess. I've never given mouth to mouth like that before."

Aware only of the tingle that ran down her spine to her curled toes from his touch, she reached up to kiss his mustache and upper lip, but he turned his head, pulling her face into his shoulder, and began to hack like a heavy smoker. His movement stirred dust from his shirt, and she sneezed three times in counterpoint to his coughing.

Blinking away grit, she really noticed where they were for the first time. She and Gard lay in a tiny space not much bigger than a large coffin, and they were surrounded and trapped by wood debris from the explosion. Dust floated on thin light motes from above.

Her heart began to pound wildly, and blind panic seized her. Losing control, she began to twist and fight against Gard and the debris.

"Shhh! Shhh." He held her in his arms and stroked her hair. "Easy, Princess. Easy."

Somehow she regained control of the animal madness in the safety of his embrace. Burying her face in his chest, she pretended they were in the open. "I have claustrophobia sometimes."

"Just hold on to me."

"Got trapped in a big wooden box when I was seven. Terrible. Hated it. Won't get into anything can't open since."

"And a junior lock picker was born."

"Mmmm hmmm." She blinked away tears and sniffed. "What happened?"

He coughed again. "Our friend the yacht bomber was here before us. It must have been timed with the front door."

"Bastard. Momma's beautiful little house. All gone?"

"I think so. We seem to be in the only place left standing. How in the world did you pick this place?"

"Architects do more than draw pictures of houses. We learn about stress and structure. Learn the secret that holds a bunch of stones together to create an arch. I know every inch of this place. Picked the best spot."

"You sure did, Princess. Anyway, I landed on you and squashed the air out. I couldn't find anything else wrong with you."

"I don't feel hurt. You okay?"

"I think so."

Her fingers holding tight to his shirt, she forced herself to open her eyes and study their location, but she couldn't see any way out of the box... the place they were in. Heaving with panic, she shoved her face back into Gard's chest.

He rolled slightly to his side, taking her with him, and caressed her head. "Your friends next door must have heard the explosion. They'll be up here soon to get us out."

Although she doubted rescue, she grunted agreement. The neighbors were almost a mile away. They'd die together in this box... coffin... this place. "Hate boxes so much I don't even want to be buried. Want to be cremated and ashes sprinkled in the open."

"I'll be sure to tell your great grandchildren when you die of old age. We'll be fine. We've gotten out of worse."

Not believing a word of it, she nodded. "So Daddy's not here, but the mad bomber has been. He must know Daddy well. Not many know about this place. Never comes much. Good place to hide though."

"The bomber certainly covers all his bases. Damn indiscriminate too about who he kills. Anyone could have walked into this place. I wonder... Maybe he was going to bomb the condo too, but we beat him there."

Her brain refusing the puzzle, she shrugged.

Wood shifted above them.

With a shriek, she squirmed tighter against him.

When nothing fell from above, the tenseness in his body eased. He nuzzled the top of her head and teased, "We can't get any closer without benefit of clergy, Princess."

His body began to respond to her as hers responded to his, but she refused to give up an inch of intimacy or the comforting heat of him.

"Your mother must have willed this place to your father as a message."

"What message?"

"If this was their honeymoon cottage... She still loved him."

"She never stopped. Even after she left him when she couldn't bear the Gingers any more. No other man ever mattered."

"Tyler, through and through." He groaned with misery. "Oh, Princess."

He throbbed against her leg, but she wasn't sure how she could help him. Her breasts ached, too, the nipples hard against his chest.

His fingers caressed down her spine and warmed themselves in the small of her back. "You're making me crazy."

"Me, too. What should we do about it?"

Old timber creaked above them, and plaster showered down. Rolling over on top of her, he shielded her with his body as she screamed into his chest.

When nothing larger fell, he lifted his head and shook away the dust. Sneezing, she tightened her arms around his waist. He was heavy, but she rather liked him where he was.

He lifted himself with his arms and smiled at her. "You okay?"

"Yes. You?"

"Dustier."

"Me, too." Gingerly, he eased off of her and onto his back. For a moment, she stared up at timbers, but they seemed to be moving closer, and closer, and closer... She jammed her eyes shut, threw herself on top of him, and buried her face in his chest with a whimper.

Holding her, he stroked her braid. "You certainly are friendly like this."

When the ceiling seemed to stop trotting toward her in her imagination, she attempted conversation. "Reminds me of the end of a Nineteenth century French novel I read in college. *Germinal* by Zola. The hero and heroine were trapped together in a coal mine cave-in."

"What happened?"

"They realized they loved each other and made love."

"And they lived happily ever after?"

"No, she died of starvation before they were rescued, and he was crippled for the rest of his life."

"Real upbeat ending there."

"It was a social novel about the injustices done to the miners back then by the mine owners. It wasn't supposed to end happily. It was supposed to make readers mad enough to change conditions."

"Oh." Gard was obviously not one to take subtle hints or answer loaded questions. Maybe she should tell him she loved him and ask if she could molest his body while she had enough energy to enjoy it before she died a virgin in this stupid hole. "What do you think of that from the mine owner's point of view?"

If his tone hadn't been teasing, she would have jabbed him in his smugly virtuous peasant ribs. "Tylers have *noblesse oblige* shoved down their infant throats from birth. We don't enjoy our money. We do noble things with it. You should see the number of foundations we have."

"And the O'Briens?"

"There aren't any O'Briens. I'm the only child of an only child of an... You get the idea. Daddy and I are all that's left, and he's now a Rountree, and I'm..."

"What?"

"Trapped in this stupid box... place until I starve to death." Tears of panic blinded her.

"We aren't going to be here that long. If help doesn't come soon, I'll get us out somehow."

"Sure thing." She dried her cheeks on his chest. "Maybe being from such a small family is the reason Daddy's so screwed up about love. His parents were ice cubes who cut him down if he wasn't perfect at everything. He didn't have cousins, and a mother who loved him, and... Maybe he never knew how to love Momma. He wanted to, but he couldn't."

"Perhaps not. Everyone's born with a need for love, but being able to love is taught by example, usually by your parents. If your mother was a tenth as fine as you are, he must have been a fool not to return her love."

The lovely compliment made her smile. "When the cabin exploded. Wherever I was when the air got squashed out... Momma was there. She was so close to me for a few moments, then you brought me back." She blurted, "Momma likes you."

"I'm glad, Princess. I would have liked her, too."

"No, I mean it. She was there."

His voice remained maddeningly sane. "I believe you. I'm not just humoring you. I felt my father when I was knocked out once."

"I'm glad... that you believe me, not that you were hurt. Was it bad?"

"Not really. A horse knocked me into a tree. No permanent damage, but the—"

"Tree died," she finished for him.

"No, it had a terrible headache for weeks."

She giggled. "You're a wonderful man. I'm sorry I brought you here. I should have gotten on that plane. You could be safe at home now instead of... I shouldn't have been so selfish trying to stay a little longer. If we get out of this, I'm going right onto that plane, no more excuses."

He lifted her chin, making her look at him, and smiled at her with his plaster-dusted beautiful face and tender hunter eyes. "I'm the one who chose to come here. I wanted one more chance to... I don't want you to leave. If things don't turn out right, I'm the one to blame, not you."

"I'm so scared. I've been scared for so long." Blinking tears, she leaned over him and nudged her lips against his. When he didn't rebuff her, she kissed him. He returned the kiss, his hands tracing up and down her ribs. Catching his right hand, she held it for a long moment entwined with hers, then pressed it against her breast. Her nipple rose into his palm.

For a moment his hand resisted hers then curved against her, and he sighed against her lips.

As her legs parted around his hips, she covered his face with kisses, her fingers tangled in his hair.

Rocking under her, he eased his hand under her waistband at her stomach then flipped the snap. "Oh, Princess."

She kissed his breast above his heart. "I love..."

He tensed, no longer even aware of her.

"Mizz O'Brien... Mizz O'Brien..." Her name floated on the wind beyond their prison.

"Help," Gard shouted. "We're here. We're here."

Nine

"Mark will be chewing the menu," Gard muttered as the worker with the stop sign finally waved them past the asphalt crew repairing the road. He drove onward through the outskirts of Charlotte.

Apprehension and hope warring inside her, Desta twisted the string handle of her pocketbook. Could this nightmare be over? Would Mark tell them the ax-faced man and those behind him were in jail? Why else would he ask to see them immediately? She prayed, "Oh, please, Lord. Please let that be it. I don't want to go into European exile and leave Gard and my life behind me."

Sun glinted across Gard's blond lashes and mustache as he watched the road and rear view mirror. After an afternoon and night of quiet at the resort after their escape from the cabin, he seemed rested, his body and injured leg in excellent shape, but undisguised by brown contacts, tension and sadness lived behind his eyes. It would be good for him when she left and freed him from the unwelcome role as her protector.

No, that judgment wasn't fair to him. He'd started protecting her because of her father's financial blackmail and that damn contract, but it had become more personal for him. He cared for her, not in the same loving way she cared for him, but he did care. That was something.

She'd been right from the beginning about him. He was a good man, a very good man, and a white knight through and through.

Why couldn't he love her? She'd examined every side of that question since he'd declared them friends. The chemistry between them was perfect, he liked and admired her, and he obviously knew how to love strongly. Everything about them seemed to click, but...

The only answer she'd come up with was her father. Gard despised Lauton O'Brien, and even though he'd said her parenthood didn't matter, it must. Why else? She couldn't change who she was, or what her father was, so Gard would never love her.

It was so unfair! But human emotions weren't fair or logical, they just were. She loved Gabriel Gardner who couldn't love her back, and neither fairness nor logic would change that feeling either.

Gard parked in the back of the lot of a busy Chinese restaurant and got out of the car. His hunter eyes examined the area and all the cars, then he walked around, and opened Desta's door for her.

Stepping out, she straightened her blue blouse, white pants, and wig. His left hand twined with hers, and they walked casually into the restaurant.

Sensing a trap, her hackles rose the moment they entered, and she almost turned and fled, but she forced herself forward trusting Gard's intuition about Mark and the situation.

The restaurant was abysmally dark, tiny Chinese lanterns lighting the tables, but little else in the restaurant. Mark slouched at a booth with a half-melted drink in front of him. The moment he sensed them, he came to his feet.

Making no comment on their disguises, he beamed and hugged Desta. "Baby Sister, I thought you'd never get here." He kissed her briskly on the lips in a very unfamilial way, then patted Gard's tense shoulder. "Hi, guy, hope you're treating Sis well."

Desta glanced around at the people at the other tables and refused to give in to her desire to clobber Mark.

She'd be nice to Gard's game playing friend if it killed her. "Hello, Mark."

With a frosty smile, she slid into the booth beside Gard.

As they ordered lunch and their soft drinks were brought, Mark remained silent, but his hunter eyes dissected them as if trying to read both their minds and their souls. Gard seemed to be the most interesting puzzle.

"Well?" Gard asked finally. "You wanted to see us?"

"Loved to see you, was ecstatic to see you, was thrilled to see you. Yes, I wanted to see you." Mark pulled a photograph out of his suit pocket and handed it to Gard. "Recognize him?"

Desta studied the police mug shot of the empty-eyed man whose facial angles were so sharp they appeared to have been hacked out by ax and shivered. "That's him."

Mark nodded smugly. "Thought so. Martin Corlich. A hired assassin of sick and efficient reputation. One of his specialties is subtle use of explosives."

Gard straightened. "Have you tied him to the yacht explosion?"

"We think so. The lab's positive the explosives are from the same batch he stole several years ago and has used since."

"He's a hard man to catch then."

"Impossible so far, but I've never been on his trail before." Mark grinned at Desta as if she were dessert. "And with such a good motive to get him."

"Who hired him?" Gard asked.

"Cal Ferret. We can't prove it, yet, but it's Ferret." As she reached for her drink, Mark ogled her hand with its wedding and engagement rings. "When did you kids get married, and why wasn't I invited to the wedding?"

"We haven't, but you'll be the first to know, Big Brother." Desta simpered.

"We've been posing as newlyweds."

"That must be fun."

"Watch your mouth. Desta is a lady. I assume you know what a lady is, or have you forgotten after all the bed-hopping fluff you spend your time with?"

Blushing, Desta wondered how Gard would have felt about her if she'd given in to strong temptation the night before and crawled into bed with him to finish what they'd started in the cabin debris.

Laughing with amusement, Mark raked back his dark hair with his fingers. "What a lifetime lease idiot you are, old buddy. But I can almost understand it sometimes." He grinned winsomely showing Desta his dimple.

"How long until you tie Martin Corlich to Cal Ferret?" Gard asked.

Hoping for a reprieve from exile, Desta held her breath.

"Maybe never." Mark shrugged, "But we've got the goods on Ferret. We've had a major break. He'll never get out of prison when we're finished with him."

"That might be months, years." Gard's voice sounded as stricken as she felt. Exile was her only choice. She bent her head.

Gard wrapped his arm around her shoulder, and she buried her face in his shoulder.

Suddenly very businesslike and professional, Mark said, "Desta, I've been sent to offer you protective custody until the matter is cleared up."

"What does that mean?"

"Strange hotel rooms and guards," Gard said.

"That sounds like prison."

"The irony of it never fails me," Mark replied.

"Desta doesn't deserve protective custody. Why?"

"I beg your pardon. She's worth a great deal."

"To me and you she is, but not to the Bureau. They don't toss out a fortune for protective custody for someone like Desta. She doesn't have any courtroom value against Ferret, and you aren't offering me anything so it can't be for witness value against Corlich." His gaze nailed Mark's. "Why?"

"I'm not at liberty to say. I have orders from higher up. It's what you want, isn't it? Desta tucked away safe, and you back to Zach?"

"I want her free, not locked in a room somewhere."

"Better a room than a grave. What about it, Desta. Do you want protective custody?"

"Who'll guard me? Will you?"

"When I can, but I can't very often."

"Oh," she whispered with disappointment. She could survive being imprisoned with someone who cared. At least with Mark, she'd get her exercise being chased around the room. "Could Gard visit?"

"Definitely not. He'll be watched."

"What do you think?" she asked Gard.

"It is your decision. If Mark assures your safety... Do you assure her safety?"

"Absolutely. Good, trustworthy people. The decision comes from very high up."

Torn, she studied Mark's face, then Gard's. Protective custody sounded even more bleak than exile, and she'd have her freedom in Europe, but... "Gard?"

As if divorcing himself from her and the decision, he shook his head.

The pain of absolute loneliness stabbed her. "Do I have to give you my decision now?"

"We'd prefer it now."

"We'll contact you tomorrow morning," Gard interceded.

Accepting temporary defeat, Mark nodded.

"What do you have on Ferret?" Gard asked.

Mark's gaze lingered on her face a moment, and he opened his mouth as if he wanted to tell her something, then he closed it. "I'm not at liberty to say."

"Damn it, Mark. It's me. It could help me protect Desta."

"I'm not at liberty, especially not with you. Special orders."

A flush of anger spread across Gard's fair face. "I didn't know you were such a toady to policy, Faulkner. You must be really hungry for a promotion."

Mark's cheek twitched, but he replied evenly, "If I were that hungry, I'd... I'm not at liberty to say."

The meal arrived. By the time the waiter had left, both men's tempers had cooled enough to be civil with each other, and Gard told a funny rendition of the battle of the dunes between him and the goon.

Desta, her shell pitching, and her dive off the dune to save the day were star features.

"I didn't do that much," she interjected. "Gard was wonderful. So brave and resourceful, and such a good battlefield scout and general."

Mark's sardonic eyebrow went up, and he said, "What a pair of unassuming heroes you are. Gosh darn it, but I'm impressed."

"Can it, Faulkner," Desta told him, "or I'll demonstrate my aim with the salt shaker and your nose."

"Don't you dare." Mark rubbed his nose. "That would be defacing an art work. My plastic surgeon considers it one of his masterworks."

"You mean you weren't born perfect?" She smiled sweetly.

"Of course I was, but a known felon with a large fist made me less perfect. I remember the bas... fellow every time I sneeze."

"My apologies to your nose, and my compliments to your surgeon."

Mark nodded, his gaze holding hers again as if trying to tell her something, then he turned to Gard. "How's puppy Godzilla? Is she being protected?"

"Barkley's fine. She's staying with friends."

"Good, a dusty little dog like that should be safe. That's an important thing for a father to concern himself with. Zach really loves that dog." Mark turned to her. "Desta, Zach's a great kid. For a kid like that, I'd settle down."

"Listening to Gard speak of him, I'd like to meet him very much. He sounds like an easy child to love."

"He is. Gard won't have any trouble convincing some nice lady of that." He turned to Gard, "Think you'll have any time to go wife hunting when this is over? Like you planned."

With a tired shrug, Gard picked at his fried rice.

Loneliness and grief stabbed harder inside her.

Mark went blithely and insensitively onward with the subject. "How will Zach feel about a new mother?"

"At Christmas he asked Santa for one. It was at the head of his list even before a puppy."

"How did you handle that?" she asked.

"Santa left a note saying he'd be looking, but it might take a while to find one special enough for Zach and me. If he found her, he'd make sure she'd meet us."

"Santa wouldn't lie about that. I'm certain you'll find some special lady." *While I'm hiding in exile,* she added to herself.

"Well, this has been charming." Mark stood. "Sorry, I can't wait for the fortune cookie, but I've got to get back to the office before Braggonier wonders what I'm up to and asks. Take care, you two, and call me tomorrow with your decision, Desta." He brushed a kiss on her cheek and patted Gard's shoulder. "I'll take care of the check."

She watched Mark saunter through the now almost empty restaurant to the cash register. "Would protective custody be better than Europe?"

Not looking up from his plate, Gard said bitterly, "Why do you ask? You've already made up your mind. You'll leave my protection for Mark's."

"What?"

"The Ivy League prince offers, and you turn your back on the captain of the guard." He stabbed at a sliver of beef. "Princes always win over toads."

She laughed incredulously. "You're jealous. You're jealous of Mark Faulkner."

"Who me? How could I be jealous? I'm not worthy enough to even be in the contest."

"You idiot," she blurted. "Don't you know anything? You aren't the toad. Being a prince has little to do with money or breeding; it has to do with having a good, caring heart. Like yours. At least by my definition of princehood. Mark's a toad through and through. If there's any prince underneath, I'm not the princess to bring it out."

Possibilities shining in his eyes, Gard stared at her. "I'm a..."

"Every inch a prince. As local princess, I should know. You don't even need kissing to improve the situation. Not that I mind kissing you." Her fingers tracing his lips, she smiled at him.

He leaned toward her, the primal pull between them intense.

"Your fortune cookies." The waiter plopped the plate on the table.

Jumping, they pulled apart.

Gard glared at the departing waiter. "Remind me to kill him later."

"Just give him a bad tip. I'll remind you to finish kissing me later."

"A woman of good priorities." He grinned at her.

With a shy smile, she picked up her fortune cookie then broke it open and read aloud, "You'll meet someone tall, dark, and handsome... who'll give you warts."

He glanced at the message. "It does not..."

"I added the warts. What does yours say?"

He cracked it open and read, "Your greatest wish will be granted."

"What a lovely fortune." She pulled apart the third cookie. "Let's see what Mark's says. 'Beware of false-faced friends. They could be dangerous.' I hope that doesn't mean us."

"Better us than someone else. We don't mean any real harm to him."

She began to nibble her fortune cookie.

"You eat those things?"

"If you can't eat the sugar you love, eat the sugar you're with. That's a sweet tooth motto."

"You're absolutely incorrigible." He pulled out his wallet and left the tip. "I know a safe place to stay in town. A garage apartment a friend rents to a grad student. It's empty over the summer, and he said I could use it if I wanted while in town. We need to figure out our options."

Depressed again at the thought of exile or protective custody in her future, she nodded. It didn't seem a happy ending was just around the corner for her, or her jealous prince.

When they walked outside, the parking lot was almost empty of cars, and totally empty of people, the late lunch crowd having returned to their jobs. Gard's rented blue sedan in the back of the lot was a solitary island in a large sea of parking asphalt. No one was in sight.

As they reached the center of the lot, she felt her hackles rising in warning. Something was wrong. "Gard."

"I feel it too. Get back into the restaurant. I'll bring the car to you."

"No. Two have a better chance than one."

A small engine revved loudly behind them at the corner of the restaurant then moved toward them.

Almost deafened by the sound, Desta turned. A huge motorcycle sped around the corner toward them, the driver in black, his face covered by a black-faced helmet.

With nowhere for either of them to hide, Gard pulled out his gun, stepped in front of her, and aimed at the figure. The motorcycle kept coming straight toward them.

Conscious of their bare backs, Desta brought out her own gun and, her back to Gard's, waited. There was always more than one of the goons.

The second motorcycle darted around the other side of the restaurant and headed toward her.

Gard's gun fired once, then again, but his motorcycle kept coming at them.

Swerving at the last moment, the motorcyclist smashed at Gard's bad knee with his foot.

Gard dodged but fell anyway against Desta's back. She toppled to the pavement, but scrambled to her feet with him. As her motorcyclist neared, she placed two shots in his chest.

It didn't stop him. He kept coming. The primitive within her wondered if he were human as the sane portion said, "He's wearing a bulletproof vest." She aimed higher.

The bullet ricocheted off his face mask.

She didn't have time to try the next logical target. He was on top of her, his arm grabbing at her.

Breath whooshed out of her as he caught her around the waist, and she was dragged against Gard who went down with her.

Stunned, she sagged in the motorcyclist's embrace as, like a horse trick-rider, he shoved her sidesaddle across the seat of the motorcycle in front of him and yanked her upright against his chest. The motorcycle wobbled violently, but the big man righted it with skill.

Gard was far behind her in the lot, the other motorcycle circling him like a shark with prey. It went for the kill.

Desta gasped with dismay. Miraculously, her gun still dangled in her hand, and with no other hope, she shot the next logical target.

As the bullet ripped through her motorcycle's engine, the driver swore as if he couldn't believe she would do anything so foolhardy or dangerous. He didn't know how desperate she was. Smiling grimly, she waited for the explosion. The engine rattled and groaned like all the pieces inside were twisting together.

The machine wobbled and slowed.

Her captor's attention now on stopping the cycle and saving his skin, she elbowed his stomach with all her strength. The motorcycle swayed. As he let her go to steady it, she jumped, hit pavement, and rolled as she'd been taught in horseback riding. Somehow, she survived. She came to rest on her belly and crawled up on her hands and knees as the cycle and rider smashed into a parked car. Groggy, she shook her head.

When her captor stayed sprawled on the ground in an ungainly black heap, she forgot him, found her gun, and staggered to her feet in search of Gard.

He still stood, barely, wavering as if he'd taken severe physical abuse. The cyclist seemed to be playing with him by darting by on the machine and smashing and kicking at him. She couldn't see Gard's gun. He must have lost it.

Her muscles ached, but she began to charge toward them.

In a run at Gard, the cyclist saw her. His black glass face turned to her and the wreck she'd left behind her then back to Gard. He lifted his gun to finish off Gard before coming after her.

"No!" She shot into the motorcycle's engine.

One or two other guns fired at that moment, then the motorcycle exploded throwing the rider into Gard. Both men went down.

Her back stung at her left shoulder, and the universe slowed, her muscles limp, her eyes dim, as she fell. She knew she'd been shot, but her last conscious thought was of Gard who hadn't moved from where he'd fallen.

~ * ~

Heat and the smell of burning gas washed over Gard as he dragged himself from under the motorcyclist's body. He crawled to his knees. The cycle burned six feet away. Swaying to his feet, he studied the battleground for his gun and Desta.

His gun lay twenty feet away; Desta lay far beyond on her stomach, Martin Corlich bending over her. Corlich flipped her over and slung her across his shoulder like a slab of unfeeling meat. Her head wobbled as if she were
dead or unconscious.

Gard reeled toward his gun.

His free arm around Desta's rump, Corlich smiled at him and fired.

Gard stared at the gun's barrel for a stupid moment then fell, his arm stinging. He stayed down.

With a nasty chuckle, Corlich dumped Desta into the back of a brown sedan at the street near their car, then slid into the passenger seat. The sedan sped westward.

Somehow, Gard came to his feet and explored the sting on his left upper arm. His fingers found a hypodermic bullet, trapped in his jacket, which hadn't penetrated fully. His left arm was already numb, and he blinked sleepily, fighting his desire to lay down.

The adrenaline surge of knowing Desta was drugged, not dead, kept him walking. Picking up his gun, her gun, and pocketbook, he tottered in the general direction of his car, fell in, started the engine, and drove westward although Corlich was already out of sight.

He prayed for a bunch of different miracles, but they were all included in one word—"Desta."

After a minute of blind driving, he remembered the directional device. He fumbled around for it in his jacket pocket as he added the prayer that Desta be wearing the homing necklace. His hand tightened around the tiny device, and he flipped it on.

Beep!

The sound was faint, but the tiny blip on the computer screen compass pointed dead ahead. He was still in the half mile range of the device. This road led directly out of Charlotte, and he was in the boondocks already. He speeded up.

After several miles, the beep seemed stronger as if he'd gained on Corlich, but then the direction blip swung violently to the north.

Studying the road map in his head, he took a left two roads later onto a two-lane road through farm country.

Sweat dripped down his back as he clinched the wheel. It would be so easy to take a wrong turn and lose them completely. It wouldn't take long for them to be completely out of range.

Somehow, his gamble had paid off. The beep was louder.

Stuck alone with a cheap Christmas present, he wished for Mark's help and the intricate electronics of the Bureau. He wished for all the hunter's luck he'd been so famous for. He wished for Desta alive and safe in his arms.

The direction shifted again.

As he turned, the faint beep vanished.

He slammed on his brakes and backed toward the last turn.

A car in his lane darted toward him, honked, then swerved just missing him.

Beep!

His heart started again, and he turned.

Hours seemed to pass as he concentrated on the tracking screen and turned, and turned, and turned, somehow always staying just in range. When the faint beeps stopped completely, he was almost too mesmerized with weariness to notice.

Pulling off the side of the road, he buried his head in his arms on the wheel and tried to remember where he'd gone wrong. There hadn't been another road for almost half a mile.

The image of a deserted motor freight warehouse shimmered like a desert mirage in his head. He turned around.

The huge flat-topped building was surrounded by an unmown field, the tall weeds already scraggly and summer brown. A large apron of grass-cracked asphalt stretched from the loading docks.

Stopping on the road, Gard examined his directional device. The beep was loud and sweet, and the directional blip pointed right at the building. Corlich and his men had come to ground.

Gard parked his car behind a stand of cedar trees, reloaded his automatic, and put three more bullet clips into his jacket pocket, then got out and crept toward the warehouse through the cover of the weeds. When he was almost at the asphalt, he paused.

No one was on guard, but the building was closed tight, all the dock doors shut. Almost at the roof on the wall beside the dock wall were several doors of recent construction that looked like barn hay doors. The warehouse must have been used recently as a storage place for hay or, more likely, tobacco. A cable still remained on the pulley above the door.

Flexing his now almost normal left hand, he grinned. Sometimes being a farm boy was damn handy.

After a quick check for guards, he trotted to the side of the building, grabbed the cable, and lifted himself hand over hand upward. When he reached the hay doors, he studied them. They seemed well oiled and should be quiet. He didn't want to warn Corlich of his approach because the assassin would kill Desta before coming after him.

With another prayer, he pulled the silent hay door open, swayed in on the cable, and landed on a second story loft that circled the inside of the warehouse.

His landing had been almost noiseless, but he startled nesting sparrows who flew upward with unhappy squawks. He threw himself to the floor.

"Damn noisy birds!" The man's voice echoed upward from across the room.

"Forget the birds."

Gard relaxed. They must be big city types who didn't understand the guard dog warning of birds. He crept toward the ledge of the loft to some rotting hay bales and peeked over.

Corlich and the goon shot during the chase from the Federal Building stood together on the floor below on the other side of the debris-littered warehouse. The goon still wore a sling. Gard could see no others. Hopefully, he'd left the other gang members lying in the restaurant parking lot.

Beyond them, a storage cage sat beside an ancient forklift.

He searched frantically for Desta.

In the shadows beyond the men on the floor, he could just spot the hem of the white pants she'd been wearing and a bare foot that was limp. Bastards.

He forced himself to remain calm. He'd love to just gun them down, but he couldn't risk Desta's life. While he was stopping them, he'd have to draw them away so they couldn't hurt her or use her as a hostage.

"Damn fools." Corlich swore. "Losing two more men getting a broad from one man."

"They went in expecting one ex-Fed and a screaming, clinging fluff, not a hellcat with a gun. She wasted both of them."

"When I told him we'd gotten her, he said there'd be a bonus. It had better be big. She's worth it. I've put down guarded diplomats with less trouble."

Obviously afraid of Corlich and his temper, the goon offered appeasingly, "That guy must have been lying, or she's a damn cop ringer. No rich, spoiled dame could do that. She must be a cop."

"This is the one we want. I look forward to killing her... slowly. She'll try to go bravely, and that makes her a challenge to destroy."

"We're to keep her alive until—"

"I know the terms of the contract. He said alive. He didn't say in what shape."

Gard shook with anger, and it took every bit of control he had not to kill the man. He crept around the edge of the loft until halfway to them, then stopped behind six moldering bales of last year's hay, and scavenged on the floor until he found a small stone. He tossed it to the floor below.

Tensing, the goon pulled out his gun.

"Ease up. It's a damn bird with the trots."

"Shhh. I hear something." The goon, his gaze toward the outside, crept toward the loft.

As he passed under the loft, Gard shoved the bales over the edge then charged to the left toward Desta.

The goon gave a startled grunt and collapsed under the hay.

Before Corlich could react, Gard jumped onto the roof of the fork lift, shimmied down onto the wheel, and to the ground. He searched for Desta, but she wasn't in the shadows where she'd been. Corlich must have her.

Corlich chuckled.

A shot smashed into the fork lift beside Gard.

He molded himself into its side.

"I have you, Gardner. You're a hard man to kill." Another shot ripped into the fork lift.

Peering around the corner of the truck, he searched for Corlich. Until he knew where Desta was, he couldn't risk a shot. A bullet whizzed past his cheek.

He crept around the fork lift.

Something thumped to the left, and he spun, but another gun went off as sparrows flew everywhere again. One bird lay dead on the floor.

That bird had given its life to tell him where Corlich was. Sighting his gun on the piled wooden boxes, he waited for Corlich to show himself again.

Something thumped to the right. Corlich's head darted upward.

Gard shot.

The head slid downward like a snake's.

Recognizing those thumps for what they were, Gard grinned. Desta was out there, alive, awake, away from Corlich, and in good pitching form.

He should circle around and try to get at Corlich since Corlich assumed he was trapped here guarding Desta's body, but if he moved, Corlich would realize Desta wasn't here and...

Rain began to pour outside and through the leaky roof, drumming and splashing loudly. Thunder rattled hard overhead.

Gard jumped. He hadn't even noticed the thunderclouds when he'd been outside. Nothing but Desta and Corlich's trail had existed for him in the last hour.

The deafening roar of the rain would mask Corlich's movement and Desta's pitching diversions. He peered around the fork lift but couldn't find Corlich.

What would he do if he were Corlich? Go up the ladder onto the loft where he could get a clear shot at Gard.

The birds flew upward in alarm.

Gard spun at the flash of human movement in the loft to his right.

Desta screamed Gard's name in warning.

As Corlich twisted, dodging a flung beer bottle, and shot toward him, Gard fired into Corlich's shoulder.

Glass shattered by Gard's head as Corlich fell off the loft to the ground below.

Gard charged around the fork lift to Corlich, but the man sprawled unconscious. Gard's bullet had struck his bulletproof vest, and the momentum had finished pushing Corlich off the wet loft ledge.

He checked the other man's pulse and his eyes, then took his gun, stiletto, a wallet, and keys.

Someone moved behind Gard. Remembering the goon, he spun and aimed.

Bedraggled and dirty, Desta staggered drunkenly toward him.

He glanced over to the goon who lay pinned and unconscious beneath the hay then folded his arms around her and squeezed.

Sniffing back tears, she buried her face in his shoulder. "Thought you were dead."

"I love you so much," he murmured into her hair. "How could I live without you?"

They just held each other for a long time, all that needed saying communicated by the fierceness of their embrace.

"He dead?" she finally mumbled.

"No, just out."

She shrugged as if the man didn't matter.

He caressed her straggling pinned hair, her wig and glasses lost in the past somewhere, and asked, "Will you be all right by yourself?"

She nodded and let him help her over to a large wooden crate, then slumped down as if she could barely sit up. Waving him away, she yawned, her eyes wide as if propped open by will alone.

He left her regretfully, returned to Corlich, picked up his legs, and dragged him over to the wire cage. The bars of the man-sized cage were in excellent shape, obviously intended for Desta's prison.

After making it Corlich's, he walked over to the goon under the hay, knelt, and put his hand on the man's throat. The man's pulse was steady, and his eyes wavered open. Seeing Gard, he began to struggle away.

"Be still, or I'll finish you off. Corlich can't help you."

Gard tucked the man's gun into the small of his back then began to toss away the bales. The hay was so sodden with moisture he could understand why its weight had held the man so effectively. A hay hook was embedded in the last bale.

Grimacing, he knelt by the man's side and gouged the hay hook's sharp end into the man's throat. "Who hired you?"

"I..."

"Who?"

"You won't use that."

"That was my woman you took and hurt. Guess again."

As he read Gard's intentions, terror shimmered deep within the goon's eyes.

"You can gut a man with this. I've seen someone put one through his thigh. It isn't pretty. Who hired you?"

"I don't know. Corlich was the only contact."

Surprisingly, the man appeared to be telling the truth. "What do you know of him?"

"His money was very good, his pockets were always full for expenses."

"Cal Ferret?"

"I don't... Maybe. I don't know. Corlich has worked for Ferret before. We were to get her and keep her alive for a while, then leave her body where it would never be found. That's all I know."

Gard eased the hook away from his throat and tossed it away. "Get up and clean your pockets."

The man staggered upright and dumped coins, car keys, a bullet clip, and a wallet onto the floor.

After frisking him, Gard motioned him with his gun to the storage cage, opened it, shoved him in, then rammed the new padlock closed. He pulled out the key.

"What are you going to do to me?"

"Leave you both here until you rot. Or maybe I'll tell the police about you." He swayed wearily back to Desta. "Let's get out of here."

With a nod, she came to her feet. His arm around her waist, he kept her in a straight line out of the warehouse. The rain had moderated, and the fields around them smelled of dampness and growth. Rain soaked them quickly.

Blinking rain out of her eyes, she kept pace with him through the field although her legs wobbled. Finally, she stopped, fell to her knees, and heaved out her lunch in the weeds. He knelt, holding her, and shielded her from the rain.

She rested her cheek in the hollow of his shoulder. "Back still aches. What did they do to me?"

"A hypodermic bullet from a gun. Like they use on wild animals. The dosage must have been too strong for your size."

"I'm a chimp, not a gorilla."

"You just fight like a gorilla."

With a laugh, she stood up, and they staggered toward the car.

"Do you need a doctor, Princess?"

"Bloody, battered, but not bent. Don't think so. You?"

"The same." He opened the passenger door and helped her inside.

Shaking rain out of his hair and face, he slid into the car and started the engine.

"Lovely car." Desta patted the dashboard. "Thought I'd never see you again."

"What about me? Don't I rate a compliment?"

"No words perfect enough for you." She curled up on the seat and rested her cheek on his thigh, the back of her head against his stomach. Her wet, matted hair was stuck to her face, her eyes were bloodshot and unfocused, and her torn, dirty blouse and pants were plastered against her frame, one foot was bare, a hole through her stocking. He'd never seen a more beautiful woman in his whole life.

Bringing the car back onto the main road, he pointed the car toward the fastest way to Charlotte.

Cold from shock and dampness, Desta shook violently against him, her fist clinched around his pant leg at his knee as if she feared he was only an illusion who'd vanish. He stroked her head to reassure her and himself about illusions.

Ten

Desta's hand trembled nervously as she daubed the perfume stopper's end between her breasts and behind her ears. She studied her image critically in the bathroom mirror, then fluffed her long clean hair around her shoulders. The black satin nightgown was perfect for her, and it didn't clash with all her bruises.

She had an insecure, jealous prince to win, and romance was hard enough without being a human road map of new and old bruises.

After taking several breaths for courage and calmness, she sashayed, her hips rotating enticingly, out into the small apartment's combination living and bedroom.

Looking out at the distant thunderstorm in the night sky, Gard stood at the open window, his shoulders slumped in sadness and defeat. Lightning shimmered across his blond hair.

Forgetting grand entrances, she walked up behind him, rested her head between his shoulder blades on his terrycloth robe, and just held him.

His arms wrapped around hers at his waist, and his shoulders straightened. "Nice bath, Princess?"

He smelled of the bath's herbal soap and the woodsy cologne she'd grown to love. "Wonderful. I'm finally completely awake. That and supper finished the cure."

His soft sound of pleasure rippled through his chest and into her arms. The tenderness inside so intense she ached, she squeezed him more tightly as she remembered his fierce protectiveness that afternoon when she'd been in danger, and his incredible gentleness when he'd found her, his hands tending her wounds and drying her body, his arms holding her so she could sleep peacefully without bad dreams.

They had come full circle back to the beginning of their relationship, and she hoped to the beginning of a more complete one.

She wanted to tell him how much she loved him, but it wasn't the right time. Tenseness that wasn't sexual held him rigid against her. "What's wrong?"

"I've gone over and over today, and I keep getting the same answers. Only three people knew about the lunch meeting at the restaurant—you, me, and Mark. Those men were prepared for us and that specific restaurant parking lot. That preparation took a lot of time, far more than the time we ate lunch in. They couldn't just have followed Mark. They knew way ahead of time, the same amount of time Mark knew. Mark betrayed us; he betrayed us to Corlich."

She'd come up with the same answer, but offered a possibility, "Maybe Mark told someone—his boss, or someone else."

"He swore he'd not. Every time we've told Mark where we were, or were going to be, Corlich has come. When we haven't spoken, Corlich hasn't been there."

"You didn't tell him about Daddy's condo."

"Not the exact location, but I mentioned Holden. It would be easy enough to connect our visit to it and find the address."

"But he warned you not to tell him of our location."

"He didn't have to know. He knew I'd meet him anywhere he asked when he was ready to finish us. By warning me, he made certain I wouldn't contact anyone else."

"I'm so sorry."

"Why did he do it? I thought I could trust him more than anyone else in the Bureau. He was my partner, my friend. He let me batter at him with all my anger and grief when I found out about Megan. He even let me beneath that smug patrician attitude of his. He cried with me."

With no answers to give, she just held Gard.

"Why? What could Corlich or Ferret give him? Mark Faulkner has everything. More money than he'll ever need, as many women. Power, family, breeding... In ten years, he'll walk into the directorship if he wants it."

"Daddy once said the only difference between the rich and the poor is the rich make a better bargain when they sell themselves."

"A typical, cynical O'Brien remark that goes right to the point and draws blood."

"Mark loves games. Maybe he was bored playing only one side of the board. He enjoys manipulating and examining you like you're a unique puzzle. He's never really wanted me except as a knee jerk reaction to any available female; he's been using me to needle you."

"And I jerk like a marionette every time he does."

Thinking of her father, she sighed. "Maybe games are the only way he knows how to react to people he cares for."

"I'm sick of games."

"Me, too. Come to bed. You've had no rest all afternoon tending me. Even when I was asleep, I could hear your brain wheels turning at high speed."

He chuckled. "I'll oil them later. I've got my plans made for Mark. I'll give him his chance to prove his honor, and if he fails, I'll give him to Braggonier garnished for trial with an apple in his mouth."

"That's tomorrow. Forget about him and everything else tonight, and come to bed." She rubbed her cheek against his back.

His breath caught, and he shuddered under her arms. "You take the bed, and I'll..."

"There are no couches, day beds, or other beds, and you aren't going to sleep on the floor or in the bathtub. Come to bed."

He sagged wearily. "My controls aren't the greatest right now, and I don't think..."

She released him. "Gabriel, would you turn around and look at me."

As if surprised by his given name, he turned. His blue eyes shimmered as he saw the sexy nightgown instead of her usual bland pajamas.

Tracing his upper lip where the mustache had been, she smiled shyly at him. "We haven't played games with each other, but we haven't been honest with each other either. I never dreamed a marvelous man like you could be so insecure, and I thought there was something wrong with me, and... But that doesn't matter. You blurted you loved me this afternoon, and..."

Gard flushed.

She rested her palm on his bare shoulder at the opening of his robe. "I love you, too, Gabriel. I enjoy being Gard's friend, but I'd very much like to be Gabriel's lover, too."

Nothing moved behind his face and eyes for a long, long moment as if she'd stunned him completely. Finally, he blinked, an incredulous smile starting in his eyes and lips. "You..."

"I love you very much. I've felt it from almost the beginning, and it's gotten stronger every hour I spend with you."

"Oh, Princess." He caught her jaws in his hands as if she were the most precious thing in the universe. "I love you very much, and it's gotten stronger every hour."

She smiled into his eyes, the light behind them glowing clear to his soul. He wrapped her in his arms and held her. Engulfed in his strength and tenderness, she buried her face in his shoulder and tried to share her own feelings in her embrace. She hadn't known until that moment how many years she'd wandered homeless and alone until she'd rediscovered home in his arms.

As if drawing comfort and healing from her, he gently rocked against her. He rested a cheek against her temple, his hand stroking her hair.

When the last of the tension and his emotional defenses fell, she realized how weary he was. Her heart ached with greater intensity for him, and she willed her own strength into him. "Come to bed, Gabriel."

"Yes, ma'am." He chuckled and nuzzled her ear.

Realizing what a pushy, wanton female she sounded and to a poor man almost dead on his feet, she blushed. "I didn't mean... You don't have to... If you're too tired, I'll understand." She blushed harder. "Oh, damn."

"What a bundle of wonderful contradictions you are, love. And nothing, not even exhaustion, will ever keep me from wanting you." He proved it by drawing her body into the crook of his and kissing her. His robe had opened, and the heat and fullness of him throbbed against her thigh through his pajama bottoms and her gown.

Moaning, she encircled his neck with her arms as she returned the slow, deep probing of his tongue. She brushed her breasts against his chest, the satin erotic black fire against her skin.

His finger tips danced in tiny circles on her nape, beneath her hair, then down her back.

Following his experienced lead in love as she had in danger, she nudged his robe off his shoulders, then explored the sleek hardness of his back and the angular wonders of his shoulder blades with her palms and fingers. A sheen of sweat touched his skin as his heart hammered against her.

His hands left her for a moment, shaking off the sleeves of his robe, then returned to her back and buttocks. He kissed his way down the cord of her throat to her shoulder strap.

She gasped in anticipation when he nuzzled her breast.

As if pleased by her reaction, he chuckled then breathed through the fabric in an openmouthed kiss. Her nipple tightened, desire exploding in lines of flame down to her belly, and she came up on her toes to offer more.

He steadied her with his hands on her hips and breathed again.

She whimpered into his hair and clutched his shoulders to stay on her feet.

He straightened. His eyes, wild with passion and tenderness, held hers, as he slid his hand under her shoulder strap and eased toward her back to untie it.

She stayed perfectly still as he wanted her to, and let him watch her as she watched him unveil her breast. His hand shook with eagerness as if he'd never seen her before. He never had with the eyes of an accepted lover.

When his fingers found the bare skin under her strap at her shoulder, she winced before she could control her face. His expression changed immediately to concern, and he turned her and pulled the fabric away. She could feel his anger as he examined the new deep bruises, which had blossomed in dark hues in the last hours.

"The bastard shot you twice, once at close range with that dart gun. No wonder you were so ill. Oh, Princess!"

"I ruined it," she said bitterly. "I wanted to be so beautiful and desirable for you, not a bruised and battered ugly wreck."

He smiled with chagrin and hugged her. "I'm the one who ruined it. I didn't mean... You're so beautiful, and every one of those bruises and cuts is a physical badge of courage that shows what a brave and splendid woman you are. Don't you know how magnificent you were fighting beside me, fighting not just for yourself but for me, too? I think you're beautiful, bruised or not. Can I start over again?"

"I love you, I respect you, I admire you, and I lust after your body." With vigorous nod, she hugged him.

"If I hurt you, tell me. I don't think you'll notice the minor discomforts soon. I never do."

"I'd rather tingle with you than take a hot bath and some aspirin. Are you all right?"

"Nothing a little tingling won't improve." He kissed her head. "I'm sorry I can only offer a dingy little garage apartment decorated in graduate school poverty for our first time together. I wanted to give you romance, candle light, and satin sheets."

"I haven't really seen anything in this place but you. You're the only real thing I remember today, or will remember."

He nodded as if understanding her need to forget all the ugliness and violence. "Tonight's real. You and I are real." He hefted her into his arms. "Come to bed, Princess."

"I thought you'd never ask, my prince." She wrapped her arms around his neck.

"I was afraid to," he admitted.

"You're not afraid of anything. You're wonderful."

His neck and cheeks turned red.

Charmed, she kissed his ear.

He carried her the short distance across the room, and perched her on the edge of the bed. She asked, "Would you cut off the lights? Bruises are more aesthetic in the dark."

The lamp by the bed he cut off, then he sat down beside her. She pointed at the dim light on the desk.

"No. I want to see you." The intensity in his hunter eyes was almost frightening as he studied her.

"I'll make a deal. I'm not embarrassed if you look, but not now. Give me two weeks to heal, then we can find a private place, an extremely private place in the sun, and you can examine every inch of me."

He grinned widely. "Sounds fun, but no deal."

"If you get grossed out, it's your own fault."

"I will never be grossed out by you or your beautiful, brave bruises." He patted her knee. "You are my Desta-knee."

She groaned at the pun.

Leaning toward her, he kissed her forehead, her nose, her lids, then her lips.

Her fingers tangled in his hair as she returned the probing gentle kiss. His fingers whispered across her back, and her gown shimmered down her breasts to her waist. He murmured his approval, "So perfect, Princess. White succulent fruit tipped with pink rosebuds. I want to hold them, worship them with my mouth, have them rub against my chest as I thrust into you."

"If that was a multiple choice question, I choose all the above."

"A woman of action, and not words."

"Just a few words. I love you, Gabriel." She pressed her breasts into his chest and kissed him.

His tongue caressed hers as they eased back onto the bed with him on her. The heat and texture of his hand curved around her bare breast, and he stroked her.

Groaning, she thrust upward. "Even my scalp tingles when you touch me."

With a sexy chuckle, he sat up, wiggled out of his pajamas, and tossed them away. Her gown had disappeared sometime during the kiss. She lay back on the bed, her hair splayed around her, and let him study her. Despite her shyness, she reveled in the pleasure and passion within his gaze.

She stared at him as frankly, not having had the sneak previews he'd had except for his chest. He was glorious—classically formed and proportioned. His untanned skin held the gold cast of his hair. His broad shoulders tapered down to narrow hips, muscular thighs, flat belly, and the full glory of his manhood.

Her stomach fluttered with nerves and anticipation.

He stretched out beside her, facing her, his head propped on his hand, and grinned.

"Nice rump," she offered, feeling she had to say something, then winced at the stupidity of the comment.

His eyes twinkling, he pouted. "Just the rump?"

"No. You're beautiful. Every inch of you is beautiful, and all together it's perfect. I love you and would think you're beautiful even if you weren't, but you're beautiful."

Red splashed across his cheeks and down his chest again.

"Why are you so embarrassed by your good looks? They're the least perfect thing about you."

"The least perfect? That was the most underhanded extravagant compliment I've ever gotten."

"And I meant every underhanded word of it." She opened her arms to him.

He eased against her and cradled her head in his arm. "I like your rump too, and every other part of your body. You're perfect. I even like that sharp-tongued mouth of yours with its underhanded compliments. I love you, Desta." He kissed her smile then each nipple.

Fire behind each breast, she gasped. "Gabriel."

Burying his head between her breasts, he nuzzled her. "Mmmm?"

"I'll need some coaching. I've never..."

His tender blue eyes glowing, he lifted his head and smiled at her. "I know, love. You told your guardian angel. I'll make it perfect for you."

"Gabriel."

He tapped her lips. "Lesson One. Making love is emotions and physical reactions. Don't try to intellectualize it. Don't talk it to death because you're nervous. Just relax, hold on tight, and trust me."

With a mental shrug, she didn't tell him she was at her most fecund time of her monthly cycle. Whatever the future of their relationship, she'd cherish and love the child, if it came, as much as the father.

"You're still thinking, love," he admonished with a smile and caught her nipple between his lips and licked.

Her brain shorted out as her back jolted off the mattress. His arms cradled her more tightly, and he began to caress her breasts with his lips. Hardening and swelling beneath his exploration, her breasts heaved as she fought for breath.

Her nipples stung and ached for him, but his lips retreated after coming tantalizingly near. When she didn't think she could bear the teasing any longer, he licked her.

She yelped with delight and thrust upward.

His lips caught her and sucked and pulled, the sensation traveling unknown routes to secret places waiting for his discovery.

Lightning flashing behind her lids, she closed her eyes and stroked the rough hairs at the nape of his neck. His fresh-shaven cheek rasped against her breast as his hand cupped her, kneading to the rhythm of his mouth.

The ache appeased in her breasts, it traveled downward. She wriggled with discomfort as it settled between her legs and throbbed.

Gard's hand journeyed downward as if he understood and rested hot, heavy, and comforting against her belly.

Her legs opening slightly, she groaned and thrust her pelvis upward. His fingers slid through her hair then cupped her. She trapped him there, the heat and pressure intensifying and soothing her ache. Her pelvis ticked upward again.

He murmured soft nonsense words of love and reassurance, and his thumb rotated against her.

Her muscles relaxed, her desire liquid, and her body blossomed under his hand. Her hips moved to the rhythm of his hand, bringing sweet languor, but the ache had gone deeper still. She clutched his shoulders.

Again he understood. Lifting his head from her breast, he slid upward between her parted legs. His weight settled on her.

Explosions popped through her where their bodies met, chest against breast, and belly to belly. She strained upward toward the branding heat of him.

Cradling her shoulders, Gard dusted kisses across her sweaty face. "Desta."

She opened her eyes. Lightning flickered across the classic angles of his face and through the gold of his hair. He smiled down at her with his soul in his sky blue eyes and whispered, "I love you."

As she smiled her own love into his eyes, he entered her. A moment of surprise and pain.

His body tensed and stilled against hers. "Are you all right?"

"It's wonderful. Don't stop."

He rocked forward with caution as if she were the most fragile woman alive. With a joyful laugh, she circled his shoulders with her arms. The slight discomfort was nothing to the wonder of the heat and fullness.

When he sensed her ease and pleasure, his rhythm steadied. Her body began to meet and cling to his in the instinctive dance of surge, tense, and pull that went on and on as the joy intensified.

She would have been lost in the dazzling newfound delights her body discovered, but Gard's presence and love held her with him. The light of his soul sparkled within becoming part of her, their spirits two stars linked as one.

She brushed back the damp hair from his passion-fired eyes and covered his face with kisses. "Oh, love."

In a roar of thunder and rain, the storm that had threatened all evening finally arrived, drowning out their hard-breathing chants of passion.

Storm wind gusted through the window across their hot bodies, and the curtain billowed out.

Panting, Desta tossed her head as ecstasy spiraled deep within. Her spirit was that curtain, and Gard was the wind that filled her. She billowed out, out, out...

When she fluttered back into existence, Gard still moved within her, his lips whispering across her forehead. He stroked her head and laughed with her pleasure as her incredulous eyes met his.

Her laughter joined his, and she met his faster thrusts, sensing his own near completion. Thunder and lightning rumbled and flashed in quick succession above them.

She became the lightning as blue-white energy flashed up her spine from their joining. Jolting, her hips lifting both of them off the mattress, she cried out his name, then vanished in a puff of white smoke as the energy melted her.

Returning to the darkness after the lightning, she found him as the thunder took him. Her name echoed above the storm, and his body convulsed against her.

She held him through his storm, wrapped her legs around him, and held him beyond as the after tremors shook them both.

She'd never felt closer to anyone or more loved in her whole life.

The rasp and thunder of his breath and heart quieted finally, and he nuzzled her throat. He asked, "Are you all right?"

"That was wonderful!" She hesitated a moment. "That was wonderful, wasn't it?"

"I thought so."

"Good. Some men have said..."

"What?"

"I didn't go crazy or straight to bed with them when they kissed me so they said I was cold."

"There are certain explosives that can be burned, battered, and dropped, but they won't explode unless they're attached to a certain detonator."

"Then you're my special detonator, my sexy Swedish prince."

He murmured a smug, "Mmmm hmmm," against her throat.

"And how did the detonator like it?"

"Mmmm! He exploded with the greatest of pleasure, too."

"I was adequate then."

"If a nuclear warhead is just a bomb, then you were just adequate. You're extraordinarily responsive, which is sexy as heck for me, and you have great reciprocating instincts."

"All hints about reciprocating would be greatly appreciated."

"They shall be given. We'll let you get comfortable first."

"I'm very comfortable with you, my love. And so happy."

He rolled to his side, taking her with him, and she nestled against him as he pulled the sheet around them. With his physical stamina, she could ask him for another detonation even though he was exhausted, and he'd comply, but she didn't have the heart even though her body had other ideas on the subject. She rubbed her face against his chest. He smelled of sexy Gabriel musk, sweat, and their lovemaking.

"You are going to be very sore tomorrow, Princess."

"The motorcycle fall and the dart gun won't get me down," she assured him.

"That wasn't where I was talking about." With a knowing chuckle, he fell asleep against her.

Deciding it was the nicest soreness she'd ever have, she settled down to sleep.

~ * ~

Gard stretched away from Desta, putting his coffee cup on the night stand, then leaned back against the bed's headboard. She snuggled more comfortably against his bare shoulder.

He kissed her forehead, his fingers fondling her hair. "We need to talk, Princess."

A sad sigh escaped. She'd known their illusion of love and safety couldn't last forever, although he'd assiduously closed himself into the kitchen with the phone when he made all his calls that morning between snuggling and making love. Forgetting and loving had been sweet while it lasted. She nodded and straightened.

His eyes glistened with passion and tenderness, and she wondered if he'd take off her nightgown for the third time that morning, but then they darkened. "I wanted to choose a better way and better time to ask, but... I wanted to give you somewhere better for your first night of love, too, but..." He caught her hand. "Would you marry me?"

She blinked with surprise. He certainly could have done a better job of proposing.

When she didn't answer immediately, he murmured bitterly, "I know you could do a lot better than me with my mortgaged house, little boy, and plebeian job, but I do love you, and I think I could make you happy."

"I thought you... Last night didn't have a price tag, Gabriel. It was a gift, a gift of love. You don't have to do the noble thing and marry the ex-virgin."

He shook his head as if she made no sense. "I had no intention but to marry you. I certainly wouldn't have..."

With a laugh, she wrapped her arms around his neck. "What a medieval, honorable soul you have, my white knight. Yes, I want to marry you. And I love your house, your job, and I especially love you and Zach. I even love your dog."

"Yes?"

"Yes! Absolutely, positively yes! I love you, and I want to marry you, spend the rest of my life with you and your son, and have your children. Is that yes enough for you?"

"Are you certain?"

She almost socked him for stupidity, but his hunter eyes twinkled with mischief so she picked up the pillow and socked him for meanness instead, pounding his chest to each answer. "Yes, yes, yes, and yes."

He yanked the pillow away from her, pinned her carefully with his chest, his legs between hers, and grinned down at her. "Was that yes?"

Her heart began to beat harder with anticipation, her body readying itself for him. She smiled and blinked tears. "When you gave me my engagement ring and acted like it was just pretend, my heart almost broke."

"I don't know whether I'm a bigger blind idiot or a coward."

His bizarre insecurity had been the culprit then as it was now as it rebuilt the wall between them, but the wall couldn't stay if their love was to last. The wall wouldn't remain if she had anything to do with it.

She wrapped her arms around his neck. "Momma would have approved of you for me. You fit her description of what she wanted for me perfectly."

He didn't seem as impressed as he should have been. "And your father?"

"What does he know about love after walking away from Momma for the Gingers. His idea of my perfect man is Dun Dubois who's made of emotional cardboard."

"Lauton O'Brien certainly won't approve of one of his flunkies as a son-in-law."

"You are definitely not a flunkey. Daddy doesn't think that. He wouldn't have trusted me with a flunkey. He would have only trusted me with an equal."

As if he didn't believe her, Gard shrugged.

"Who cares what Daddy thinks. He ruined his life, and he can keep his manipulating fingers out of mine. Let's seal this engagement with a kiss." She lifted herself and rubbed her nose against Gard's.

His brain elsewhere, he didn't react.

She let him think sad, deep thoughts for several long moments then captured his ear lobes between her fingers. "I've got you in a Billy Bob death grip, and you're in my power."

Returning from wherever he'd been, he blinked and tried to shake off her fingers. They wouldn't shake off. "The famous cousin Billy Bob who taught you how to shoot?"

"That's him, William Robeson Tyler the Fourth. He also taught me how to French kiss, drive, and... some other things. We were twelve and thirteen and decided French kissing was yucky."

"I'm relieved about that. Let me go."

"No, you're at my mercy, slave. Do my biding, or I'll finish you off with the death grip." She grinned triumphantly.

He detached her fingers from his ears.

She stared in disbelief. "That never happened when Billy Bob did it."

"You can't kill anyone through the ear lobes either."

Sighing dramatically, she slumped. "I'm disillusioned. Billy Bob swore it would work."

"His anatomy information wasn't accurate."

"I hope it's improved. He's an intern in neurosurgery at John Hopkins."

As she'd hoped, her silliness eased the tension behind his eyes, and he laughed. "Oh, Princess. You and that tongue of yours." He rubbed his face against hers. "What did you want of your slave?"

"The future Mrs. Gabriel Gardner wanted a kiss."

"Yes?"

"Yes! Yes! I'll marry you. Would you like it written in blood?"

He nudged her gown upward with his leg until his knee rested intimately against her. It rotated gently.

She almost jolted them both off the edge of the bed.

He kissed her slowly, his tongue exploring her, and his hands feathered up and down her hips. "Want something more than a kiss?"

Stars sparkled overhead even in daylight as her body exploded with tingling. She slid her hands around his chest to his bare buttocks and assured him huskily, "Oh, yes."

This third time, the nightgown never came off.

Eleven

Noonday heat wavered above the country road's asphalt and the young corn in the fields, and shimmered as mirage pools in front of the sedan's nose. Desta stirred restlessly in her seat. She was sick of the car, sick of the constant tight knot of fear in her stomach. This morning, she'd become engaged, and she should be home calling friends and family, or making plans and love with her future husband, not meeting treacherous Mark, and baiting him into attempting the murder Corlich had botched.

Gard glanced to her then back to the road. "It won't be long, Princess."

Smiling wanly, she squeezed his hand. He had the agony of Mark's betrayal to accept and prove; she shouldn't complain. "I love you, Gabriel Gardner."

"I love you, Desta O'Brien. Desta Gardner has rather a ring to it." He smiled happily.

"It positively sings."

"I've never heard the name Desta before."

"It's an old family name from the Tylers. I don't know what it means."

"Short for Desdemona?"

"Perhaps."

"I don't fancy the role of Othello. I'd never kill you but with kindness, but Mark would make an excellent Iago."

Fear goose bumps streaked down her arms. "A man without a conscience who manipulates for the sake of manipulating."

"And who shall be manipulated in turn and meet his just ends." Gard turned off the road onto an empty meadow by a stand of elderly oaks, and parked in their shade.

A big man, wearing hunting camouflage and a sophisticated rifle with a giant scope over his shoulder, materialized out of the shadows.

It took several moments for Desta to recognize Bubba Henson out of his Swedish chef's apron. Here he appeared positively dangerous.

Gard didn't seem alarmed so she relaxed and followed him as he limped over to Bubba and shook his hand.

Bubba tipped his cap. "Howdy, gal. Nice seeing you looking well."

"Hello, Bubba." She smiled at him.

Bubba's hard little eyes flashed over them, and he grinned. "You going to remember me for that buffet smorgasbord for your wedding?"

With a shy nod, she showed him the engagement ring.

Chuckling, Bubba clapped Gard on the shoulder, almost knocking him down. "About time, boy. Nice gal, must have some Swedish in her, too. Will one day anyway with some Swedish babies."

"Did you get the equipment?"

"Easy as pie. Just used your name like you said. Even got the van with the recording equipment and a technician aboard. Got it stashed over there." Bubba pointed toward a thicker stand of trees, then handed Gard a man's wristwatch.

"This is a radio transmitter. A bug," Gard told her and slid it on his wrist, then asked the other man, "Are you certain the unit is active?"

"Say something." Bubba lifted a headphone from his neck and settled it over his ears then backed away.

Gard whispered, "Do you have any Swedish blood, Princess?"

"No, but I'm willing to convert."

Bubba snickered and pulled the headphone off his ears. "Every word. It's being recorded in the van, too." He took the rifle off his shoulder. "Got something neat here. Works as both a telephoto video camera and as a sniper rifle. I can plug the bastard, and take his picture at the same time. I've got a nice perch in one of those trees."

"No. I don't want you to take the chance. This is my risk," Gard protested. "Mark's a Federal agent. If I can't prove he's crooked, you'll never get out of jail."

Bubba patted his shoulder. "Only as a last resort, boy. If thing's go bad, and you can't handle him, I will. A simple clean shot with the tapes and the video as evidence in my favor. I don't want you and that pretty little gal dead, and me just watching. I'll take my chances."

"The risk..."

"I'm good at this. During the war, I potted a lot of Nazis with a sniper gun not a tenth as good as this one, and I've gotten a few deer since. Heck, this is returning to my glory days. Fun. It also makes us about even for my boy."

"I didn't do..."

Bubba's eyes hardened even more, and he said stubbornly, "He'd be dead now if you hadn't helped. Hush now about this, or I'll trot through those woods and talk to Mr. Faulkner myself, and I won't do it so polite as you."

"Very well. Remember, though, that I have no proof yet, besides logic and surmise, he's anything but an honest agent."

Bubba shrugged.

To ease the tension, Desta asked, "Did you get your restaurant damage paid for, Bubba?"

"Sure did, gal. That lawyer of yours shelled it right out, no questions, but he sure did bend my arms about you." Bubba beamed. "Asked all about you. How you was doing, whether you was hurt, what happened, what was said. I think he must be sweet on you as upset as he was."

"He wants Daddy as a father-in-law more than me as a bride. I don't think his heart will be badly damaged when I marry Gard."

Bubba turned to Gard. "I'll be right over there so position yourself out of my line of sight so I can get a clean shot and photo of Faulkner."

Gard studied where he'd pointed. "Very well. You know where to meet us if we walk away from the meeting?"

Bubba nodded again.

Desta shivered at Gard's "if we walk away."

"Thanks, Bubba." Gard shook his meaty hand.

"Get out of here now." Bubba patted Desta's shoulder. "Take care, gal."

"Thank you, Bubba." She brushed a kiss on his cheek and got back into the car.

Gard slid into the driver's seat and started the engine.

"What happened to his son?"

"He's an importer." Gard backed and returned to the road. "He got caught in a messy political problem in the Middle East and was jailed. I used my contacts to light fires under some bureaucratic tails in the State Department to get him out. They did. It was just a few phone calls."

"Mmmm hmmm," she offered, unconvinced. "The shine on your white knight armor is showing. I bet a string of knightly deeds trails behind you to the horizon."

"Are you sure you don't want to stay with Bubba?"

"No, and you couldn't keep me there. It's back to back like in the parking lot, or it's nothing. I won't let you face the danger alone."

"I didn't think so, my little hellcat with a gun."

"I'm even getting good reviews from the goons."

"If you can't earn the respect of your enemies..."

"Nothing like the respect of a sadistic killer," she assured him dryly.

On the other side of the oaks, he turned off the road again into a fallow grassy meadow of last year's hay. A new black Ferrari, obviously not of Government Issue, sat in the middle of the meadow with Mark Faulkner lounging against its side, his arms crossed. Gard stopped a distance away. "We'll walk to keep the car out of Bubba's line of sight. Stay away from my gun hand. I don't know when he'll try for us."

Her heart hammering with panic and stage fright, she stepped out of the car and walked beside Gard at his awkward limping pace, but she wasn't able to maintain her easy facade long on the hard uneven dirt as she had earlier. She began to hobble with all the grace of Great Aunt Toot on a bad day of arthritis.

A groan of distress rattled inside Gard's chest, and he wrapped his arm around her waist to help her. "You sneak. Why didn't you tell me you were hurting?"

"And be put to bed alone for the duration? No, thank you. It only hurts," she winced, "all over. Damn motorcycle."

From his lazy, disinterested slouch, Mark jerked upright and rushed to them with seeming genuine concern and caring. "My God, are you injured?" He studied them both as if trying to decide which battered victim needed medical attention first. "Let me..."

Desta would have been touched by his intense concern for them both if she could have believed it. She waved him away. "I just feel like the hockey puck at the end of the season. Bruised and sore, nothing else." She winced again. "The day after is supposed to be the worst. I hope."

Mark rested a hand on Gard's shoulder. Gard nodded reassurance.

Agitated, Mark raked his fingers through his hair, and she noticed his bloodshot eyes and exhausted face for the first time. "When I heard about the attack at the restaurant and talked to the eyewitnesses... My God, I thought you'd both been taken, and your trail was nonexistent like you'd vanished off the earth, and I knew..." He shivered. "Corlich's file about what he does to victims isn't pretty." He blinked back into the present and asked Desta, "Would you like to sit in my car?"

"I stand good," Desta assured him. "It's the walking I have trouble with."

"What kinds of news reports are there?" Gard asked.

"We've kept you and Desta out of it. The two motorcyclists and the attack are being called a gang war attack by the press. Neither of them is in any shape yet to be interrogated, but they have records a mile long. What the hell happened after I left?"

Gard gave a quick sketch of events in the parking lot.

Mark's brown eyes flickered with disbelief, and his eyebrow rose with its normal sardonic arch as he listened. "Desta wiped out both men herself? Why don't you hire her to guard you?"

"I had the advantage of surprise," she said. "They didn't think a spoiled, rich broad could defend herself, and they didn't even attempt to protect themselves from me. They were scared silly of Gard."

"Why did you shoot into the motorcycle you were on? That's crazy."

As if interested in that answer himself, Gard examined her face.

"I preferred public incineration with Gard to private death at the pleasure of..." She shuddered. "You don't have to read the files of his sick killings if you've looked into those inhuman eyes of his."

"Our greatest advantage, beyond their disregard of Desta, was their own natures," Gard said. "Sadists make lousy, inefficient killers. They were so eager to hurt and humiliate me before they killed me they missed their opportunity to get me, and we got them."

Mark shook his head with understanding. "What happened next? Corlich had Desta, and you were on your face in the parking lot."

"Desta was wearing a small homing device. I followed her with that. They, Corlich and his remaining goon, finally stopped near here at a deserted warehouse. I went in after them. Desta was awake by then, and she distracted them by tossing debris. I captured them both. They're in a cage there all ready for you." Gard grimaced. "I hope you have better luck than I did getting information about who paid them for the job. They wouldn't even tell me who's been feeding them inside information about Desta."

Mark stiffened, and Desta waited for him to pull his gun, but he asked, "Inside information?"

"Don't be stupid. How do you think they've found us so easily? Someone has been feeding them the information. Yesterday at the restaurant was a well prepared setup. We walked into a trap like mice, and you were the cheese."

"But I didn't tell anyone at the Bureau. Who have you been talking to?"

Gard's voice was unruffled. "You."

With nervous fingers, Mark mangled his styled hair again. "And you have Corlich ready for arrest?"

"Yes, I've called Braggonier to pick him up. He should be here in," Gard glanced at his watch, "twenty minutes."

"And Corlich is near here?"

"Less than a mile. A deserted warehouse on the intrastate east of here." Gard smiled as if he didn't realize he was giving Mark a motive for killing them both, then freeing or killing Corlich to cover his trail of duplicity.

"I guess I'd better get over there soon. Have you decided on protective custody, Desta?"

A whimper of distress caught in her throat. She hadn't even thought of protective custody or exile since the restaurant. Leaving Gard now, perhaps forever, after a few hours of love and happiness...

"She doesn't want protective custody," Gard said. "Right after we leave you, I'm putting her on a plane for Europe before Ferret finds out he's lost her and his assassins. She has contacts there and can remain underground indefinitely. I'll only let her come home when Ferret and our informant are in jail for good."

A chunk of her heart died, but she knew Gard was right. She was dangerous to Gard and especially to Zach now; exile was the best choice.

His face twisting with thought, Mark tensed suddenly as if aware Gard had just given him a second excellent motive for killing them.

Gard's body became still in response as he waited for Mark's attack.

"Well, I offered." Mark studied her. "Are you sure you're all right?"

Her voice was hoarse with strain. "Fine."

He brushed a kiss on her cheek and whispered, "Take care, Dusty. Give my love to Paris." He patted Gard's shoulder. "I'll be seeing you soon, old buddy. I'll get your statement then. You didn't say a word about Desta's itinerary to me, not a word. I don't know she's leaving."

Gard nodded. "Thanks."

"I figure I owe you for my leaving that restaurant instead of staying. We could have wiped out Corlich together. Night, Day, and the dangerous damsel would make a good team." He sauntered back to his Ferrari.

As he drove toward the road, dust pluming behind, Desta shook her head. "He didn't kill us."

"He didn't even make the first try." Gard's shoulders sagged with strain, and he lowered his head. "Thank God."

She hugged him. "I think that game-playing idiot really cares for you."

Gard buried his face in her shoulder. "We're friends. He couldn't kill me, but maybe he thought freeing or killing Corlich would be enough. Let's go see."

When he picked her up, she squeaked with protest.

"Hush. I'm less gimpy than you are." He carried her to the car and put her in. "We'll meet you at the van, Bubba."

For a moment she thought he was crazy, then she remembered the microphone on his wrist.

Gard started the car and drove across the meadow to another road.

"Short cut?" she asked.

"Short cut." A minute later, they pulled off the road behind a dirty blue van. Beyond, Desta could just see the warehouse where she'd been held prisoner the day before.

Rubbing away the memory goose bumps of fear on her arms, she limped after him to the van, and he lifted her up into it. The wall areas behind the driver's seat looked like an electronics store. Several television monitors and a tape recorder she recognized, but all the other equipment was a mystery. A stranger sat at a huge control console. She asked, "What—?"

Feedback blared at them. Yanking off his headphones, the stranger swore and hit switches silencing the din. The man studied them with sharp foxy green eyes from a forest of bushy red beard and long Brillo hair. "Forgot to cut off your unit."

"What's happening?" Gard took off the bugged watch and handed it to the other man.

"Bubba reports Faulkner's car approaching. Where did you get that guy, Gardner? He's like a B war movie."

"His real war record makes John Wayne look like a sissy. What have you set up, Jack?"

"I have a camera in the loft of the warehouse." Jack tapped the left monitor. "The jokers in the cage didn't even hear us come in and set up. They were too busy bitching about sharing that cage. We have clear pictures." He flicked it on.

The camera showed a long shot of the cage. Corlich and the goon sat on its floor. Desta's hackles rose even though she was in the safety of the van, and she nestled against Gard's side and wrapped her arm around his waist. He brushed a kiss on her forehead and rested his arm around her shoulder.

Gard asked, "Do you have audio?"

"Yes." Jack flicked another switch. The sound of the warehouse sparrows filled the van. Corlich and the goon weren't speaking, and the goon sprawled against the cage as if asleep.

Jack wiggled the headphone at his ears. "Bubba reports Faulkner's circling the building and reconning for danger."

Several tense minutes passed as they waited for Mark to enter and free or kill the men who could expose him. Finally, he came. They could hear his steps on the concrete floor of the warehouse.

Corlich must have heard him, too, because he stood up and shouted, "Help! Help!"

Mark sauntered into view and stopped in front of the cage. "Troubles?"

All outraged innocence, Corlich smiled. "I'll say. Some men are holding us hostage. Could you free us? They'll be back soon." The goon grinned like a schoolboy.

"I'm afraid I can't help you, Mr. Corlich." Mark pulled out a badge and I.D. and flashed it. "FBI. You both are under arrest." He began to read them their Miranda rights.

Gard laughed with disbelief. "Are you sure Corlich doesn't know the camera is there?"

"Positive."

Gard's voice trembled with puzzlement. "Mark has no way of knowing he's being filmed. Why shouldn't he free them if he's working for the same man?"

"Maybe he thinks he's safe because he's only spoken to Ferret, and they don't know he's been supplying the information," Desta said.

"They would still be dangerous to Mark. They lead us to Ferret, and Ferret would lead us to Mark. Plus, Mark knows we suspect an informant so he's got an even stronger motive to keep Corlich out of our hands. It makes no sense if Mark's betrayed us."

"Then he didn't betray us." Desta smiled happily for Gard's sake.

"Then who did? No one else knew our plans but Mark."

"Bugs."

They both jumped at Jack's voice. Gard asked, "Bugs?"

"Why not? An office, a phone. Simple enough. CQureCo makes most of its money sweeping for industrial bugs. We find them, too."

"FBI headquarters? We do routine sweeps."

"Damn government budget cuts."

"True enough."

"You called Mark this morning," Desta said, "yet, no one tried to kill us in that meadow. If there was a bug, why didn't Ferret send someone to our rendezvous? A drug lord shouldn't be short on hired muscle."

"Mark wasn't at the office. I got him on his cell phone." Excitement lit Gard's face, and he hugged her, his lips finding hers.

Encircling his neck with her arms, she returned the happy, passionate kiss. Her muscles limp, her nerves tingling, she forgot the reason for the kiss, she forgot their audience, she forgot their location, she forgot...

"Oh, Princess."

She smiled dreamily up at him.

His hand captured her braid sliding it through his fingers, then he released her, his sky blue eyes becoming a hunter's again. He asked Jack, "Can I use your phone?"

Jack pointed toward the driver's seat. "Help yourself. I'll add it to your bill."

Gard disengaged himself reluctantly and limped to the front of the van.

Her hands shook when she smoothed her perfectly smooth hair. Pointing to the monitor, she asked Jack,
"Anything happen?"

"Faulkner read them their rights. They offered some obscene comments on his ancestry. He walked back outside. Bubba reports he's leaning against the front door waiting for someone."

Sitting down at another console, she tried to get her brain functioning again on the new information about Mark. She thought about Mark's conversation with them in the meadow, about game playing, and about men who won't admit feeling love.

~ * ~

Gard murmured in her ear, "I told you the hot water would help the sore muscles."

Mellow from heat and happiness, she wiggled in his lap, laughed huskily, and rubbed her cheek on his chest. "Is that the only reason you got me in here?"

With a sexy chuckle, he stroked her spine, bath water sloshing around them. "Not the only one, Princess. Am I so transparent?"

She caressed down the hard smooth muscles of his chest and belly, then circled and stroked the growing evidence with her fingers. "Your motive is quite apparent."

His hips ticking upward lifting them both, he groaned. Water splashed over the side of the tub onto the floor of the tiny garage apartment bathroom. "If we keep this up, I'm going to make you a parent."

"Mmmm. You're keeping it up just fine. I once swore I'd only have the children of a man who punned worse than I did." She turned in the tub so that she faced him, her legs straddling one of his. A relaxed, sexy smile on his face, he leaned back in the tub, his head against the wall. Sadness that this could be their last time together before she left for

Europe stabbed at her, but she forced herself not to think of endings, only of making perfect memories and love to this wonderful man.

Her nipples already painfully hard, she slithered her breasts against his wet chest and nibbled her way across his forehead, his silky blond hair tickling her nose. Tiny explosions ricocheted through her breasts, and she ground herself against the hardness of his thigh.

"Oh..." His hands caught her buttocks pulling her more snugly against him, and he rocked against her, the sloshing hot water a second whole body caress. "It doesn't take a great detective—"

"Like you."

"Like me to figure out you aren't using any birth control."

"Not a one." She licked his ear discovering structure and texture. "I'm as healthy as a horse, and the doctor says I can have lots of easy, healthy babies. Not a genetic problem in either bloodline."

His heart beat erratically against her breast, his pulse under her lips. He tasted like sea water. "Me neither."

She gently nipped the skin where shoulder and neck joined and rubbed her thumb against his nipple. It rose to her touch, his body shuddering. "Blondes on both sides, too. Just might produce some more golden Swedes."

"Nothing wrong with chocolate-eyed little Madonnas." His fingers slid up her thigh, stroked, then probed. She undulated against him, her femininity blossoming like a water lily. He nuzzled her head. "You smell of sunshine."

Hotter than the water, his manhood throbbed against her stomach. Caressing it, she kissed him. He closed his eyes, his golden lashes against his tanned cheeks. Arching and rubbing, she kissed his lids, lashes, and cheeks. "I love you, my wonderful guardian angel."

"Oh, Desta..."

As his fingers danced within her, she threw her head back in ecstasy. The water seemed to slow and intensify the sensations until she thought she'd go mad with them. "Are you ready?"

His chuckle was so deep it seemed painful. "If I were any more ready, I'd embarrass myself."

"I know the theory of this, but please help me with the details."

His hands steadied and guided her as she sheathed herself on him. Her eyes widened with the miracle of their joining, the joy still as great as it had been their first time. "Oh..." She arced as they cleaved completely together. Two bodies now one and perfect.

He lifted his knees behind her and clutched her hips.

Quakes shattering her, she inhaled sharply and sagged forward. He buried his head against her breast, keeping her still on him, and suckled as his other fingers found their joining and danced against her.

Writhing, she exploded again and again and again...

When she returned from wherever she's been, he held her against him and on him, his hands stroking up and down her back. He nuzzled her hair and her ear. "My love?"

"Oh my!"

"Your waves about emptied the tub on that one."

He'd exaggerated, only several inches were missing, but the remaining water had gotten considerably hotter. Intending to get it hotter still, she rotated her hips, then experimented with a lift upward then a thrust back down against him. When he sighed and his hip ticked up to meet her, she wrapped her arms around his neck and kept repeating it, using the rhythm she'd learned from him. She kissed his head, bent backwards in pleasure, his eyes half-closed like a sleepy cat.

When he began to move faster, she danced to his hungrier rhythm until he exploded within her taking her with him.

When all their fragments of self floated back down and rejoined, he chuckled and pulled her tightly against his chest. "There went the rest of the water."

The tub was almost half empty. "What a way to go." She rested her head on his shoulder as reality and remembering returned. "Was that a farewell performance?"

"Whose?"

"Mine. On a jet plane to Europe."

"Oh, what I told Mark. No, not if I have my way about it. I'm not beaten yet. I have no intention of being beaten. You're mine." He squeezed her tightly. "I won't be parted from you ever again."

"And if I have to leave?"

"I'll find a way to get you back. Even if I have to kill Ferret myself."

"Don't you dare, Gabriel. You could get killed. You have to think about Zach."

"You're a special lady, Princess." He massaged down her back with a soapy hand.

Purring happily at the tender gesture, she found the soap herself. With soapy hands, she stroked down his chest then up his shoulders, the muscles tight and smooth, then to his arm pits.

He skirted gently over bruised ribs above her waist. "Here's a nice one. I've never seen that shade of green before."

"You wouldn't recognize me without them, or me you."

"I'd like to."

"Mmmm hmmm. What's a courtship like without someone trying to kill you?"

"Quieter. Much quieter. But the feelings don't change."

"This isn't just a danger aphrodisiac I'm feeling."

"I didn't think it was." He nuzzled her face. "Something strong, deep, and permanent ties us together."

"Love." She smiled happily. "Mark..."

"Throwing my rival in my face already?"

His sky eyes sparkled with teasing so she "riveted" her best toad sound instead of protesting.

He chuckled. "What about Mark?"

Leaning toward him, she soaped his back. "I've had this crazy sense Mark's been trying to tell me something for our last two meetings, but he won't say it straight. For his own reasons, he's been hinting in his own bizarre code."

"He usually doesn't care what he says, or how cruel it sounds as long as it's clever and patrician smug. What is he trying to say?"

"He's seen Daddy since the boat explosion. He called me Dusty, and said something Daddy says. He wanted me to know Daddy was all right."

"Are you certain it wasn't just a coincidence?"

"No, he was giving me a message from Daddy. Daddy knew I intended to hide in Europe if it was dangerous, and he always says 'give my love to Paris' when I leave for Europe. It isn't something anyone else knows about us. I was too scared of Mark killing us to even think what he was saying when he said it."

"How could he have seen..." As Gard absently soaped her hips and thighs, she could almost see his brain wheels whir with activity. "Lauton left the resort Wednesday. He'd been there since the day the boat blew up, so Mark couldn't have found him before that. What happened Wednesday to spook or force Lauton out of his safe hiding place?"

"The goons attacked us at the beach, and you dislocated your knee."

"Mark didn't know that, and your father certainly shouldn't have. He left the resort before the attack anyway." Gard groaned with understanding. "The photos in the paper, and the story about those men trying to kidnap you!"

"He was worried about me so he went to Mark."

"Why Mark?" Gard soaped her tummy and breasts and thought some more. "Damn!"

Her errant thoughts on his palms and fingers on her breasts, she jumped at his sudden expletive.

"Of course! Lauton's in protective custody. He intends to testify against Ferret and stop him before he kills you." Gard's face twisted as if he were puzzled by Lauton's uncharacteristic behavior.

Her father's love no surprise to her, she smiled softly. "That's why the government offered me protective custody. Daddy insisted that be part of the deal."

"He must have thought I'd leave you helpless and alone when I thought I'd earned my money."

"No." She rinsed off his arm with the wash cloth. "Daddy knows white knights better than that."

Gard's eyes brightened as if a light bulb had just gone off over his head, and he untangled himself from her and stood. "I've got to use the phone." He stepped out of the tub.

"You're soapy," she protested, but he was already out of the bathroom.

Sighing, she rested her arm and chin on the rim of the tub. "Maybe not deserted, helpless and alone, but definitely cold and soapy. I wonder if Watson ever had this problem with Holmes?" She giggled. "I guess not."

In his full naked glory, Gard had stopped by the phone. She stared at his long lean silhouette of legs, hip, buttocks, manhood, and chest, and the clean lines of his face capped in damp blond hair. "Gosh, he's beautiful!"

After ten minutes, she gave up hope he was coming back. She splashed herself off with cold tub water then wrapped herself in a towel and cleaned up the sloshed water. When she came out of the bathroom, he still stood, the phone at his ear. She found his bathrobe and draped it over his shoulders. He nodded absentminded thanks and shrugged it on.

Berating herself that she had no right to complain, wait until Gard saw her in one of her creative clouds, she slipped on her robe, and explored the almost empty kitchen shelves and the freezer for dinner ingredients.

She was stir frying the sweet and sour tuna with the rice when he finally remembered her existence. He
sauntered into the kitchen. "That smells wonderful."

"Jeri taught me the recipe. Chinese cooking was one of the only vices of hers I acquired."

"Well, I'm happy for that."

"What have you learned, oh great Swedish detective?" She cut off the unit.

"I talked to Braggonier. " He beamed smugly. "His people found the bug on Mark's phone. He's definitely innocent."

"I'm so glad, Gabriel."

"Me, too, Princess. Mark has his faults, but he's a good agent, and a good friend." He cleared his throat as if preparing for a speech. "I've also arranged an appointment for you to see your father."

Lightheaded with the awareness she'd never expected to see her father alive again, and the relief that wasn't true, she laughed and hugged Gard exuberantly.

Twelve

Lauton O'Brien was the most dangerous man Gard had ever met, and Gard was afraid. He could stop Martin Corlich, or another like him, from killing Desta, but he could never stop Lauton O'Brien with his fatherly wiles from taking her heart away from him.

On the hotel room sofa across from Gard, Lauton smiled smugly as if knowing exactly how dangerous he was. Although tall like Desta, he had none of her features, but he was a strikingly handsome man with broad forehead, deep, intelligent blue eyes, chiseled patrician features, full, sensual and ironic lips, and a statesman's gray hair. He had the hard, lithe body of a man half his age.

Desta curled beside her father on the sofa, her head on his shoulder, fast asleep. Lauton had a possessive arm around her shoulder, his hand stroking her braid. Desta and Lauton had talked themselves out after several hours together of small talk and Desta's narration of her adventures, and she had drifted off while they waited for Mark to come so they could speak of serious official matters.

Jealousy stabbed Gard that it was Lauton who held Desta.

Lauton brushed a kiss on her head. "Poor little Dusty's had a rough time of it."

"She didn't sleep much last night." Gard winced at how that had sounded. "She was so excited about seeing you this morning."

"I'm certain you found something else to entertain yourselves with."

Gard bristled at the innuendo. "I love your daughter. I intend to marry her when this mess is all over. If this had been a normal courtship, you can be damn sure we'd have seen a minister before..."

"Noble sentiments, Robbie." Lauton stretched lazily. "I'm certain you would have. I'm also certain Desta has a mind and heart of her own, and won't be coerced into any man's bed. She's like her mother— spirit, love, intelligence, and loyalty. She's chosen you. Her story of your grizzly adventures positively reeked of her love and infatuation for your manly bravery and honor."

"She is the extraordinary one. I'm a professional trained for this. In a totally foreign situation, she handled herself with more style, courage, and aplomb than most professionals do. You have a very special daughter."

"That is one point we can heartily agree upon."

Gard took a deep breath. "I don't want to be your enemy. We both love Desta. We both want what's best for her."

Lauton studied him as if he were a particularly unimpressive variety of amoeba. "But are you best?"

"As you said, Desta chose me. I intend to live up to her expectations."

"Silly child. I promised her dying mother I'd see her properly married to a good man. Desta yawned at my prime choice, Dunlap Dubois. I'd found her another when this nonsense started. I'd already arranged their meeting. A good man, too. Dun was my choice, and he wasn't acceptable, so I found a man her mother would have approved of, one like she should have married... But that's done." Lauton shrugged. "Perhaps, we can be... Not friends, but not enemies either."

"I respect you."

"The plaster saint respects the sinner. How ever did that happen, Robbie?"

"Desta's safety and life meant more to you than your own. You chose to come back to testify for her. That earns my undying respect."

"And you've just won mine by saying that."

Gard wasn't certain whether he was serious or not.

"We shall be equals then, not friends or enemies, but equals in respect and love for Desta. I warn you, though, that if you keep her, you must keep her safe and happy. If you can't, I'll take her back."

"I'll keep her safe and love her and your grandchildren."

Lauton's dark blue eyes twinkled for a moment with genuine feeling before returning to shallow mirrors. "I'm too young for grandchildren. However, I may make an exception in Desta's case."

At this most tentative of cease fires between them, Gard felt his heart lightened. Lauton could so easily change Desta's impression of him— remind her of his peasant farmer roots, his lack of money, his limited social ambitions. He struggled for a safe topic. "Her mother means a great deal to Desta. She must have been a fine woman."

Lauton's eyes flickered again with feeling. "Fine in the sense pure silk is fine—beautiful, elegant, ephemeral, and strong. I was a fool with her. She was better than I deserved. Love is all well and good, Gardner... Gabriel, but love doesn't change human weakness. I let my weaknesses rule me. Don't be a fool like I was and let weaknesses destroy the love."

"I don't have the same... predilections you have."

"Predilections?" Lauton chuckled. "A passion for beautiful young women is only one of these weaknesses. I have to keep proving myself with each conquest. Belief in an inferiority and a desire to prove ourselves wrong is a flaw most of us have had since Adam."

"Perhaps. Does Desta know you still love her mother?"

"Robbie, your sharp eyes continually amaze me. I doubt she knows."

"You should tell her. It would mean a great deal."

"Perhaps."

The hotel room doorknob jiggled, and the door flew open.

Gard jumped and reached for his gun as Lauton flinched and threw himself down shielding Desta's body with his own.

Mark sauntered in and stared at drawn gun and hiding protected witness. "Oops. It's me. Didn't mean to upset you."

Gard holstered his gun as Lauton sat back up bringing Desta with him. She blinked sleepily in Lauton's arm and brushed back her hair as if used to being squashed awake. Lauton appeared as unperturbed. Gard wondered if such panache was a trait of the blue blood wealthy or only of the O'Briens.

Grinning cheerily, Mark handed Gard a stack of mail in a rubber band. "Someone picked this up at your place. Everything's fine."

He accepted the mail. "Thank you."

"Your mail, my lady. Same report." Mark gave her another pile.

Desta nodded, yawning, and dumped the mail into her lap then snuggled back against Lauton's shoulder. He wrapped his arm around her.

"Well, I guess we can begin." Mark plopped down in the chair beside Gard's and across from the O'Briens' couch. "Everyone been good while I've been gone?"

"We didn't speak of the situation," Gard said, "beyond the personal, as we agreed."

"What good little boys and girl you were."

Gard grimaced. Mark, at his most snide, was unpleasant to live with. "I'll start then. Lauton, why did this mess start?"

"The mistake of an idiot accountant. I was supposed to receive Cal Ferret's business books to study for his racketeering charges. Well, I got the books all right. The wrong ones, or I should say the right ones, the undoctored ones. I had Ferret's whole crime empire in my hands. When I realized what I had, I knew I couldn't just return them and pretend nothing had happened. Ferret would kill me. I took the books and ran."

Lauton stroked Desta's braid. "I heard about my fatal boat explosion, and when Gard told me Dusty was unhurt,
I decided to stay dead."

Wondering about Mark's reaction to his lies, Gard studied Mark's serene patrician face. If he were hurt or upset, he didn't show it as he returned Gard's stare and said, "Braggonier wanted to cook your ass for withholding information, but I pointed out you were the prime witness for the government against Corlich and friends, and charges against you would ruin credibility. I assured him you were suffering from brain seizures caused by romantic heart problems and weren't responsible for your actions."

"Thank you."

Mark shrugged. "I've always had a soft spot for the mentally deranged."

Lauton continued, "I remained in hiding until I saw Desta's photographs in the *Observer* and the story about the kidnap attempt. I contacted Faulkner and came in out of the cold, so to speak, with my evidence to stop Ferret before he got her."

"How did Ferret know you weren't dead?" Gard asked.

"A leak in the Bureau, now very plugged," Mark said. "Our people within Ferret's organization are certain Ferret found out three days ago when the leak learned O'Brien was alive."

"You knew Lauton was alive before he came in?"

"He called last Wednesday."

"But Corlich came after Desta last Tuesday. He had to know Lauton was alive."

"He couldn't have," Lauton insisted. "Ferret thought I was dead until... He didn't contact me through the leak until yesterday morning. I've been in protective custody over a week. He offered me a million dollars and safe conduct if I'd keep my mouth shut."

"This makes no sense. Did he tell you he had Desta?"

"No, she's never been mentioned. Not the first threat."

"But he knew Corlich had her. He couldn't have discovered I rescued her because Corlich was in that cage. Why would he kidnap Desta then not use her as leverage?"

"The bug?" Mark offered.

"I called you on your car phone. It isn't bugged. He couldn't have known Desta was rescued."

Mark chuckled. "I have another variable to throw into the equation. The hood Desta put into the car in the parking lot regained consciousness about six hours ago. He's Corlich's number two man. Guess which lawyer he groggily called when he was arrested. Dunlap Dubois."

Lauton's brutal expletive cut the air. "He must have sold his loyalty. I thought I could trust him. I even told him Desta was..."

"What did you tell him about Desta?" Gard asked.

"I told him I was sending her to you. I had him check the boat. Damn!"

"He knew Desta was on the sunken boat, but he told no one. He knew you weren't dead, but Ferret didn't seem to know until much later, but he had to because Corlich knew. Corlich had a bug on the phone so he had to know you were alive, but Ferret didn't do anything for a week. None of this makes sense."

Like a sane voice in all the madness, Desta offered, "Dun told Corlich, but he didn't tell Ferret, who learned from another source. Corlich and Dun must not work for Ferret."

"Who then?" Mark asked.

"Dubois knew we were on the way to the Federal Building, and no one else did," Gard said. "Corlich was waiting for us there."

Desta rubbed her cheek against Lauton's shoulder. "He also knew we were keeping in contact with Mark."

"He volunteered his presence in my office right after I sent you off together from Bubba's restaurant," Mark said. "He could have left the bug then."

"Who is Dubois working for?" Gard asked.

"Himself," Lauton answered. "Do you know how much money he's handling from my trust? Millions. All to play with as he chooses."

"What if we've got all this wrong," Gard said. "Dubois knew Desta was going to be on that boat. Maybe he paid Corlich to kill her. What if it's Desta Corlich has been after the whole time, not Lauton. Corlich's goon told me they were to keep her alive a few days, then kill her, and hide her body for good."

"And you need proof of death to close an estate," Mark said. "Dubois could handle the estate as he chooses for years before she's declared legally dead."

Desta shivered violently. "So the boat explosion was meant for me."

Lauton hugged her. "But the explosion would be proof of her death."

"He chose a specific time to kill her," Gard said. "The time you left for good. Why? What did that mean to the estate?"

"Before I left, I signed a document releasing the trust from Dun's into Desta's care. It wouldn't take long to take effect."

His prey almost within his grasp, Gard grinned with hunter's glee. "Then Dun was already tinkering with the funds, and he didn't want Desta to find out, so he arranged her death. When the boat explosion, disguised as Ferret's attempt on Lauton, failed, he decided he'd not just hide his earlier embezzlement, he'd go for the whole estate. He's used Ferret to camouflage his own crimes. The bastard. He almost did it, too! We've been looking right past him."

Mark drawled, "Wonderful theories, guys, but can we prove it?"

"Yes, I think we can." Gard lifted a manila envelope from his mail and handed it to Lauton. "As Dubois promised, a copy of the trust, and an accounting of funds, probably very embezzled. Prepared for me, not for the knowing eyes of the man who wrote the original."

Hours later, Lauton looked up from his copy of the trust. "Here it is. Or isn't. I've got the bastard now."

Mark jerked awake in his chair and rubbed at his eyes.

Gard put down his own papers and stood. He came around the sofa and leaned over the back between Desta and Lauton's shoulders. "What is it? Or isn't it?"

Lauton tapped the paper under section fifteen. "The dowry is missing."

"The what!"

"Dowry. When Desta marries, her husband gains a half a million dollar chunk of the fund. I wrote it in as an incentive for Dun to marry Desta. He wasn't trying hard enough."

"I told you what you could do with that dowry and Dun, too," Desta said. "I'm not such a bad deal as a wife I need money dangling around my neck to gain interest."

Lauton patted her knee. "Now, Dusty. I just wanted the right man for you."

"Perfect choice, Daddy. A man who sends a hired killer known for his sadistic brutality to murder me."

"My second choice is much better, honey. You'll have to let me introduce him."

"No thank you." She smiled up at Gard. "I did just fine on my own."

His heart filled with love and longing, Gard smiled back.

"Well, Gard," Mark drawled in his most sardonic tone, "will you leave her at the church door now that the half a mill dowry is gone?"

Gard winced but replied evenly, "I love her so much, I'd marry her with the damn dowry."

Desta giggled with appreciation. "That's true love for one of the smugly virtuous."

"Now my work begins." Mark stood. "I have to prove that Dubois has tampered with the trust and embezzled the funds, then I can tie him to Corlich and the murder attempts. A simple enough matter and soon done so the smugly virtuous can live happily ever after, and the evil rot in jail." He beamed like a cat with a live mouse under its paw. "I love my job."

Lauton stretched. "My records are in my office, and my original of the trust is in my safety deposit box."

Mark nodded. "I'll get someone else to guard you and begin."

Gard rented a room in the same hotel for Desta and himself, and they spent the evening alone together in each other's arms. They even had enough hope in Dubois' destruction to speak of the future and make practical plans about their marriage. Desta's easy acceptance of life in an ordinary home with a little boy, dog, and mother-in-law surprised him, and he kept expecting her to come to her senses and walk out on him, but she hadn't.

The next morning after breakfast, Mark called them back to Lauton's room. Lauton sat on the sofa. With unshaven chin and weary eyes, he'd obviously been up all night studying the trust, but he'd regained a warhorse's eagerness from work that his enforced captivity had drained from him. Mark appeared as sleepless, but he'd shaven, and his eyes lit up with appreciation when Desta strode into the room with her businesslike but willowy graceful walk, her pastel, floral dress swaying around her hips.

Gard fought back his instinctive surge of jealousy. Mark had behaved around Desta since they'd announced their engagement. His friend had many faults, but wooing another man's woman wasn't one of them.

Desta slid onto the couch beside her father and pecked his cheek. "Good morning, Daddy."

Lauton hugged her like he'd never see her again.

Gard's hackles rose as he sensed very bad news, and he sat down in the chair beside Mark's. "What's wrong?"

"We've gone through Lauton's originals and compared them with Dubois' changed copies."

Lauton swore bitterly. "Every one of my originals isn't mine. He's gotten to everything and changed it. The dowry doesn't exist on paper anymore."

"We have nothing but Lauton and Desta's word to prove Dubois has embezzled the money," Mark added. "We can't build a case on that. Maybe if we sic our accountants and the IRS on him, we'll be able to pin it on him after a year of accounting drudge work, but not now. We have no way to stop him from killing Desta to protect himself completely."

With a moan of anguish, she bolted into the bedroom of the suite. Lauton chased after her, with Gard only a few steps behind him. Tears streaming down her face, she stood in the middle of the bedroom. Lauton pulled her against his chest and held her.

Stopping at the door, Gard watched them, feeling useless, but he refused to leave.

With a tenderness that belied his normal behavior, Lauton stroked her braid and murmured endearments until she sniffed back tears.

"Oh, Daddy! Why did this happen? I didn't even want the stupid money. I just want to be happy. I don't want to hide the rest of my life."

"Honey, this doesn't mean you have to be unhappy. Remember all the wonderful times we had in Europe? We could do that again. I can walk away from testifying against Ferret, and you and I can go together. I have enough money in Switzerland so we can live like royalty for years. Just you and me. Like it used to be. Safe, and happy, and together."

"But Gabriel..."

"He can't protect you forever. You can't stay." Lauton stepped away from her. "He's right here. I'm certain he'll know the sensible, safe thing for you to do."

Gard's muscles from his throat down to his heart constricted so violently he couldn't breathe. He knew
what he had to say, but he'd give his arm not to say it.

She stared at his stricken face and threw herself in his arms. They clung to each other as if someone wanted to tear them apart.

Her voice was tiny against his throat. "What should I do?"

"I can't offer you the life your father has. I can't even offer you safety."

"I don't want to traipse around Europe playing jet setter. None of that matters to me anymore. I want to live in your house by the lake with your son. I want to share my life with you, and have babies with you, and grow old with you."

"I can't keep you safe."

"Then come to Europe with me. You and Zachary."

"I can't. He's so emotionally fragile. He can't handle that kind of enormous change yet."

"No, he can't. You have to stay, and I have to go." Tears rolled down her face. "Damn, Dun Dubois. Damn him." She straightened. "No, I'm not going. I refuse to go. I'd rather die here now, than die of a broken heart over there."

"That's not sensible," Lauton said.

"No, it's not sensible. Love isn't sensible, but I prefer it to cold empty logic and self-absorption." Brushing away her tears, she stepped away from

Gard. "I'm going after Dun Dubois, and I'm going to stop him. Dangle myself in front of his nose until he has to strike and hook himself."

From the door, Mark said drily, "Worms are usually eaten."

"I don't care. It's quicker than dying of loneliness in Europe. I'm going to do it if I have to do it by myself."

All three male voices protested in unison, "No!"

"Yes!"

~ * ~

As Gard opened Dubois' office door, Desta strode confidently into the stuffy, elegant office. His own face carefully neutral, Gard followed close behind. At work on papers in his shirt sleeves at his pretentious mahogany desk, Dubois glanced up at the interruption and, seeing his supposed dead victim, almost jumped through the desk in shock.

"Desta, I didn't know..."

"Sorry to come in without an appointment, but I just had to speak with you."

"You never need an appointment, honey. You know that." He brushed back his premature gray hair then motioned expansively to chairs. "Have a seat."

She settled into a chair.

Gard sat down beside her.

Dubois finally deigned to notice him. "Gardner."

Despite his urge to wrap his hands around the man's neck and break his windpipe, Gard nodded politely.

Dubois sprawled back in his chair, picked up his brass unicorn paperweight, and twisted it in his hands. "How are you? I've been so worried about you; your father's death, and those criminals after you. I've been worried sick. The FBI assured me you were safe, but..."

"I'm doing well, Dun. I've been through some very scary moments, but I've come through unscathed thanks to Gard."

"I'm glad you've finally come in. We have things to discuss. You know that the divers never found your father's body. We really must have a memorial service. It would be unseemly not to."

"I don't think that's necessary." She smiled. "I've got some wonderful news. Daddy isn't dead. He wasn't even on the yacht. I was. Gard pulled me off before I was killed."

Dubois' pretend shock wasn't nearly as realistic as his earlier performance. "He wasn't..."

"No, he's alive and well. I've seen him. He's under protective custody, I can't tell you where or why, but he's alive and well. I'm sorry I couldn't tell you before. I know how you've grieved."

"That's marvelous news. I'm so pleased."

"So am I. Don't tell anyone. It's to remain secret for a short time until the government is ready to use him as a witness."

"I won't say a word. I really can't tell you how pleased..."

"I have some more wonderful news. It's wonderful to me and Gabriel anyway. We've gotten married." She extended her hand and showed her engagement and wedding rings.

Gard's death gleamed in Dubois' eyes a moment, but he stammered like a heartbroken schoolboy, "I'd hoped you and I still had a chance."

"I'm sorry, Dun. I'm very fond of you, but as a brother. I've never been able to think of you in any other way."

As if heartbroken, Dubois lowered his eyes.

Gard fought a wave of nausea.

The gallant, heartbroken lover, Dubois offered softly, "I'm very happy for you both. I do want you to be happy, Desta."

"I'm very happy, Dun. I'm certain you'll get over this soon. I've always felt your desire to please Daddy was the real source of your feelings for me. I'm certain you'll realize I'm right, in time."

"Perhaps."

"Gabriel and I have had some difficult times from those evil men after us, but we've finally come to the end of that. The killer who was after me..." She glanced over at Gard.

"Martin Corlich," he supplied.

"That awful man and his gang are in jail, and they'll never come out again, but the government feels that until Daddy testifies against...the man he's testifying against, I won't be safe. Gabriel and I have decided to hide in Europe until then. We'll leave in a few days with his little boy. That's why I wanted to see you."

Dubois prompted, "Yes?"

"I want to transfer one hundred thousand dollars out of my trust dowry into Gabriel's bank account for our living expenses in Europe."

"Dowry?"

"Of course. You remember that awful thing. Daddy and I had a terrible fight about it." She beamed fondly at Gard. "Gabriel and I have had a few fights about it, too, he's such an old-fashioned, honorable type, but I've convinced him it's only fair to use Daddy's money to live on while we're hiding. After all, it's Daddy's fault we're in this mess, and Gabriel won't be able to practice law either."

"I see." With a smug snobbish expression he must have learned from Lauton, Dubois studied Gard as if he were a degenerate slug.

"Can you do that? He is my husband now, and according to the trust, the money belongs to him."

"I don't remember the dowry, but I will look into it. If the dowry exists, you can be certain I'll transfer the money."

"It exists. I have a copy of the trust with me."

Dubois jerked slightly. "May I see it?"

"I meant I have it where we're staying. Not on me." She handed him a bank slip. "Here is Gabriel's account and bank. Can we have the money within a few days?"

"I'll do my best." Dubois accepted the slip. "How can I get in touch with you?"

"We'll be at Gabriel's home until his son... *our* son Zach returns from the mountains Sunday evening. We didn't think anyone would look for us there since we've been gone so long."

"An excellent stratagem." Dubois stood. "My congratulations to you both. I hope you have a long and happy marriage."

"We intend to," Gard assured him coming to his feet.

"Bye, Dun. Thank you." With another sweet smile, Desta turned and sashayed out of the room.

His sense attuned to attack, Gard followed behind her. He didn't speak or lower his defenses until they were in the car, and he'd driven a block.

"I've never had a greater desire to commit cold-blooded murder than I did with him."

"That's why I did all the talking. He's nauseating. I always knew he was cardboard, but I didn't realize how phony and rotten that cardboard was. He barely flinched."

"Your performance was magnificent. You were the most delectable, seductive worm I've ever seen. Throwing in having a copy of the genuine trust was brilliant when he was so busy denying the dowry existed. How will I know when you're telling me the truth? I would have believed every word you said."

"Not counting the little white social lies, I'll never lie to you, love. You know I don't play games."

"I know." He was silent for a moment then asked, "Would you like to get married now? I can have a judge and special license in a few hours. It's not the church wedding you deserve, but..."

"I love you, and I want to marry you, but it wouldn't be right without our families, especially Zach, there. Besides, I feel married already."

"I do, too. In the eyes of God." He squeezed her hand. "I just want it permanent in the eyes of man."

"Me, too."

"We can wait then," Gard said. "I'd hate to miss you in that white gown."

"Oh, I thought we could have a skydiver's wedding, and everyone would jump out of the plane, and I'd wear purple, and you pink, the minister would be in a clown suit—"

"And we could land in a giant wedding cake and eat ourselves into sweet tooth heaven."

"Perfect," Desta said. "How about making love in a vat of chocolate for our wedding night?"

"I don't even want chocolate between us there."

"I don't either. I didn't think it was possible, but you've shown me something I love better than chocolate."

"I'm honored."

"As well you should be." Desta grinned at him.

Suddenly serious, he said, "I want to tell you about something I learned this morning when you said Europe and jet setting didn't matter to you; when you didn't blink about losing half a million dollars, but grieved about leaving me and Zach. I've been a terrible fool.

"When I was in college, I got dumped by the wealthiest girl in town. We were engaged, and she left me for the wealthiest boy in town."

"She certainly lacked discrimination in men," Desta said.

"I thought so. No, I thought I was nothing. I realized how important money was to people, and that America, the classless country, had classes after all, and I wasn't very high on the scale. I've been carrying that wound and that belief around for my whole life."

"I can't say social class doesn't exist. It does, and some people are so stupid and snobbish about it. But it really doesn't matter what class you were born in, if you have genuine class. I've met Mayflower descendants who are appalling, without any redeeming style or qualities. I've met the poorest of the homeless who shine like royalty from inside with their natural dignity.

"You have genuine class—intelligence, breeding, goodness, dignity..." She kissed his palm. "I told you before. You are a prince, Gabriel."

"I didn't feel like one until now."

"Don't let snobbery, someone else's or your own, destroy what's between us."

"I have been an awful reverse snob, haven't I? I couldn't trust your belief in me. I do now, and I won't expect you to walk away from me.

"Your father tried to warn me about my weakness. He said that belief in an inferiority can destroy love. I thought he was talking about himself, but he was warning me that I could ruin us."

She nodded.

"I love you, Desta... What's your middle name?"

"Tyler, naturally. It's an old Southern tradition to use the middle name to show the matriarchal line. What's yours?"

"Bennet, after my father's late brother."

"Well, I'm glad it isn't Lunderson."

"Me, too. I love you Desta Tyler O'Brien. Long may your blue blood survive."

"I love you, Gabriel Bennet Gardner, long may your red blood join my blue blood for some all-American purple children."

"True royalty." He paused. "You don't have to stay at my house. You can stay with your father, and Mark and I can spring the trap around Dubois."

"If he doesn't see me, he won't come. And you know full well you two can't survive without me to protect you."

"I can almost agree, my little hellcat with a gun."

"I want to get this over with. Dun isn't going to ruin my life or yours. Besides, I've got a son to meet in three days, and no money hungry, amoral jerk like Dun Dubois is going to stop that."

Thirteen

With Barkley trotting attendance at her side, Desta strode down the hall from Gard's bedroom into the living room. Wearing black jogging trunks and a faded black Harvard tee shirt, its worn red insignia almost invisible, Mark sprawled across the living room couch with his arm over his eyes. She stared.

He was an extraordinarily handsome man with long muscular legs, broad shoulders, and narrow hips, and he exuded masculine sexuality. She could understand why he had no problems attracting women. From the lessons in sensuality and her own body she'd learned from Gard, she sensed he'd be an intense, satisfying lover.

Despite that, sexy Mark didn't hit her tingle button. Gard had discovered it and had exclusive rights for life, his and hers. She had proven to be more Tyler than O'Brien emotionally, and she was glad.

Before Mark noticed her gaping at him, she walked through the living room and into the kitchen. Peeping from under his wrist, he watched her stride by, her white lace gown swaying under the hem of Gard's big blue terry robe.

"Would you like a bedtime snack?" she asked politely.

"No, thank you," he replied in an equal tone of politeness. "Where's Gard?"

"He's showering before bed." She rooted around in the kitchen for a snack while Barkley nibbled at some dry dog food out of a bowl by the counter. She poured herself a glass of milk and counted six Oreos from the cookie jar onto a plate. "My sweet tooth has been just dreadful lately. I hope Dun goes to jail soon, or I'll weight two hundred pounds."

Mark chuckled. "That is the most unusual motive for catching a criminal I've ever heard."

Something about the relaxed, unguarded chuckle made her return to the living room instead of fleeing back to the bedroom as she'd planned. Sitting down in the chair near the sofa, she placed her cookies on the end table near Mark's feet.

His brown eyes twinkled as he studied her. "I wouldn't be concerned about the extra food. You're burning it with all your activity."

She blushed a hot red.

"I wasn't referring to... I meant worrying and fear. Although lovemaking is an excellent way to burn calories. Much more satisfying than running, and just as good for the heart."

"I'll remember that."

"Relax, Desta. I won't eat you. I would never lay a lascivious finger on Gard's chocolate-eyed Madonna."

"Gabriel wouldn't let you, and neither would I."

"I'm well aware of that, and of how dangerous either or both of you can be. I'm not interested even if you aren't dangerous. There are enough mares running wild for me without messing with any of the branded ones. Much safer and less complicated."

"A stallion with a harem of mares. Is that how you see yourself?" She shook her head. "I'd rather be a paired hawk and spend all my days with my mate, or a paired wolf."

"To each his own."

Barkley trotted over to Mark and licked his cheek then rested her chin on his chest and stared adoringly at his face, her tail thumping against the sofa.

"I can see how charming you are to women."

Mark sputtered a moment and swiped away the doggie kiss, but his hand settled gently on Barkley's head and stroked. "It's merely the respect one guard dog shows another. A young amateur's respect for the seasoned professional."

"Sure it is," she said disbelieving. "You'd better watch yourself. Gabriel and Zach will demand marriage if you steal her heart."

"A shotgun wedding. I've avoided that with great care. I think I'm safe though. Barkley only has a bad case of puppy love."

She laughed with delight, pulled apart an Oreo, and licked off the icing. She felt Mark's eyes on her, but when she glanced up, he was assiduously studying the top of Barkley's head and scratching under her ear.

"Ever have a dog?" Desta asked.

"When I was twelve. A collie. Lassie was popular and fashionable then. My father had her put to sleep so they wouldn't have to transport her to D.C. when we moved there."

"What a rotten thing to do to a little boy and the dog."

"I survived. I always do."

"We poor little rich kids have to. Just because we're kept in luxury everyone thinks we don't hurt the same way other people do. We end up with good, kind parents or insensitive jerks like everyone else. Money and nice toys don't make those hurts go away either."

"F. Scott Fitzgerald said that rich people were different. He should know."

"The less rich always think they do know." She drank some milk and ate the outside of her cookie. "What game are you playing with Gabriel?"

As she studied his face, Mark's sardonic eyebrow went up, and he replied blandly, "Game?"

"He's your friend, but you've been playing with his emotions since I've met you. You threw yourself at me when you weren't that interested. You kissed me in the parking lot, but your eyes were on Gabriel. You've tossed the innuendoes and ogling stares at me, but they were meant as knives aimed at your friend. I don't understand why you've done them. I'm incompetent at these games so I have to ask."

With a chuckle, Mark crossed his legs at his ankles. "Even ingenuousness is a game. You play that game well."

"Why, Mark? Don't you feel friendship for him?"

"I am capable of friendship, scummy game player that I am, my straightforward little Madonna. I consider him my friend. I also consider him a major enigma, a puzzle to be understood. You learn the meaning of an enigma by worrying it and seeing how it will react. I don't understand what makes Gard tick. Why he's so different from me. I upset him just enough to examine the reaction."

His eyes flickering with thought, he paused. "The moment you walked into my office, my radar went off. Something was between you two, something I couldn't understand. Something more than sexual attraction, or that bloody gentle paternalism Gard shows every female and kid he comes in contact with. I probed around a bit and watched where he flinched. I never expected Saint Gabriel to be lying to me and the Bureau. Lying with a straight face."

"He was trying to protect me. Can't you understand that?"

"The scope and splendor of the lie were absolutely elegant. A wonder to behold. But he could have told us the truth, and we'd have protected you. Maybe not as well as the lie would have if Ferret had been after you, but he didn't have to lie. Besmirch that virgin integrity of his. Why?"

Gard's voice boomed behind Desta, "Because some things mean more than integrity." He slid into her chair and wrapped his arm around her shoulder.

Barkley nuzzled Mark's cheek in farewell and curled up on the floor at Gard's feet.

"I thought nothing meant more than your integrity," Mark insisted. "You've never been bought or swayed away from what you thought was right."

"Sometimes right doesn't agree with company policy. Nothing matters more to me than the people I love. That's what love is all about."

Mark shook his head in confusion.

"Why did you kiss me in the parking lot?" Desta asked.

"An acid test. Despite all that flirting you'd done, you were as disinterested as my sister in my manly smooch, and you were always conscious of Gard. Gard wanted to punch me out, but he didn't. He had that same dopey look in his eyes over you he has for Megan and Zach, and he was jealous as hell, but he did nothing. You were smitten with him; he was smitten with you, and you both were avoiding the other like crazy. Fascinating."

"Idiotic." Chuckling, Gard nuzzled her ear.

She gave him a cookie to distract him from other plans and asked Mark, "And the other times?"

"A few brief tests at how the relationship was progressing, and a little healthy jealousy to motivate him."

"Why, Mark, you're a matchmaker!" Desta beamed.

"Never call me pro-marriage. It might give someone the wrong impression about me. I merely pushed the game to its logical conclusion."

"Oh, you were a matchmaker," Gard said with understanding.

"If you keep talking dirty, I'm going home." Mark's wristwatch alarm beeped. He picked up the remote control and cut on the television. The eleven o'clock Charlotte news had just started.

Deciding Mark was more than a news junkie and was awaiting something special, Desta watched the news, and Mark watching the news. He practically quivered with excitement when the anchorman said, "In a freaky piece of luck today, Charlotte police stopped a car on a routine traffic violation, and arrested Paul Rector, a well-known hitman who's reputed to be responsible for last September's slaying of a local union leader. There are more than thirty arrest warrants for Rector in the state of North Carolina alone, and many more from surrounding states."

Mark thrust his fist upward. "Yeah! We've got him. We've got him."

Gard rubbed her temple with Oreo-scented lips and asked Mark, "Would you mind explaining?"

Mark cut off the TV. "We've got people watching Dubois. With a lot of string pulling, I was also able to get a court order to wiretap Dubois' home, office, and cell phone."

"It takes a nuclear emergency these days to arrange a wiretap," Gard explained to her. "Civil liberty problems make judges very leery of them."

"It wasn't easy." Mark smiled like a sated tiger. "We knew Dubois would hire another killer to finish Desta after her stellar worm performance. He apparently did, and we tipped the Charlotte police who arrested Paul Rector on a seeming traffic violation."

"So Paul Rector was my new Corlich."

"Yes. He's as charming a jackal as Corlich. I bet Dubois is crawling the walls after losing another killer."

"I hope he doesn't sleep tonight worrying about it. Do you have enough evidence to nail Dubois for hiring Rector?"

"Not really. We need more, but we didn't want to risk the men meeting. Rector could have slipped our net and come for Desta."

"Well, thanks for that," Gard replied.

"We're pushing Dubois into a rash move. He knows you and Desta will leave the country and get out of his reach in two days, so he'll have to come after Desta himself. If he tries to hire another killer, we'll pick that killer up, too."

"Oh," Desta said, "you want to catch him with the smoking gun rather than for just conspiracy to commit murder. It would be much more conclusive."

"They promised me they'd get Dubois the moment he tried anything," Gard said coldly. "They won't wait until he attacks."

"I told you we wouldn't," Mark insisted.

"Dun will need a good strong push to try for me himself. Daddy always thought he was too fastidious to be a great criminal lawyer. He didn't like to get down and dirty. Of course, he wasn't supposed to have the backbone to embezzle the funds and kill me either."

"Why did he hire him then?" Mark asked.

"He wanted to buy me a husband."

"Hey Gard, do you suppose O'Brien offered you a partnership to marry you off to her?"

Desta stiffened in horror.

"If O'Brien was looking for another Ivy League type to replace Dubois as husband material, he'd have asked you, not me. He doesn't think I'm worthy of his daughter."

His sardonic eyebrow up, Mark opened his mouth for another snide remark, but Gard glared him into silence and stood. "Let's go to bed, honey."

As she came to her feet, Gard asked Mark, "You'll be comfortable on the sofa?"

"I've spent stakeouts in worse spots. It's very comfortable."

Desta pointed. "Zach's bedroom..."

"Is not central enough to hear a break in," Mark explained. "Goodnight."

Gard's arm around her shoulder, Desta and Gard strolled back to the bedroom with Barkley walking sleepily behind them. The puppy curled up in the corner of the bedroom by the closet as Gard closed and locked the door behind them.

She slipped her robe off and tossed in onto the chair. "I guess I should brush my teeth again after those cookies."

"Oh my..." He gaped with appreciation at the nightgown.

Beaming, she pirouetted. The white gown was pure antique lace and subtly displayed most of her curves and valleys.

He dragged his gaze from the game of peekaboo her nipples played with the lace. "That's incredible."

"I thought we should celebrate our first night in your bed."

"*Our* bed."

"Our bed."

"That's so beautiful and seductive, but the only thing I want to do is take it off you."

She turned around displaying a bare back. "It unties in the back."

Stepping up behind her, he chuckled and nuzzled her neck. "I love you, Princess."

As his hands cupped her lace-covered breasts, she leaned back against him. Her nipples rose into his palms.

"I need to explain what Mark said." Gard brushed a kiss on her shoulder. "I don't want you to get the wrong idea."

"It doesn't matter."

"It must matter. Your heart picked up speed, and you stiffened when he said it. Lauton offered me a place in his firm right after I left the Bureau. It had nothing to do with you. He wanted me so he could smirk at me under his thumb. My careful evidence defeated him in court a number of times, and he never forgave me."

"You were an equal opponent. He has so few of them. He loves a good fight. He's taken several cases because he knew you would oppose him. If he wanted you in the firm, it was a compliment to you, and another arena for game playing."

"I feel like a catnip-stuffed cat toy sometimes." Gard laughed wearily. "Mark and Lauton love to jerk me around and play their games with me." He kissed her head. "You're not a game, love. I swear it. Lauton had nothing to do with my wanting to marry you."

"You wouldn't be my Gabriel if he had lured you. I knew you would never do that. I was just upset Daddy's game playing extended to us. I feel like a cat toy myself."

"Their games will never touch us, or what's between us. I promise you."

"Me, too." She lifted her hair away from her neck.

He took her hint and untied her gown. It drifted downward like a snowflake and landed around her feet. "When I get sated of you, in about four or five hundred years, I'd like to see you in that gown for more than five minutes. If I can hold off making love to you that long." He wrapped his arms around her waist under her breast and hugged.

"I'm so happy to be home." She savored the word "home" by repeating it aloud.

He rubbed his face in her hair. "For all its good points, something was lacking until you arrived."

"Explosions, killers, FBI men on the sofa..."

"Someone besides a little boy with bad dreams to crawl into my bed at night, a woman who smells of gardenias and Oreo cookies..." He lifted and placed her on the bed, her head on a pillow, then shucked off his robe.

She studied him. From blond, handsome head to broad, muscled chest to rampant manhood he became more beautiful the better she knew him and learned his body. He clicked off the lamp and crawled onto the bed on his knees.

In the light from the bathroom, she could see the exultation on his face as he gazed at her. She opened her arms to him.

"I never thought I'd see you here, Princess. I thought that was only a foolish dream."

"A dream's arms don't tire. Come here, my sexy Swedish prince, before they fall off."

Chuckling, he stretched out beside her on his side and leaned over her. She lifted kissing him, her fingers wandering across his temples and into the blond silk.

He slid his arm under her neck, holding her up, and returned the slow exploration of tongues. His hand curved against her breast, his thumb feathering her nipple.

The tingle spreading from her breast all the way down to her toes, she sighed happily against his lips and melted under him. He nibbled down her throat to between her breasts then found the breast his hand didn't caress.

She moaned as his lips caught her nipple and pulled, the tingle becoming a series of tiny explosions like firecrackers on a string. She thrust against him and encircled his neck with her arms.

A thud and loud *whump* shook the house.

Someone must be trying to break into the house. Jerking, she stiffened beneath him and whimpered with panic, her nails biting into his back.

He lifted his head, his eyes holding hers. "It's all right. That's the hall bathroom door. You'll get used to the night sounds soon. He won't come tonight. He might not even know he's lost another hired killer."

"Oh."

Gard kissed her sweetly and stroked her head, but her body refused to relax, and her heart chugged with panic instead of passion.

"I'm sorry." She blinked tears. "I talked a brave role this morning, but I'm so scared."

"I am, too, love. I am too. We have so much to gain, and so much to lose." His voice broke. "I love you so much. I couldn't bear to lose you." His tears splashed her cheeks.

"Oh, Gabriel." She clung to him comforting and comforted, her own tears blending with his. Experiencing his hurt and fear as intensely as she'd shared his passion, she ached. Although her own tears refused to stop, she kissed away his, the salt bitter. "I love you."

"Don't leave me. Please don't ever leave me. I couldn't bear that emptiness again," he pleaded and rocked against her.

"Never, never, never..." she chanted hoarsely and opened her thighs around his hips. Unready, she winced, but lifted her hips and enclosed him.

He would have pulled free, but she clasped his thighs with her legs. He stilled, and his hand slid between them, his callused palm against her stomach. His fingers danced and soothed.

Her muscles relaxing and becoming liquid, she sighed at the heat and fullness of their bond and arched completing their joining. Her arms around his neck, she lifted kissing his closed eyes, his face tense with control, and the tears streaming down his cheeks. "Never," she promised again and again through her own sobs.

He began to thrust within her.

Their spirits joined, consoling, healing, and banishing fear.

The intensity of their feelings fueled their bodies' reaction, and they met, clung, and parted with white hot passion, their bodies striving to attain the oneness of their spirits. Finally, they could bear no more. An inferno exploded within burning away self and body, and they were one spirit, incandescent and eternal in the dark night.

Then they became two tiny lights again. Desta moaned and brushed away her tears on his shoulder. When she kissed his collarbone, he sniffed and rubbed his tear-streaked face against the pillow under her head. "Did I hurt you?"

"No."

"I've never been so close to anyone before. I love you sounds bland after that, but I love you."

"I love you, too. We'll survive somehow."

"Somehow." He nuzzled her throat.

They made love again, this time gently and slowly, all the pain and hurt burned away, but the pleasure and love were as intense as it always was between them. At peace, they curled in each other's arms and fell asleep.

In the deepest blackness of the night, Barkley growled.

Desta's hackles rose at the primal sound of danger, and she stiffened. Under her ear, Gard's heart thudded loudly, and he slipped his hand under the pillow and pulled out his gun as he lifted slightly and studied the room.

When he didn't fire, she sat up in bed. Her head stiff with concentration, her hackles upright, Barkley stood staring at their curtained window and growled again.

Gard slid off the bed and pulled Desta with him to the floor so the bed was between them and the window. As he pulled on a dark running suit and shoes, he whispered, "Stay here. Keep the door locked. Mark and I will circle the house and get him. Stay here until I come for you."

She nodded agreement and pulled her gun off the night stand.

He brushed a kiss on her head then left.

Her heart ached with the fear of never seeing him again, and she almost followed him, but she locked the door as she'd promised. He whispered, "Mark," then everything was silent.

She found her own dark clothes, which she'd laid out earlier on the chair, and wiggled into them behind the bed. Listening with her whole body, she zipped up the black jacket over her bare breasts and tied her tennis shoes then pinned her sleep-tangled hair out of her face.

On her knees, she peeped over the bed toward the window. The lack of noise was unnerving. Certainly Gard and Mark had found their intruder by now. Barkley sat on the floor with her head resting on her front paws and watched the window.

The dog's lack of urgency told her Dubois or whoever was outside was no longer trying to break in through the window.

Barkley's stillness bothered her. The puppy should be reacting to Gard's presence outside, but she wasn't. Could the animal have gone to sleep, or had Gard been stopped by Dubois before he reached the window?

She whispered, "Barkley," but the dog didn't respond. With a quick glance at the window, she crawled on her knees over to the dog and shook her. "Barkley." The dog sagged under her hand.

As she bent to see if the puppy was breathing, she gagged and coughed at the odor of natural gas near the floor. Natural gas? That made no sense. Gard's house was all electric.

The air conditioning! Dubois was leaking gas into the air conditioning. If Barkley hadn't wakened them, they'd have died in their sleep from gas poisoning.

Desta shivered. Gas was heavier than air so it clung to the floor. It would rise upward as more gas entered the house. Poor Barkley had been closest to the floor.

The puppy's heart beat against her hand so she hefted her in her arms and wobbled to her feet. Barkley was too heavy to carry far, and she couldn't keep her gun in her hand either. She dumped the puppy on the bed. Maybe she could stop the air conditioning before the gas reached the bed and killed the dog. She certainly couldn't stay in here and wait patiently to be gassed to death.

Desta picked up her gun, and strode to the door. Putting her ear against the door, she listened, but could hear nothing except the motor chug of the air conditioning through the skeleton of the house. She unlocked the door, peeked out into the empty hall brightened by a tiny night light, then stepped out. Her gun ready, she walked to the air conditioning controls across from the hall bathroom. The temperature was turned down as far as it would go. She reached out to cut it off.

A gun muzzle probed the small of her back, and an odd, hollow voice whispered, "Be still, or I'll pull the trigger."

Her heart threatening to bang out of her ribs, she stopped. A hand grabbed her right wrist and forced it back, and her gun was pried out of her fingers.

The muffled voice ordered, "Turn around."

She turned and jerked backwards in surprise as she saw what looked like a giant black humanoid insect, but then she recognized the black jumpsuit, the gas mask, and the man behind it. "Hello, Dun."

"Nice tea party we're having, Ms. O'Brien," he mocked. "Get back into the bedroom."

Praying like mad for Gard to come to her rescue, she wobbled back toward the bedroom with Dun's gun prodding her back. Dun reeked of terror, and frightened men were more dangerous and unpredictable than seasoned professionals. That made her more afraid. As she reached the door, he caught her left arm and twisted it behind her. "Try to escape, or warn him, and I'll kill you."

He didn't know Gard was outside, not in the bedroom. Dun pushed open the door and shoved her forward as a shield. His gun trailed across the bed and Barkley, then he scanned the room. He shoved her to the bathroom and checked it. "Where is he?"

"He told me to stay here. He was going to look for intruders."

"Outside then. I guess I'll have to wait for him to come back in."

Gard and Mark would be sitting ducks walking into the house, but they had the upper hand outside. "A gun going off inside the house will set off the gas. You, me, and the house will go up if you pull the trigger."

"You're lying."

"Am I? Haven't you ever seen a diagram of how a bullet works? It has gun powder inside, and it explodes when the hammer hits. You'll explode, too, in a fireball of gas and flame. Poof! Burning to death is an ugly way to go." She wasn't certain he believed her, but she'd made him even more nervous. The arm that held her was now wet with sweat, and it shook slightly.

He force marched her to the bed. "Lie down."

"Gabriel will kill you if you touch me."

"He won't be around long enough to protest. Lie down, you stupid bitch." He kneed the small of her back, and gasping with pain, she collapsed face down on the bed. Pinning her to the bed with a knee on her back, he forced her arms up against headboard. Something cold stung her wrists.

His weight eased off her. She spun and kicked at him, but her arms were chained to the bed. Off balance, she fell before the kick connected. Half-twisted on her back in the bed, she glanced up at the handcuffs, then back to Dun who loomed over her. Underneath his bland patrician breeding and civilization, she finally recognized the emerging sadistic bully. "Why, Dun? What did I ever do to you?"

Pulling off his mask, he shrugged, his eyes shallow gray mirrors. "I needed some money for an incredible stock opportunity. I borrowed the dowry since I knew it would be mine eventually. The stock plummeted, and I couldn't pay it back. You weren't as agreeable as I thought to marriage. I had no other choice but to take advantage of Lauton's disappearance. I didn't want to kill him, but you didn't matter. When the boat didn't get you, I decided to go for the whole trust fund."

"How did you get in?"

"Corlich set up window entry and the gas when we couldn't find you. We figured you'd come back here sooner or later, and we'd be ready for you." His hand slithered up her chest and caught her zipper. He yanked downward.

Her skin flinching, she kicked at him, but he pinned her legs, pushed open her jacket, and stared at her bare breasts. "Not bad." He reached under the elastic waistband of her pants.

She cringed again as his cold hand met her stomach, and she twisted against the handcuffs and his legs. "Don't touch me."

He chuckled, and his hand journeyed around her waistband. "Don't give yourself too much credit. I was looking for weapons. You're not even my style. My taste runs more toward your pretty blond husband."

She laughed.

His fingers wrapped around her throat, and he squeezed. "You find my preferences funny?"

Hysteria touching her voice, she laughed again. "No, I was just thinking Daddy made a wonderful choice for my husband."

"So he did. After I've killed your husband... If the gas hasn't finished you off, I'll come back and discover what I've missed in your marriage bed. Unless, of course, you cooperate with me."

"How?"

"Where is the original copy of the trust fund?"

"The FBI has it."

"If they had it, I'd be sweating in jail. Where is it?" His fingers tightened around her throat again, and he shook her.

"They just got it. You expect bureaucrats to act immediately?"

"You're lying. It's here in this house." He smiled like a cadaver. "Well, when I'm finished with you both, I'll light the gas and burn you, this house, and the original to hell."

"You'll get yours whatever you do to me, Dun. You'll get yours. Daddy will see that original, and he'll make Martin Corlich look sane when he gets his hands on you."

"He sure does love Daddy's little girl." Dun fluffed a handkerchief from his pocket and tied it around her mouth as a gag. "Bye, Desta. I'll see much more of you when I finish with that pretty husband of yours." With a nasty chuckle, he pulled the gas mask back over his face and left.

As the door closed, Desta jerked the cuffs against the headboard with her complete strength, but nothing gave. Her wrists burned with pain, but she yanked again.

Images of Gard being shot when he walked into the house tormenting her, she fought the cuffs and the headboard that must be solid oak.

Swearing, she thought hard then remembered "Chapter Ten" of her favorite book on lock picking.

She rolled back over onto her stomach, crawled closer to the headboard, and pulled a bobby pin from her hair. Biting her tongue and forcing herself to forget Gard, the gas, and Dun, she poked the bobby pin into the left cuff lock and probed.

Sweat streamed down her face despite the frigid air conditioning, and she wriggled her nose as the gas smell became stronger. She imagined the house as a bottle, the gas as water filling it up slowly; she imagined drowning when the gas reached the top of her bed. Minutes passed disguised as hours.

Click! The cuff sprang open.

Sliding the cuff off her left wrist, she stood up, pulled out the gag, and glanced at the right wrist where the cuffs still dangled but decided to forget it. She hefted the unconscious puppy into her arms, carried her into the bathroom, and put her on the counter by the sink, then cut off the air vent, grabbed towels, and closed the door. She knelt and covered the floor crack in the door with a towel to keep out the gas, then closed the bedroom's air vent and covered the crack to the hall door. "Good luck, pup. I've got to go warn Gabriel."

She shoved open the bedroom window, forced up the screen, and crawled through head first. As she hit the ground outside, she did a forward roll.

A man's weight pinned her on her back before she could sit up. Hands clutched, and the man came upright with her. Her nose was pressed against male chest, and a hand clamped her mouth. "Shhh, Princess."

Although the endearment was Gard's, the voice and male scent were Mark's. Relaxing, she didn't struggle against his arms that were now more a comforting embrace than prison. His hand left her mouth. She whispered, "Dun's pumping in natural gas through the air conditioning. He's in the living room waiting for Gabriel to come in so he can kill him. He's wearing a gas mask. He has my gun, and his own. He doesn't know you're here."

"Excellent report, scout," Mark whispered. The handcuff hit his bare leg. He jumped and explored with his fingers discovering cuff and open jacket. His gaze flashed down at her bare breasts, then his eyes flamed with anger as he quickly averted his gaze. "Did he?"

She fumbled her zipper closed. "He threatened, but he wasn't really interested. He prefers boys."

"His great loss. Gard's circling the other way in the upper yard. We'll pull the plug on the gas, find Gard, then he and I will go in from the window and finish him."

"He has an easy entrance from some other window. Probably the study. He came in behind me. I tried to convince him a gun would set off the gas to get him outside, but I don't think he believed me."

"It will. One shot will take the whole house. Stay behind me." His gun at ready, he crept forward. She captured the dangling end of her cuffs in her hand to keep it quiet and followed him.

The moon was three-quarters full above the lake beyond them, and its light and the reflected light on the placid surface of the lake silvered the landscape. Like a night shadow, Mark floated from shrub to shrub that surrounded the house. Always a shrub behind, she copied his movement and his body placement but knew she could be seen while she could barely see him.

He paused at the corner of the house, peeked around, jerked back, then peeped around again. He motioned her to him. She scooted up behind and against his back. Despite the seeming effortlessness of his scouting, he was breathing heavily, and she could smell his sweat. Even in the cool June air, sweat streamed down her back and breasts, too.

Mark pointed with his head then went around the edge of the building. Using his body as a shield as he intended her to, she followed. They flitted around three tall azaleas and reached the outside pump unit of the air conditioning. He thumbed toward it then darted around it to scout territory ahead.

She knelt at the unit. The air intake panel was pulled away slightly exposing the heating and cooling coils as well as the air duct. Tucked against them was plastic tubing with a cutoff valve that had been inserted into a drilled hole in the air duct. The tubing seemed to run back through the unit. Apparently, a large bottle of gas was hidden under the house and the tubing led to it.

The smell of escaping natural gas made her nose wriggle as she closed the small valve, then the aroma vanished. The gas was off.

With a brief smile at that tiny victory for the house, the puppy, and them, she stood and glanced around for Mark. His back was just visible against the next corner of the house. With as much stealth as she was capable of, she crept to him and gave a quick thumbs up.

He nodded, peeked around the corner of the house again, then darted to the holly bush just past the corner. She followed. Her face against his back, she waited for the next shrub run.

His body quivered suddenly like a dog's when it caught a scent, then he became dead still as he watched something.

Like a night hunter, Gard flitted from tree trunk to tree trunk in the upper yard. She could barely see him he moved so secretly, but something in her hummed in resonance to his presence, and she could feel him.

Mark, however, studied something else. On the porch at the back door, someone lay flat on his stomach. The moonlight glinted on premature gray hair and a revolver's barrel. Dun watched Gard, his gun following him as he neared the house.

Her heart landed in her stomach, and she wanted to tell Mark to do something before Dun killed Gard, but she dared not break his concentration. She prayed instead.

Mark's gun pointed at Dun but wavered. At their angle, they could just see Dun, but it would be impossible to shoot him. Unless Dun sat up or moved, Mark couldn't shoot him, and they couldn't get any closer without giving themselves away. The holly bush they hid behind wouldn't provide any protection from bullets.

Mark reached backwards and nudged her toward the house wall. Taking the hint, she burrowed further into the bush out of sight as he motioned she stay.

Gard was close now, but they couldn't warn him without exposing themselves to Dun's gunfire. Desta prayed harder.

Dun lifted his gun to take steady aim.

Mark bolted out of the bush, shouted "Dubois," spun, and shot above Dubois' position.

Twisting around, Dun shot.

Mark fell, clutching his left shoulder.

Gard's gun flashed in the darkness, and brick shattered near Dubois who dived over the side of the porch, and dashed toward her and Mark.

Covering her mouth in horror, she shrank into the darkness.

Dubois pulled up Mark who swayed drunkenly, his bloody fingers pressed against his shoulder, and used him as a shield against Gard who hid behind a large oak. "Try anything, Gardner, and I shoot him." He began to back away, dragging Mark with him.

Gard spoke as if to a frightened child, "Give it up, Dubois. The FBI knows all about you, Corlich, Rector, and the trust fund. You don't have a chance. You're an amateur, and it shows. Give up before the charges are even worse. If Mark bleeds to death, you'll be on the Ten Most Wanted List in every post office in the country. Every agent in the country will be after you. No one gets more attention than a cop killer. You know that. Give up now. You're a great lawyer, but a lousy criminal. Turn yourself in, and you'll have a good chance in court. You have no chance here."

Dubois answered by shooting into the tree Gard hid behind.

Mark's face was ghost pale in the moonlight, and she thought frantically of a way she could stop Dubois, but nothing came to mind. She'd be little help as another victim or hostage if she gave away her position.

Mark's eyelids fluttered, his head fell back, and he collapsed, jerking out of the other man's grip. Swearing, Dubois darted away from the house.

Gard glanced toward Dubois then back at Mark.

Desta bolted out of the bushes to Mark and urged Gard after Dubois with a wave of her hand. With a nod, he charged off in pursuit. She knelt by Mark's chest. Deathly white, he slumped on his back with his hand still clutching his bleeding shoulder. He seemed to be breathing.

She moaned with despair and untied the handkerchief gag from around her throat.

One of his eyes opened slightly as he examined her, then the other opened, and the sardonic eyebrow went up. "Do you think the Academy saw that Oscar-winning performance?"

"You idiot."

He sat up.

She pressed the handkerchief against his shoulder. "Are you hurt bad?"

"Just a fleshy wound. The fleshy part of the upper shoulder." He groped around on the ground and found his gun, then handed it to her. "Go on. I can take care of myself. I'll go call for reinforcements."

"You sure?" At his nod, she took it then tucked the dangling handcuff into her sleeve to keep it out of the way.

"Go on after your paired hawk."

She brushed a kiss on his sweaty forehead. "Thank you for saving Gabriel. There is a prince in you after all."

Before he had a chance to ask what she meant, she began to trot into the woods where Gard and Dun had disappeared.

Fourteen

In the woods, the moon shone dimly, flickering across fallen leaves in a mosaic of light and nothingness, dancing across tree trunks in slats of brightness, and fluttering like giant fireflies on the leaves around Desta. The lake smell of water, fish, and humus clung to the woodland near the water, but no raucous lake insects sang. The woods were silent, expectant.

Desta's heart trembled in her chest like leave-prismed moonbeams as she stopped at the edge of the woods and listened for the sound trail of human hunter and hunted. The silence told her nothing moved.

She imagined Dun hiding in the darkness, and Gard listening for him, both men's guns drawn as they waited to kill the other. The woods and the darkness made that hunting both sinister and primitive.

The silence was terrible.

She wanted to shout to Gard to tell him she was here, but she dared not give her location away, dared not break the terrible silence.

Crouching like a hunting cat, she listened and waited.

Leaves above whispered in the strengthening breeze, and a soft-winged hunter passed over her, but nothing large moved through the fallen leaves.

Finally, something moved. The rhythmic pat of running feet on the lawn grew louder and louder, then leaves crunched almost obscenely under feet. The feet didn't sound right. They seemed...

The harsh noise was almost on top of her. Damp cold touched her cheek. She choked back a scream.

Thump, thump, thump. Barkley's tail battered the ground as she threw herself into Desta's crouching half-lap.

Desta hugged the puppy's shoulder and buried her head in Barkley's neck hair. Relief and terror warred inside her. Relief that Barkley was safe, she was safe, and she was no longer alone in the darkness won.

Mark must have reached the house, called for help, and opened it up to release the gas. Visions of him fainting from blood loss in the gas-filled house had haunted her since she'd left him. He must be safe, too. Now, if only Gard could be safe.

The paralysis that had held her since she'd entered the woods left, and she now knew how to find Gard. She wrapped her fingers around the dog's collar and whispered into her ear, "Find Gabriel. Find Daddy, girl."

The puppy's ears went forward as if she understood, and she got up with Desta and led her deeper into the woods.

Not wanting to walk into an ambush, Desta held on tight to the collar and her gun and listened. With six feet, they trampled like a herd of elephants.

As gentle-footed as an Indian, someone advanced toward them.

Desta lifted her gun toward the sound, and her finger tightened on the trigger. The sound materialized into a human shadow.

Barkley's tail thumped wild circles in greeting.

Desta's finger eased off the trigger as she lowered the gun. The shadow became Gard who hugged her, Barkley happily between them, the cream stuffing to their Oreo cookie. He nibbled a kiss to her ear before whispering, "Okay?"

Including Mark, Barkley, and herself in the answer, she nodded and smiled into his hunter eyes.

"I've lost him. He must be heading back to his car. It will be next door or on the road. Want to do to him what that goon did to us at Holden?"

With a wicked grin, she nodded.

"Come then. We'll take the faster, quieter route of the lawn." He stroked the puppy's head and tapped her muzzle. "Barkley, shhh."

Desta released the puppy and followed him out of the woods. He began to run when they reached the lawn, Barkley loping beside him. Wildly happy to be flying with her mated hawk again wherever he led her, she matched their easy pace. They skirted the woods and the shallow tongue of the cove that marked the end of Gard's property.

The wind carried sound toward them from the lake *Luffa. Luffa. Luffa.*

Her stride faltered. She'd heard that sound before. Somewhere. Dun's face and that pretentious white captain's hat of his fluttered in the memory of the sound. *Luffa. Luffa. Luffa.*

Remembering, she bolted after Gard and caught his arm. He stopped and studied her curiously. She motioned toward the bay. "He's not in a car. He came by sailboat. I can hear the empty full sail fluttering in the wind."

Gard's head cocked as he listened, then he nodded agreement. "The dock next door. Same plan." He began to run again.

They reached the road, bypassed the first end of the driveway next door, then quickly entered the other end of the drive loop that circled the house. The house was dark, untenanted by the weekenders.

Pausing at the corner of the house, Gard studied the terrain. The lawn from the house sloped briskly downward to the water with few trees or bushes to hide behind. At the waterfront, two docks extended out into the water from both end points of the crescent-shaped shoreline. The furthest was a short fishing pier, the nearest extended far out into the bay with a floating boat dock at its end. Dun's long motorized sailboat was tied to its side.

Gard motioned toward the small boathouse on the shore not far from the short pier. "It has a ladder up and a sun deck on top. Position yourself up there. Don't make a move against him unless it's absolutely necessary. I'll watch the dock with the boat from behind that knoll. I'll make the first move."

Although her safe position and role were minimal in catching Dun, she nodded and didn't protest. She'd be there to keep him from slipping past them. Gard was the professional hunter, and she'd trust his expertise. She caressed his cheek with I love you, take care in her fingertips.

He answered with a smile then motioned that she take her position while he guarded her back.

Raising her gun parallel to her chest, she winked then darted like a silent almost invisible luna moth from tree to bush to tree across the lawn until she reached the boathouse, climbed upward, and settled on her stomach on the flat surface.

~ * ~

Gard fought to ignore his surge of love, admiration, and fear as he watched her. Emotions clouded the senses, and he'd need all his senses to finish Dubois. He stroked Barkley's head, "Heel, girl," then began his own dash toward his lookout spot. With the puppy at his side, he followed the night shadows to avoid the moonlit patches of lawn, circled behind the knoll, then crawled up on his hands and knees and settled on his stomach facing the dock. He patted the ground.

Barkley sank down beside him with her own gaze on the lawn and dock before them. Her ears perked up with interest.

He smiled. His and Zach's games with her had been meant as training to find Zach and protect him if needed, but they had proven handy tonight. As serious as he and Desta, Barkley sensed this was no game, and a real enemy to her family pack existed.

Gard concentrated on the night and the landscape. Wind fluttered creating ripples in the water and in the full sails of Dubois' boat. The lake insects had begun to sing again in the cove in the woods. No human disturbed them. Dubois wasn't in the woods.

The lawn shadows didn't shift or vary with human movement, and he couldn't feel Dubois near. Barkley, too, seemed relaxed but alert. Where could Dubois be? Could the boat have been a false escape route? Could he have doubled back to the house in search of Desta? Gard had heard no gunfire from his house.

Desta wouldn't have left Mark if he weren't capable of fending for himself, and Mark knew where Gard's gun cabinet key was. He'd have replaced the automatic he'd given to Desta. Why did she have Mark's gun and not her own? She'd had her gun when he'd left her in the house. Why had she left the safety of the house?

He shook away unimportant questions. He'd ask later. Mark was or had been in the house. Lights now glowed through curtained windows in all the rooms. If Dubois tried for the house again, Mark would stop him.

If he were Dubois, he'd be getting the hell away from here. The police were surely on the way now, and he'd told Dubois enough to let him know the FBI knew of his embezzlement and attempted murder of Desta. Dubois had nothing left to hide, and nothing to gain by killing Desta or him. Why wasn't Dubois making a run for his boat?

Barkley quivered and crept forward slightly. She bumped his shoulder with her nose to get his attention then gazed toward the water.

He looked toward the short pier where her nose and ears pointed. The water! Dubois had left the woods and gone into the water to reach the sloop. A shadow and slight splash under the far pilings were all that gave away Dubois' presence. He must be an excellent swimmer.

Gard patted Barkley in thanks and considered his options. Unless Desta showed herself, which she wouldn't as long as he was safe, Dubois had no reason to suspect he was swimming past her hiding place, and he'd keep going until he climbed aboard his sailboat. Gard had positioned himself where he could stop Dubois when he came onto the dock, but he was at a lousy position to get Dubois now so he'd have to move.

He pulled off his black jogging suit and his tennis shoes then glanced down at the waistband of his briefs. He'd lose the gun if he kept it there, and he'd prefer not to swim with it in his hand. That made too much noise. After a moment's thought, he yanked out the cord threaded through the hood of his jacket, strung it through the trigger guard, and tied it around his neck.

After he motioned to Barkley to stay, he crawled back off the knoll and crept toward the water behind the knoll.

He gingerly chose his footing down the piled loose large stones, which protected the shoreline from wave erosion. Several wobbled under his weight, but he balanced himself to prevent a fall or a noisy rock slide, then he strode into the shallow water and waded out until waist deep.

The miserably cold water and the slimy lake mud made him grimace. He began to swim toward Dubois' sailboat. The distance wasn't great, but the tension of remaining silent stretched the distance interminably. When he reached the stern of the boat where Dubois couldn't see him, he caught his foot on a rudder bracket and his hand on the taffrail, and climbed up.

The sloop was large enough for four to six people, but seats were formed in the fiberglass sides of the cockpit. As he'd expected, there was nowhere for him to hide.

He slid back down into the water and anchored himself against the dock at the stern where Dubois shouldn't see him when boarding. He pulled his gun from around his neck and waited.

After several minutes, the water rippled with a moving body, and the boat rocked gently then rolled as Dubois clutched the side of the boat and pulled himself aboard. Before the boat finished its violent movement, Gard hoisted himself up and onto the boat.

Bending over the bow cleat and the rope that moored the boat to the dock, the other man didn't notice Gard's weight addition to the boat's rolls.

"Hold it, Dubois. Don't move, or I'll blow your head off."

The other man didn't turn. Instead, he scrambled off the boat and onto the dock, then began to run toward shore. Gard's finger tightened on the trigger, but he didn't pull it. He wanted the miserable jerk alive and around a long time to enjoy prison.

Vaulting off the boat, he charged after Dubois who'd already gained a sizable lead. The dock planks burned Gard's bare feet, but he kept moving. Dubois jumped off the dock onto the shore and bolted toward the fishing pier and Desta's hiding place.

Two gunshots echoed around them. As Desta's bullets landed, sand blew upward in front of Dubois. He spun around and headed back toward the dock.

Stopping, Gard watched his headlong flight.

Obviously trying for the boat again from the water, Dubois jumped onto the otter slide against the dock. His bare feet hit the wet mud that caked the slide at water level, slipped, and he fell feet first, his body smashing into a dock piling.

Gard ran down the pier, jumped onto the shore below, and searched for Dubois. His body wasn't by the piling he'd hit. He'd kept moving.

His gun ready, Gard waded into the water by the pier. Parallel pilings on both sides of the dock extended at six foot intervals into the deep water. The other man must be hiding behind one because he couldn't hear swimming sounds. Did Dubois still have his gun, or had he ditched it when he'd first gone into the water? Well, only one way to find out. Gard waded out further.

The water rose from hip deep to chest deep so he lifted his gun over his head as he circled cautiously around the first piling, ducked under the cross beam, and crept under the dock.

Moonlight didn't penetrate much through the board cracks above, and he had to feel his way with feet and cop radar. He stumped his big toe on something large and hard but bit his tongue and kept moving.

The water was so murky and mysterious he could easily believe terrible things lived in the water. Alligators, creatures from the Black Lagoon, and sharks would love a place like this.

A minnow nibbled his bare shin.

He jerked and concentrated on the next piling and the gunman who could wait behind it. Conscious of his vulnerability during the action, he ducked under the next cross beam and floated around the piling into moonlight and open water. Where could Dubois have gotten to?

The dock shook with the patter of four large feet. Barkley peered over the side of the dock at Gard and wagged her tail then, her hackles upright, walked a piling down on the other side and peeked through the boards.

Gard silently promised the puppy fresh meat instead of dry food for the rest of her life. He'd been right. The puppy was smarter than some humans he knew and had a much better nose for creeps.

Ducking back under the cross beam and into the darkness under the dock, he crept forward to where Barkley had pointed.

Something smashed into his chest, and he crashed into the piling.

Water rocked and splashed around him as Dubois pulled himself up onto the dock.

Barkley growled and snapped.

With a yelp of pain, Dubois fell backwards into the water.

Gard surged toward Dubois and hit him on the chin as he cleared the surface.

Coughing water, Dubois jerked away, glanced toward the dock and his boat where Barkley barked and growled on guard duty, then floundered back toward shore and away from Gard.

Hanging his gun back around his neck, he took off in fast pursuit as Dubois came up out of the water and began to wade.

With a lunge, Gard shoved him into the water face first. The other man twisted free and punched at his face, but he dodged and punched back. Dubois doubled over, and Gard aimed precisely for the chin.

Dubois' head jerked back, and he toppled backwards, landing with his upper body half out of the water, and crawled like a crab away from Gard and the water onto the sandy, gently sloped shore.

When he came to his feet, Gard swung again, but Dubois ducked and jabbed with a surprisingly good left. Blocking it with his right, Gard clipped him across the chin.

Dubois kicked at his groin, but Gard dodged.

Smiling grimly, he let some of the anger he'd capped deep inside since the boat explosion erupt. This stinking, smug bastard with his love of Desta's money had caused them a lot of pain and misery, and it was time for this creep to start paying for it.

They were evenly matched physically, and Dubois seemed as well trained with his fists, but the lawyer was a manipulator and a bully, not a hunter and front lines fighter as Gard was. Nor was he as angry.

Avoiding his blows and dirty tricks, Gard battered at him until he swayed drunkenly on his feet, then clipped him across the jaw. He fell backwards. Gard backed away and waited for him to get or give up. Dubois floundered a moment then threw sand underhanded into his face. Gard ducked, but grit blinded him anyway. Blinking hard, he swiped at his face then stared tearfully at where Dubois had been. The other man was running toward the house.

Gard charged after him.

A shadow solidified in front of them and aimed a gun at Dubois. "Stop, or I'll shoot."

Dubois stumbled to a stop and gaped at Desta and her gun. Recognizing her, he started forward, but her grim face and burning eyes stopped him again. She appeared very capable of shooting him and sleeping well afterwards.

Gard trotted up behind Dubois and tapped him on the shoulder. When he turned, Gard smashed his fist against his chin.

Like a tall, thin willow, Dubois toppled and stayed down.

Kneeling, Gard frisked him.

Desta extended her right hand. A handcuff dangled from her wrist. "If you find the key, I've got the handcuffs."

The bastard had put his hands on Desta! Gard struggled with his inclination to murder him. Instead, he found the key in a hip pocket of the black jumpsuit and tossed it to her then grabbed Dubois by the wrists and dragged him over to an oak.

She handed him the cuffs. He circled Dubois' arms around the tree trunk and cuffed his wrists together, then pulled out the key, handed it to Desta, then stood.

"Did you enjoy beating him to a pulp?"

"Very much."

"Men!" Smiling, she hugged him.

He engulfed her in his arms and buried his face in her sleep-knotted hair. She smelled of gardenias and Barkley.

"Are you all right?" she asked.

As the adrenaline faded and the pain began to be felt, he considered his condition. "Bruises, a few cuts, and splinters, but nothing worse than what I've seen. You?"

"I'm fine. Now." She glanced down at Dubois. "Is it really over?"

"Everything but the questions and the courtroom."

"I won't regret a minute of them if he and his goons never get out of jail."

"Me neither." He nuzzled her ear.

"You're like an ice cube." She rubbed her hands along his bare ribs down to his wet underwear. "Where are your clothes? You'll catch pneumonia."

Except where her hands and body touched him, he felt like an ice cube. His skin positively glowed there. "Behind that knoll." He wrapped his arm around her shoulder, and they walked across the lawn no longer avoiding the moonlit patches.

Her tail wagging with puppy exuberance, Barkley trotted over to them, and began to heel by his side. He stroked her ears. "Good dog. Very good dog, Barkley. The very best dog in the whole world."

The puppy pranced with delight at his warm praise.

When he had dressed, they began to walk back toward Gard's land. The sound of someone whistling *Our Love Is Here To Stay* drew them toward the lake side of the house.

Whistling soulfully, Mark was stretched out in the hammock between the oaks. "'Lo," he offered and finished the song.

Gard asked, "How is the bleeding?"

Mark peeked under several wash cloths piled on his left shoulder. "About stopped. You enjoy smashing him into paste?"

"How did you know?"

"I watched the whole drama from your dock. Good cast, splendid action, and great plot ending with happily ever after."

"You should try a happily ever after instead of a quick goodbye," Gard said.

"If I ever figure out what love is, I'll think about it."

"You're so busy trying to puzzle out Gabriel you haven't considered your own puzzle," Desta said. "Why did you deliberately get shot to save him?"

"It seemed the stupid, noble thing to do." Mark's sardonic eyebrow went up then went down again as he met Desta's glare. "Okay, so I like him. He's my friend."

"Oh, you mean you love him. Friendship is a form of love."

Mark actually blushed.

"Think about it," she insisted gently. "Think about it, and don't hide behind that uncaring veneer you show to the world and to yourself. Maybe one day, you'll find a woman you feel friendship for, and much more."

"Fat chance."

"A very likely chance if you give it a try."

The sardonic troublemaker eyebrow went back up, and Mark attacked again. "Well, Desta, you handled yourself really great through all this. Want to leave architecture behind and join the Bureau? Ordinary life will be pretty dull now."

Contentment and commitment in her eyes, she wrapped her arms around Gard and smiled up at him. "No, thank you. I'll be perfectly happy being Gabriel's wife, and Zach's mother, and living here for the rest of my life."

Knowing he'd been a fool to think she could never love him, Gard held her. He was a prince, after all, and she was his loving princess.

In the distance, police and ambulance sirens screamed. Help, it seemed, had finally arrived.

~ * ~

The smorgasbord Bubba had produced for the wedding reception was as incredible as he'd promised. Guests still raided the long tables under the trees near the house's front door, and Bubba had just made another trip to his catering truck for more champagne, Swedish cookies, and meatballs. Other guests wandered around the lawn or were down by the water lured by the late afternoon July breeze and sunshine. Happy children's shrieks and Barkley's friendly barking echoed from the shore.

Standing under a nearby tree with Gard, Desta smiled at the joyous, large clutter of people. Even with only two weeks warning, Tylers, Gardners, Lundersons, and special friends had poured in from all over to help them celebrate their marriage. Her family and friends and Gard's blended as well together as she and Gard did. Sam Braggonier, local head of the FBI, chatted with her uncle Judge Tyler who'd given her away since her father couldn't, her partner was flirting with a tall blonde beauty—one of the real Eric Lunderson's granddaughters, and several of the lake locals were discussing fishing with Great Aunt Toot Tyler, her cousin Sheila, and Gard's wonderful mother Rebecca.

Despite Jeri's mouth being agape at all the blond, handsome kinfolk of Gard's, and tall, dark hunks of the Tylers, she remained demurely at Andy's side. Even Billy Bob, doctor and Tom Cruise look-alike, hadn't drawn her attention away from Andy while they discussed medicine. It must be love.

Most touching of all was the presence of Megan's parents who'd wished Desta and the marriage well with their whole hearts. She'd accepted the wonderful couple as completely. She had no real grandparents to offer their future children, and she was thrilled to have discovered such perfect replacements.

Pushing back her veil a bit, Gard brushed at a tear on her cheek and teased, "Standard Desta post-disaster hysteria?"

She smiled at him, so impossibly handsome in his white suit, and so impossibly tender with his sky-blue angel eyes. "Happy tears."

"I am, too." His fingers tightened in hers, and he squeezed. "So very happy."

"Thank you for the church wedding, and your beautiful little country church. It was so perfect."

"No regrets about the cathedral in Charlotte?"

"Absolutely none. It wasn't worth the extra wait, and it couldn't have equaled what we had. That church was us."

"Absolutely. You were such a beautiful bride. I couldn't believe my luck that you were walking to my side." He smiled his incredible smile, light streaming from his soul through his eyes.

Her own spirit quivered in response, and she lost herself in his eyes. She leaned toward him.

As his lips met hers, someone tugged at her dress, and a young voice asked, "Will you show Bobby how to throw a curve ball?"

She smiled down at the nine-year-old miniature of her husband. Zach grinned back, and his furry shadow wagged her tail.

"It's not polite to interrupt people when they're kissing," Gard said softly.

Fondling Barkley's head, Zach made a slight face. "You're always kissing."

"And we shall continue to kiss. Married people do that sometimes."

Zach's eyes rolled as if he thought his father was drastically downplaying the amount of kissing that went on. "Momma?" His voice hesitated slightly at the word.

Neither was totally comfortable yet with the word or her new role, but they'd taken to each other as strongly and as immediately as she and Gard had taken to each other. There would be adjustments to be made, but, already, a strong foundation for being a complete family had been built between them. "Momma, will you show Bobby how to throw a curve ball? I told him you knew how." Zach beamed as if proud of having a new mother with such wonderful talents.

Desta rotated her arm experimentally. "I'm afraid this dress wasn't made for throwing balls. Tell Bobby that we'll get together some Saturday with any of the other Tyler cousins who want to after we come back from our honeymoon, and we can throw curve balls."

"After we finish our honeymoon." Zach beamed as if pleased with the idea and trotted back toward the lake with Barkley loping along as escort and companion.

Gard chuckled. "Very nicely done, Mom."

"I'm glad. All hints will be greatly appreciated."

His laugh was low and sexy in his chest. "I'm a great one for hints."

"I'm a great one for taking them." She wiggled her brows in a comic leer.

"Mmmm hmmm! I'm glad we're legal. I don't think I could stand staying away from you another day."

"I thought I would die sometimes. If we hadn't..."

"Rendezvoused without Zach's watchful eyes on us?"

"Exactly. I agree completely we have to live certain high standards in front of Zach as well as teach them, but..."

"Parenthood can be heck."

Their son had stopped by a group of young Tylers he'd made friends with and began to circle his arm as if explaining about the curve balls and her dress.

Desta chuckled. "I'm glad I'm bringing something of real value into this family besides myself. Zach's never had cousins near his age. Cousins are wonderful friends. They stay when all the other friends disappear."

"They teach you to shoot, pick locks, and French kiss."

"Better a cousin than a stranger."

"True."

Dashingly handsome in a tailored brown suit, Mark sauntered toward them from the house and saluted them with an elegant flip of his hand from his brow. "'Lo."

"Having fun?" Gard asked.

"All those exquisite blondes with their long legs in your family. I don't think my heart can stand it. But I can't find one who isn't attached, or doesn't have that damnable fondness for lifetime leases. Does this emotional aberration run in your family?"

"Afraid so."

"Now those dark, beautiful Tyler maidens. Oh my!"

"I'm afraid Tylers are even worse than Gardners and Lundersons," Desta said.

"Playboy hell. Wall to wall beautiful marriage-minded females." Mark bit his knuckles in frustration.

They laughed.

"I'm afraid you've got a lot of competition," Desta said. "Tylers, Lundersons, and Gardners seem to have an affinity for each other. They're already beginning to pair off. I imagine this weekend will cause a lot of expensive phone and airplane romances. And maybe a few more weddings."

"Better them than me." Mark pulled out a white-wrapped gift from under his arm. "Lauton asked me to give Desta this present today."

Desta accepted it. "He's already given us our honeymoon."

"If you call a week in a cabin at a mountain resort for a couple, mother-in-law, dog, and little boy a honeymoon." Mark's face brightened. "Lauton told me about the swinging half of that resort. Those great rooms with their—"

"Victorian bordello furnishings," Desta finished for him. "It's a lovely place with tennis courts, swimming pools, and horses. Zach will love it. He needs to know he's gaining a mother, not losing a father in this marriage. We can wait a little while for a private honeymoon."

"What strange creatures these married people be."

"You got the address of the photographer?" Desta asked.

"Lauton will receive the photographs and videotape of the wedding. I wouldn't dare forget that. He's been a bear in protective custody since he found out he couldn't give you away."

"I'm just glad he's not publicly dead anymore. You've definitely got Ferret?"

"Completely. After your father testifies, Ferret will never be able to threaten him again. The cases against Dubois and Corlich grow stronger each day, too. They'll never get out of jail. We've even found a copy of the original trust without Dubois' changes." Mark explained to Gard, "Lauton's secretary is a pack rat and a duplicator addict. She has copies of copies of copies of things stashed in odd places."

"Bless her." Gard grinned, his hunter eyes gleaming.

"Yep. Well, I shouldn't talk shop to the happy couple. Have a nice family honeymoon if I don't see you again. I want to try some more of those Swedish goodies, then I might try the food, too." With a wink, he strolled away toward a cluster of chatting young Lunderson blondes.

Thinking of her father and his fondness for manipulating her life, Desta stared uneasily down at the present as if it were a bomb. "I guess I'd better open it."

"The size is right. Maybe it's just another silver picture frame." Gard looked no more pleased than she did.

"The favorite present of this year. I guess that beats all the woks a friend received last year, but not nearly so good as the lock pick kit I got from the groom." With a sigh, she pulled at the wrapping. "Well, here goes. It's the right size for a coffee table book."

She dropped the wrappings and pulled off the top of the box, then brought out the card from on top of the tissue paper, opened it, and read aloud, "Dear Dusty, Your mother asked me to see you well married and happy. I'm sorry my first choice was such a poor one." Desta laughed harshly. "What an understatement. A gay embezzler who tried to murder me for my money."

Her gaze returning to the card, she read aloud, "For my second choice, I asked myself what kind of man your mother should have married. What kind of man would have made her as happy as she deserved to be. I figured a man like that would make you happy since you're so like your mother. I think I've found this man. I intended to introduce him to you, but this mess started instead. I've enclosed his dossier. Love, Daddy."

With a furious groan, she thrust the unopened dossier into Gard's hand. "That stinky, manipulating... On my wedding day. How could he?"

"So much for the truce between us."

As Gard stared down at the box, the hurt on his face made her ache. "Oh, Gabriel. I'm so sorry."

"It's not your fault. I knew from the beginning he didn't think I was good enough for his little girl."

"You are," she insisted.

"Yes, I am." The pain vanished as he smiled at her, the magic between them reasserting itself. "Aren't you curious?"

She glanced down at the dossier he offered her but didn't take it. "Kind of. Yes. Not because I don't think you're perfect for me, but... What kind of jerk did he pick out for me? A Hungarian ax-murderer? A deposed Arab sheik with eight wives?"

Gard pulled away the tissue paper and opened the file then blinked with astonishment. "It's me."

"You?"

"Me. All the time he wanted us together." Gard began to laugh at the great joke on them.

She joined his laughter until they were breathless.

He handed her another card with her name. "It was inside the dossier."

She opened it and read aloud, "Dearest Desta, I want you to be very happy. Please be happy. I've learned my lesson. I'll never manipulate your life again. I promise. I'll be home in time to hold that first grandchild. I'll always love you and your mother. Daddy." Desta blinked tears. "P.S. Sometimes manipulating a romance does work even if the circumstances become real instead of pretend. Tell Gabriel he should consider his fee your dowry."

"What a monumental manipulator."

"He was right though. You are what Momma would have wanted for me." She sniffed away happy tears. "I'm glad he loves her."

"I'm glad he told you. I'm especially glad he promised not to play with your life anymore."

With a nod, she wrapped her arms around his neck. "I love you. I don't need anyone else but you. You're all the guardian angel I'll ever need."

"I think someone higher up than me or your father helped arrange this. Whatever that guardian angel's name is who brought us together, I thank him."

Zach's voice insisted directly below them. "It was Santa. That's who did it. He promised me he would." Zach patted Barkley's head. "Right, girl?"

The puppy woofed agreement.

Meet

Marilynn Byerly

Marilynn Byerly's writing passion is romantic adventure stories. *Romantic Times* called her an author to watch. *Affaire de Coeur* named her an outstanding achiever in romance. Her books have won major awards including a Sapphire Award, The National Reader's Choice Award, the Affaire de Coeur Award, and a Write Touch Award.

Marilynn is happily single and, when she is not writing, spends her time with her extended family, her garden, and her cat.

www.ingramcontent.com/pod-product-compliance
Lightning Source LLC
Chambersburg PA
CBHW061031120726
47910CB00006B/2191